Assault on the Senses

A Novel

Michael P. Ferrari

Blue Room Publishing
Conshohocken, Pennsylvania, USA

Assault on the Senses is a work of fiction. Names, characters, places and incidents either are the product of the author's imagination or are used fictitiously. Any resemblance to actual persons, living or dead, events or locales is entirely coincidental.

To Mom and Dad. Again.

Prologue

Booze, Broads and Balls

"Give me a fucking cigarette!" I yell across the three people crowded between Barry and I.

"I thought you were quitting..." he mentions, standing still as I wiggle through the three people—three short, chubby blonde girls—trying to make my way in Barry's direction.

"Fuck quitting," I tell him. "One isn't going to kill me."

"I don't got a lot left," he tells me. His voice shrinks into the blaring music as he yells to me.

"I'll buy you a pack tomorrow," I reassure him.

"Fuckin' A-right you will," he says, dragging a crushed pack of smokes out of the front pocket of his jeans. Barry is like a cigarette loan shark: if he gives you one when you really need it, he expects a pack back in return.

"Feeling old yet?" I yell to him, slurring on my last word and lighting my first smoke in two days.

"No...why?"

"This is your first party of your last year in college," I scream to him, glazing my eyes across our crowded living room. The room is filled with freshman girls covered more by their drunken smiles than their clothes. I love freshman girls in all their slutty, underdressed goodness.

"Thanks for reminding me, douche!" Barry yells back with a smile. "I'll be sure to come up for your last year just to rub it in your chubby, degenerate face when it's your turn!"

Turning away from Barry, the first thing I notice is a squad of freshman girls huddled together in a corner, protecting themselves from every sexual predator in the room with just an awkward smile. They hide from would-be drunken conversations with their half-full, plastic Silo cups propped up in front of them as if they were crucifixes warding off vampires. It's a shame these girls don't know the truth: they aren't in high school anymore. The minute they get drunk, they're going to be dancing all over anything with a cock, prepping to go home arm-in-arm with the first guy smooth enough to convince them that the Liquor Control Board is in town, and the safest place to hide from them is in his dorm room. God bless freshmen.

"There he is!" I hear in a cheerful voice. I do a swaying, drunken spin to face the voice.

"Molly, Lana," I say, tipping my head and greeting the two girls I've known since I came to this school several years ago.

"Kalvin," Lana says, drunk and pretending to be a lady, "how are you?"

"Pretty damn good."

"Okay," Molly says, "I'll admit it: I'm kind of impressed."

"With what?"

"This is actually a good party you guys have going here."

"First weekend of the year, darling," I respond. "Had to start the year right."

"Yeah, but this actually looks like a real frat party," Molly says.

"Well, we are a real fraternity."

"But you never had parties before."

"That's just cuz we were lazy in the past," I say. "This year? It's a whole different fuckin' can of worms!"

"Kal?" Lana asks in a half-concerned, half-playful voice. "Are you fucked-up already?"

"Lil' bit, Lana," I say, pinching my index finger and thumb together to show them the teeny, tiny degree of how drunk I am. "Only a lil' bit."

"You got an extra one of those?" Molly asks, looking down at my cigarette.

3

"Don't you got your own?" I ask.

"I forgot to stop on the way here."

"Well, that's too bad, because I can't help you," I tell her. "I don't smoke anymore!" I smile like a dick when I take the next delicious, almost delirious drag. "I'm quitting."

"You?" Molly asks.

"Yup!"

"Why?"

"For a girl," Lana responds with a casual smile.

"What?!" Molly exclaims, yelling more than asking.

"Fuck you!" I yell to Lana over the music. "You weren't supposed to tell anyone!"

"What girl?" Molly asks.

"Yo, dickface," I hear as I turn around to see Doug, drunk and squinty-eyed, stumbling around like the poster child for Down's syndrome.

"Yes sir?" I ask, wrapping my arm around him in the typical drunk fashion.

"Some broad was looking for you in the kitchen," he slurs out.

"She hot?"

"I don't know about 'hot,'" he mumbles, "but she's definitely too good-looking to be asking about you."

"Sweet…" I say, letting Doug out of my grasp.

"Is that her?" Lana asks.

"I don't know," I say, crushing my dropped cigarette butt between my foot and the carpet. "How's my breath?" I ask, opening up and urging my breath out in the direction of Molly's nose.

"Atrocious."

"Dammit! Gimme some gum!" I stumble my hands in front of her.

"Give me a cigarette."

"Fuck you! I told you I quit!"

"Here…" Lana says, handing me a peppermint Life Saver. "It's the closest thing I've got."

"Awww, Lana!" I yell, being as over-the-top as I can.

4

"You're *my* life saver!"

"I know," she says sweetly as I fumble my fingers, forcing the mint out of its tight, plastic wrapping.

"Now," I say, popping the mint into my mouth, "if only we can get you to keep that large, whorish mouth of yours shut!" She cringes as I pinch both of her warm cheeks with my index fingers and thumbs.

"Kalvin!" Molly yells. "Don't be a dick!"

"What? She knows I'm kidding!" I turn to Lana, who's still smiling. "You know I'm kidding, right?"

"Go..." Lana says, sweet smile still intact, "knock her dead." I smile and pat her back as I walk away.

I leave Molly, Lana and Doug to the fate of the party as I merge into the tightly packed crowd occupying our living room. Thick smog covers the low-hanging ceiling of our place, which we've inhabited for only a little more than a week now. It reeks of smoke, sweat and spilled beer. The hot September humidity hangs off of the people I push by, spreading across their drunken faces in the form of glimmering sweat smears. I wedge behind a girl in tight black pants—a trademark fashion statement of slutty freshman girls. My hand subconsciously glides across the small of her back as I pass by.

I push through a few more people before I almost forget why I'm doing it in the first place. Then I see her, waltzing out of the kitchen and slowly pacing into the crowd. Her deep black hair hangs straight off of her head, blowing gently every few seconds as small gusts of wind from the only fan in the room blow by her soft face. She has her arms folded insecurely over her chest. A flimsy, tan blouse barely hangs off of her shoulders revealing a white tank-top underneath. The room goes silent in my head as I see her inching slowly into the living room. I can almost hear the clapping of her sandals as she approaches; her short, denim skirt clings to her thin legs with each step.

"Jill!" I yell, standing maybe 10 feet away from her at the most. She snaps out of a neutral stare and jerks her head in my direction as she hears her name carried over the noisy drunks and obnoxious dance music.

"Hey!" she says, stepping towards me. "There you are!"

"Here I am!" I say. "Find the place all right?"

"Yeah…it wasn't very hard to find," she says with a curved, flirty smile, "you are only a few houses down from me."

"Yeah, that and I give kick-ass directions!" she softly chuckles and looks at me before coming in for a hug.

"Looks like a heck of a party," she comments.

"Yeah, it's all right," I say casually. "Want something to drink?"

"Sure!" A smile beams across her face as she steps towards me, expecting me to take the lead. I grab her by the hand and lure her towards the less crowded kitchen she just emerged from. We find a crevice in the corner by the fridge, the one spot in the house right now where nobody seems to be lingering.

"I know you told me before that you don't drink beer," I say to her as I open the freezer door. "So I got you this." Her eyebrow rises as she accepts the clear, chilled bottle I hand her.

"Banker's Club, huh?" she scoffs. "You know what a girl likes." Her voice is layered with a fake, snide tone. "I can't imagine how you stayed single for so long before you met me."

"Before I met you?" I ask. "Are you implying I'm not single anymore?"

"Well, we have been kind of 'seeing each other' for a while now," she says, putting the bottle aside and drawing herself closer to me. "And, to be honest, I don't know if I can easily resist a guy so willing to buy me a $10 handle of vodka." Her head bobs in slowly as she drops a soft kiss on my mouth just before she pulls away as slowly as she approached.

"If it sweetens the deal, I've got some cheap cranberry juice in the fridge." She smiles at me again before giving me another short, sweet kiss.

"So," she says, pulling away again. I guess she doesn't want to be that couple that sits around making out at a party. "Aren't you going to introduce me to your friends?"

"Now?"

"That's why I came here, wasn't it?"

"It wasn't for cheap booze and rough, awkward sex?"

"Ha, ha," she says. "Funny."

With that, I feel a slow, slithering hand on my shoulder. It's soft at first, and then it digs its fingers deep into my shoulder. Jill makes a weird, almost disturbed face when she looks behind me.

"Yo..." I hear slurred silently into my ear. "Gimme a smoke..." I turn my head to be greeted by Dutch's sloppy drunk face and giant red ears resting on my shoulder.

"Okay," I say with a deep breath. "Jill, this is my friend, Dutch. Dutch, this is Jill."

"Hi!" Jill says, her smile beaming bright and sincere.

"Tonight," Dutch slurs at me, his eyes dead set on mine while he totally ignores Jill. "Tonight...I will drop my balls on your forehead while you sleep."

"What?!" Jill exclaims.

"My balls and your forehead, Kal..." Dutch says cryptically as he slowly pulls his drunken mess of a face away from me. He stumbles a few feet from us. "Sleep with one eye open, fucker!" he yells as he walks away, pointing at his balls just before he points at my head.

"Ooooo-kay..." Jill says with a shocked smile.

"Yeeeeeah..." I say, having no other words to explain the moment. "That's Dutch. He likes to put his balls on things when he's drunk..."

"Like your forehead?"

"Ummm..." Fuck! This was a stupid fucking idea. I just started dating the girl and she's already repulsed. "Well, he puts his balls on all kinds of things. He hasn't put them on my head yet though. I think that's why he wants to. It's like a challenge to him. That's why I lock the door and sleep with a

7

shotgun and…"

"Kal?" Jill says, interrupting me. "You're rambling."

"Sorry about that…"

"Well, since he's so hell-bent on dipping his balls on your head tonight," she starts, "why don't you just stay at my place?"

"Tonight?" Jackpot. Something tells me I'll actually enjoy waking up tomorrow morning.

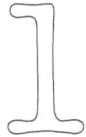

A Day in the Life

Six Months Later...

Nobody enjoys waking up. It's the worst part of the day.

I'm still asleep, but I lift my head up anyway. I crack my eyelids and let the light burn in. It always takes about 45 seconds for me to get re-oriented. The day feels half-over when I come around, but then I get really depressed because I know it's only started. Out of habit, I look to the right side of my bed—the part pushed against the wall—and look to see if anyone is there. Nobody ever is. Ever. All I see is fake wood paneling against the stained end of my mattress with no sheets.

Morning breath is sitting thick and hot in my mouth, waiting for me to blindly sway my arms around, looking for something to drink. I only find near-empty water bottles, the bottom halves stained a tarnished yellow from cigarette filters and whatever shit they put in them to keep us coming back for more. My chest pounds; the wear and tear caused by smoking a pack and a half the day before makes me feel like a tank was just dumped onto my rib cage. This is how I wake up. This is how I feel every morning.

This semester, every day starts at 9:30 a.m. I'm used to sleeping until noon before I have to go anywhere. Wally, the housemate I share a bedroom with, always wakes up before me—sometime around 8. This always throws me off. Whenever his alarm goes off, I spend 15 minutes whacking at my alarm, trying to get the noise to stop. I hate that alarm clock noise. Each loud, piercing beep feels like napalm spreading through the back of my skull.

When this little ritual is done, I awake to an empty room. Well, almost—the only other creatures in my room are flies. Flies don't normally fester a place in early February, at least not in Pennsylvania. We have the only house in this frozen state that has fly problems in the winter—a constant testament to how disgusting our hole of a house is. To make things weirder, I swear the flies have sex on my alarm clock. I watch them every morning while I sit on my bed and spin my head in circles to get the kinks out. It only takes a couple of minutes for a pair of flies to land, one pouncing on the other from behind. I watch as one fly forces a strangely sensual display of power onto the other. It doesn't look any different than two people going at it doggy-style. I've been seeing them do this for months. Dried specks of brown, sticky stuff—fly run-off, maybe?—get all over my hand every time I slap onto the snooze bar.

Almost every morning, I trip on all the shit we have spewed upon the stairs, and every morning I barely save myself by clinging to a piece of fake wood paneling that is hanging on the wall. The entire downstairs of the place looks like it's in a state of constant hangover from the long night before. Crumpled, ripped papers are common, so are half-empty cans of beer and soda loaded with cigarette butts. Usually, at least one ceramic plate is broken in the corner of the room, with leftover grease and ketchup stains on the shattered pieces. Old newspapers, junk mail and used wrappers make up the rest of the mess.

I swear to myself every morning that I'm going to make a good breakfast for myself—toast, eggs, maybe some juice—I never do. I'm a lazy shit. Even if I do find some motivation, most of the stuff in our fridge is half past dead. There are stains painting the walls and floor on the inside of the fridge as if it were a crime scene. The only things that stay alive in that fridge are soda, beer and bottled water.

This is the part of the morning where I get enraged. I realize, for the first of many times though out the day, that I am a fucking cliché. The binging, the messy house, the rotting fridge—I've become nothing but a novelty poster a freshman would hang in his new dorm, right next to a mixology chart, a random naked chick and a list of multiple empty shot glasses cleverly titled "What I Really Did in College." And there I would be. A poster. Standing in my wasteland of a house, wearing my fraternity letters, buried in broken bottles and empty beer cans with some stupid look on my face and something retarded like "What's class?" printed in bold white across the bottom. This is my life. This is what I've become. I hear the snooty 16-year-old I used to be crying out from inside of me. He sits there in a constant protest, resenting what he'll ultimately become. The only rebellious, unique part of my being, and I repress and ignore it. I have to. If I don't, I'll fall into depression, and with depression comes "The Stare." The Stare is an occurrence that manifests at times when my brain just isn't there. The most common time is in the early morning hours while I sit in my heap of a vehicle, waiting for the inch-deep coating of frost to melt away from the hood and windshield. Lately, The Stare comes a lot more often. I caught myself doing it yesterday when I was eating dinner. It happened again when I was driving. It happened at the bar last night for probably a good 20 minutes before I even realized what was going on. The problem with The Stare isn't the fact that I look like I fell off the short bus. No, the real problem is that I have no idea what's going on while I'm staring. I usually don't know what I'm staring at, and I'm usually so zoned out that I have no idea what's going on around me. When The Stare is over, I usually act and sound more depressed than a Radiohead CD.

This is my regular morning. These are just some of the broken pieces of my crappy life.

I don't exactly feel like scraping the ice off my car this

morning. Laziness is becoming a regular part of my life. Luckily, I have a back up plan: Jay—another component of the quartet that dwells in our place on Cohen Street. We have class at the same time everyday, and on cue, he comes outside just in time.

"I need a ride again," I say.

"Your car still broken?"

"It's not broken."

"Oh, God!" he exclaims. "I mean, why the hell would I think that? I just assumed that was the reason for you acting like a lazy shit, sitting in my car smoking cigarettes while I scrape the hell out of my windshield."

Jay is a tiny, bitter man. Measuring a diminutive 5'7, he often feels like he's getting the short end of the stick, pun intended.

"I just don't feel like driving."

"I know, because you're a lazy shit," he says, once again, as he unlocks the driver's door of his '91 Beretta. He's looking at me with beady, little eyes peaking out from the bottom of a knit hat.

"I had a long night, and I really don't feel like driving this morning." I hope he doesn't remember that I used that excuse yesterday.

"You said that yesterday. Besides, you didn't have a long night. You went to bed at 8. I know this because you decided to sleep with every fucking light in the house turned on."

"I know. It was…really dark." He's staring through me like I'm invisible. He opens up the door and throws his backpack onto the back seat. "Okay, you're right. I had no real reason. I just forgot to turn them off."

"You have to say more than that, or I won't give you a ride."

"Like what?"

"You know what I want to hear."

"I am a lazy, worthless piece of shit."

"Yeah, I know," Jay stands there looking at me, waiting for more.

"Do you want me scrape the windshield?"

I finally get Jay to crack a smirk underneath those beady, little eyes. "Scraper is in the glove box."

My bare hands blister and chap as flakes of shaved ice fly against them with each scrape. If I knew I'd be doing this, I would have just fucking done this for my car. The back door of our house slams again as Barry, the fourth member of our group, exits the house.

"Sup?" he asks with a casual nod, approaching his car right next to us. His burly shoulders hold steady as he waltzes towards us with a lazy swagger.

"Yo," I respond while continuously slashing at the ice. Jay responds with a nod in Barry's direction.

"Why are you scraping his car?" Barry asks, confused as hell.

"Because he's my boyish man-bitch," Jay responds.

"Oh," Barry says, surprisingly understanding of Jay's answer. "Only a little more than seven hours left," he says, reminding us that Happy Hour is fast approaching.

"Nice..." Jay says, keeping his eyes on me, assuring that he can continue to enjoy the spectacle I provide while doing his grunt work.

The slamming of another door rings from a short distance. The big, fat kid who lives next door wobbles out silently, glaring at us as he slowly approaches his massive pickup truck.

"Morning!" Barry yells, throwing an arm to greet the goliath as he moves forward like a sloth. Fats gives him no response.

"The fuck's up with that guy?" Jay asks. "He's got some kinda hate on for us or something."

"Yeah, that's probably my fault," Barry says, unlocking his car door.

"Why?" I ask.

"I think he's still mad about me passing out and puking in the back of his pick-up," he says, sliding his large, massive, ex-high school linebacker body into his car. The car bounces

13

slowly on the shocks as he fits himself in. "Some people, huh?"

"When we gonna start drinkin'?" Jay asks just as Barry's about to close the door.

"Patience, darlin'" Barry says as he closes the car door. "Patience."

"Your steed is ready, sire," I say, throwing his scraper across the hood of the car. Barry's muffler coughs and puffs like a cancer patient as he drives away.

"Hey!" Jay yells. "Watch my fucking paint job!"

"What paint job?" I ask. "The thing's got more scratches than a fucking cat toy."

"And you missed some of the ice…" he says, evaluating the windshield.

"Will you just get in the fuckin' car already and take me to my fuckin' class?"

*   *   *

It's not a long trip to Stanley Hall, the building where we have our first classes of the day. We don't have time to get into any real conversations. Even if we did have that kind of time, it's too early and neither of us are "morning people" enough to start yapping. I just sit there with a cigarette, blowing smoke out the side of my mouth.

The longest part of the trip begins only a few houses down from ours. This is where Jill lives. Every Monday, Wednesday and Friday at this time, we drive by her house on the way to class. I see her walk outside with Fernando, her Latin lover. I see her kiss him deeply, the butterflies in her stomach visible while she does it. This is one of the hardest parts of my day. My jeans have marks around my knees from squeezing so hard while I watch. I know he slept over again. I know he fucked her again. Jill and I may not have a future, but our history is enough to keep me occupied. I'm really pathetic like that.

"I feel like drinking tonight." Jay says. He doesn't realize

14

I'm only half listening to his attempt at small talk. "I think I might get a case after class. Get an early start."

"Well, it is Friday," I reply. I'm on autopilot when I talk. I'm too busy concentrating on Jill and the Spanish Fly over there. Standing on the front door step, rubbing noses and baby talking. I watch them do this, watch as they ignore the musk that's probably hanging off his body from a night of throwing his dick in her. Every Monday, Wednesday and Friday, I swallow hard and try to hold back the vomit caused by the nerves bouncing around in my stomach—the kind of nerves you only get when you see lost opportunity cuddle and woo with someone else right before your eyes.

Learning Curve

We climb up the stairwell of Stanley Hall, reluctant as always. It's so early in the morning that I'm convinced the cold has frozen the water in my muscles. Each thigh feels like it weighs three times what it should and moves as slowly as sap dripping down a pine tree. Each step up the stairs is a challenge while trying to heat up in the lukewarm building. Berkshire University is one of those places in the world where lukewarm is the best you can hope for. Jay was kind enough to park about a mile away from the building—dickhead. I've never seen anyone get such a hard-on for pissing people off. We split up at the top of the steps, going into different directions, barely a word exchanged when we do.

Advanced Communications is my first class of the day. I've had better classes. Chip is our professor. Everyone has met Chip before, they just may not realize it. Chip was cut from a mold, which was made in a factory out in Ohio before he was shipped out to universities across the country. Chip has a head of lush hair that's barely tainted by the gray that comes with age. He has one of those scalps that have only given up in certain spots. In this case, it's in the front— just atop his forehead—leaving only a peninsula of hair on what used to be a widow's peak. The other Chips of the world are known for having similar hair, give or take an extra inch of length. Like this Chip, they have the mentality of a quickly aging 26-year-old in the body of a pot-bellied, 55-

year-old. Yeah, the Chips of the world are everywhere. Ours is fortunate enough to fit into his old clothes from the 70's, giving him the look of a washed-up, cowboy porn star. The Chips never use chairs—they always sit on the desk instead. And, of course, it's hard to forget one of the most endearing qualities of the Chips: they always insist against formalities. After all, "Mr. <insert your Chip's last name here>" is his father's name. The world never gets sick of that little gem.

Chip, as usual, is late. He feels that wearing a watch makes you uptight. Probably. I don't know. I'm just assuming that he feels that way. I take my regular seat behind the fat chick that always leaves class early to get to the cafeteria before they stop serving those Egg McMuffin knock-offs that they sell. She says she leaves early so she can make it to her next class in time, but we all know the truth.

I can't help sitting with my head rested in my arms staring at the seat cattycorner from me. This is where the Hot Liberal Arts Chick that doesn't date frat guys sits. I always dig girls like that. Maybe it's that whole "I hated you before I met you" style she walks around with that turns me on. Either that or because she gives off that mystery vibe that sucks you in and leaves you baffled over little details like what her underwear looks like or if she sleeps naked. Maybe I want her because I can't have her. She seems like one of those girls who probably weren't given much attention in high school. I'm betting she didn't start looking really hot until the summer after she graduated. She probably dates some guy who's studying civil engineering at MIT. She probably sits around with her roommates in tight little cut-off sweat shorts and talks about how it's hard being in a long-distance relationship, but it's "so totally worth it" because he wants to change the world and that's so romantic and blah, blah, blah. I'm betting she's either like that, or she digs bad boys. I'm neither.

When I see her walk in, hair in a ponytail, thong sticking out of her sweat pants when she sits down, I get shifted into thinking about time travel. I think about going back in time a lot. I think all people do secretly. It'd be so nice to know what I know now back when I started college. I'd go back and tell little, wide-eyed Kalvin L. Gray all the right things to do and say. I would have definitely been able to lie and work the whole "noble diligence" or "misogynistic bad ass" angle perfectly, and I could've spent the better part of my college years banging girls like her. That'd be so friggin' hot.

While leering at the Hot Liberal Arts Chick, I notice she's giving me a bit of a stare back, which is hot. The bad part is that it's not so much of a "yeah, daddy, come and tease me" kind of stare. It's more of a baffled, "what the hell?" kind of stare. I'm not really surprised by it. I just woke up—I probably look and smell like an elephant's ball sack. Whatever.

A funny feeling comes over me. I look around the room and realize that aside from the fat chick and Hot Liberal Arts Chick, nobody is sitting near me. There's a circle of empty desks around me, like a buffer zone. I look over to my left and see shy, blonde girl. She turns her head quickly. Behind her is retarded stoner guy, who's just looking at me with glazed eyes and a sneered lip. Whatever. They can probably smell the gas I just squeezed out of my ass. I hope it burns their nose hairs.

Five minutes later, and Chip still isn't here. I'll be pissed if he doesn't show up. I hate waking up for nothing. I notice that the stares are starting to get more constant. In the corner of my right eye, I keep catching emotionally misdirected jock aiming his big, heavy brow at me. I get the feeling that he's planning on taking me out to the bar and date-raping me in the mouth like he probably has to so many guys in the past. This class is annoying enough without having to worry about being subjected to the wonton desires of Berkshire University's third-string cornerback. Three seats right of him is some really short girl that I've never seen before in my life, who is also staring at me. Only her stare kind of freaks me out, probably because she's cross-eyed.

Finally, Chip walks into class a total of 10 minutes late. That goddamn "seven-minute rule" joke has been said seven times—I counted. It's Friday, which means it's donut day. Under his right arm are two boxes of donuts. In a constant effort to prove he's not a typical college professor, Chip always brings donuts for his class on Friday. My fat ass has yet to find a problem with this.

"Wha'sup guys?" Chip's typical greeting. Ugh. "As you know, it's donut day, so help yourself." Chip drops the boxes on his desk and opens one of them. He opens his backpack—yeah, he wears a backpack since he rides his bike to work—and pulls out his grade book. He starts gliding his eyes back and forth, from his book to the audience in front of him. "Perfect attendance," he mutters, putting down his book. "That's just awesome. Y'know, I got no problem buying donuts for you guys if you come to class. Believe me, I remember how hard it was coming to class this early on a Friday. Anyone have any idea how many times I used to say 'Fuck it' and turn off my alarm on days like this?" Chip admits with a chuckle. That's right—like all the Chips of the world, he's the cool teacher who curses.

"Probably about six times less than I did this morning!" says the douche bag suck-up who lives to clean Chip's dick with his tongue. He chuckles some more before saying "I fuckin' hate your class, Chip!"

"Ha! And this is coming from one of my advisees!" Chip chuckles a little more before he hands a box of donuts to the suck-up. "Take some and pass them around, you lil' sonnuva bitch."

Chip reaches into his backpack and pulls out an empty plastic jar. The label has been peeled off, and the cap has a slit in it, obviously carved with a knife. I don't know what the fuck he's collecting for, but my poor, broke ass will have nothing to do with it.

"As some of you may have already heard," Chip begins, his voice suddenly grim and low, "Connie Ward, one of my advisees, was assaulted and nearly raped last week behind Dill's Bar. Connie should be getting out of the hospital later this week. Since the incident, she's missed about a week of

19

work. For those of you who don't know Connie, she works full-time in the cafeteria in order to pay for her time here at Berkshire. The other professors in the department and I all agreed that it'd be a nice thought to start up a collection to help cover the money Connie won't be able to make while she's recovering. I'm just going to pass this around the class right now. If you want to leave a donation later, you can find donation bins in the teachers' lounge and my office."

Chip passes the jar to the suck-up, who puts in about 10 different bills. Even in charity he kisses ass. While the jar goes around, I focus my attention on something much hotter: Hot Liberal Arts Chick holding onto the box of donuts that have been passed around for the last five minutes. She takes out a plain glazed and puts it down on the top half of her notebook. She whips her ponytail around as she turns to me and hands the box my way. She puts her index finger in her mouth and starts to suck on it, lowering her lips halfway down, and then dragging her smooth, puffy lips back up. She drops her jaw slightly, circling her finger around the inside rim of her lips just before she dips the finger further in her mouth. Keeping her mouth open just enough to show her tongue grinding against her moist finger, she mutters out one of the hottest things I've ever heard:

"Here you go, Kalvin."

The rest of the class is fixated on Chip's little "Ode to Connie." I only feel kind of guilty about not paying attention while I mentally masturbate to the little show Hot Liberal Arts Chick just put on for me. I have to admit, I don't even care that much about watching her finger her mouth; I popped half a chub just hearing her say my name. Hell, I didn't even think she knew my name. Wow. That was incredible. That's just another thing I love about girls like her: they all have these hot, devilish, just plain slutty sides to them that they are itching to show. Part of me wonders if it's normal to be damn near creaming my pants just because I heard a hot girl saying my name. Another part of me tells me I'm a completely love-starved pussy for acting this way. A third part of me tells me not to get worked up over her. The forth tells me that I shouldn't care about this because someday Jill is going to come back to me. The fifth and final part is my favorite: it doesn't tell me anything at all—it just focuses on ripping at her clothes with my claws and teeth before I throw her against something and have vulgar, demeaning sex with her.

Of course, she's already turned around towards the front of the class again by the time I finish digesting all this. I notice the fat chick in front of me is turned around. She's sweating—who the hell sweats in the middle of the winter? She's eyeing the donuts.

"You planning on sharing them with anyone else today, sweety?"

"Are you?" I reply. I don't think she likes me much as I hand her the box.

"Listen, I don't want to be here. I have to leave soon to make it to my next class, and I just want my damn donut before I go."

"Sure. Wouldn't want to starve you before you have a chance to dig into a breakfast burrito." Hot Liberal Arts Chick snickers as I say it. I think I just felt my dick jitter a little.

"Jesus Christ!" yells the fat chick. "I am so fucking sick of you elitist frat guys going around acting like you're fucking better than everyone!" Whoa. "Just because you think you're so damn perfect doesn't mean you have to hold everyone else up to your standards!"

"The hell you talking about? I'm 15 pounds overweight, and I'm wearing a stained undershirt! How the hell could I be an elitist?" By this point, Chip and the rest of the class have stopped what they're doing to listen to us. "I mean, Jesus, look at me here! Do I look 'elite' to you? For fuck's sake, my shoes have holes in them!"

"Oh, so now you want everyone to feel sorry for you?"

"No..."

"Awwww! Poor little guy can't afford shoes! But you can

21

still afford a pedestal to stand on while you spit insults on people!"

"What the fuck?!" I exclaim. "I've never even talked to you before!"

"Of course you haven't!" she says, flailing her arms towards me. "People like you can't be bothered talking to little 'peons' like me! All you have time for is making remarks about how we're ugly or fat or not as well dressed!"

"Whoa, whoa…wait a sec," my face is chilly with sweat and red hot with embarrassment. "Aren't you being a little melodramatic here?"

"Who are you to sit there and bark out derogatory remarks about people like me?" Clearly, she can only hear herself at this point. "I'm friggin' tired of people like you! You, and everyone like you, can go and fuck yourselves in the ass with a hot iron rod!"

With that, everyone in the class, including Chip starts clapping for her while she walks out of the room with a tear in her eye.

"What the hell just happened?" I ask.

Everyone looks at me, expecting me to make some kind of rebuttal in my defense, and I wish I could. But honestly, what the hell can I say to that? Each person's look of expectation begins to sour into a look of anger and resentment. With a speech she probably knocked off from *The Breakfast Club*, Fat Chick has just completely demonized me to a class of my peers—during a speech about an attempted rape victim, no less.

"Here ya go, sweetie." I look over to see Hot Liberal Arts Chick handing me the plastic donation jar. Everyone is still staring at me. Either they still haven't cooled off from seeing me destroy an overweight girl's self-esteem with just a few words and no actions, or they're giving me a small chance to redeem myself. They're sitting there in wait, looking to see the extent of my guilt. They want to see if I'll make it up to all the downtrodden masses of the world with a small donation. They want to measure my worth in pocket change.

"Um…here," I mutter to the person closest to me as I pass the jar. "I don't have any money on me…" The room immediately fills with angry moans and venom-soaked hisses. The girl I'm trying to pass the jar to stares at me with a look so mortified that it could peel paint from the wall. "Seriously! I really don't have any money on me!" The hisses get louder. Any chance I convinced myself of having with Hot Liberal Arts Chick evaporates. Chip just leans against his desk and shakes his head. On this day, the devil invaded Berkshire University, and his name is Kalvin Gray.

The rest of the class drips by slower than hunks of wet sand out of a beach pail. Chip, as usual, didn't lecture, teach or even bring up the topic of Advanced Communications. He mostly sat on his desk and talked about a time he got drunk at a wedding and got two separate blowjobs from two of the bridesmaids in the same bathroom stall. Two girls from the Women's Empowerment Club left after hearing about the first bridesmaid.

The class ends, and immediately a small crowd bottlenecks towards the door. Even this early in the morning, people are able to summon up an amazing amount of energy to get on with the rest of their day. People crowd along the inside of the room, lining the walls along the door. Constant glares and stares keep coming my way. Everyone looks at me like I'm the "Dickhead of the Year." Guess I can't blame them. I had a chance to prove my worth by donating to the Connie fund, and gave shit. My opportunity for looking good in their eyes has sunk like a fat guy in a kayak.

Chip is leaning casually against his desk, arms folded, a cocky glare painted across his face. His eyes set on me and stick like flies on a donut. Everyone else thinks I'm a douche right now, why shouldn't he?

"Kal?" Chip calls, as I approach the crowded doorway. "Have a nice day." His voice is creepy and leering, like a child molester. Why did he say "nice" so weird?

"What?" I ask. He doesn't respond. He stares at me, smirking as if he just pulled off the crime of the century. I shrug at him, and still no response. Creep.

In the hallway, I feel like a million stares are glued to my body and eating away at my skin. It's getting stuffy in here. I feel like taking off my coat, but I only have a white under-shirt on, and the armpits are caked a shade of piss-yellow from profuse sweating. The back of my head burns. It feels itchy underneath my fingernails. Little beads perspire from my forehead. What the hell is going on?

"Hey, Kalvin." I turn around and see Hot Liberal Arts Chick, in all her slender glory. "How's it going?"

"Hey...you. What's up?" Weird just got weirder.

"Not much. You look like you're having a rough day."

"Yeah, kinda," I reply. "And it's only 10 am." What am I doing? I don't even know her name.

"I'm really glad you told that girl off. I hate that girl. She lived down the hall from me my first semester. She's always been really self-righteous like that. I thought it was cool how you stood up to her though."

"Yeah, I guess...if you consider that standing up to her."

Crap. I've got nothing here. What the hell am I going to say to her? This is my chance to "wow" her, and I don't have shit to say. I hate these weird moments. She's going to think I'm autistic unless I say something soon. Either that or she'll leave. Yeah, that's what'll happen. And then I'll blow any chance with her. That sounds about right.

"Hey, you and your friends usually go to the bar for happy hour, don't you?" she asks, with one of the sexiest smiles ever recorded by human eyes. "I'll probably be there tonight, if you want to talk about all this...get it off your chest..." she says this while putting her hand on my chest. Holy shit...Hot Liberal Arts Chick is flirting with me! As long as I don't sweat or pop a wood, I should be okay.

"Sure. Sounds cool." That's right, playa. I want to ask how she knows what my friends and I do on Fridays, but I should keep it simple. Chicks dig the whole "man of a few words" routine.

"Allrigty! See you then." She starts to walk, but then stops after a few steps, whips her ponytail around, and faces me again. "By the way, my name is Katie, in case you forgot to ask." She smiles, "See ya!"

"Okay. See you later, Katie," I say while I wave goodbye. My hand feels heavy and numb as I sway it back and forth. Is it bad that she knew that I didn't know her name?

People whisper and stare some more as I pace down the hall. I walk through a gauntlet of whispers and appalled faces armed with pointing fingers. My ears pick up waves of incomplete, whispered sentences.

"...looks really creepy," I hear in a hushed girl's voice.

"No, the one from the poster..." I hear from another direction.

I'm starting to feel sick, and I don't know why. I feel acid in my stomach climbing up and sliding back down again as if it were a water slide. I feel the heat from each of the florescent lights I walk under as they burn the top of my head while I rush further down the hall and around the corner. Room 214. That's where Jay had class. I think. I could just walk the mile home, but I want to get far away from this place as quickly as I can. Not only do I want to get out of here fast, but it's fucking cold out—I don't want to walk in that.

Before I turn the next corner, I hear the muzzled roar of a small crowd. It doesn't sound like it could be more than 10 people. On top of the low whispering, I hear a familiar cackling. It layers itself above the noise of the crowd. It sounds like a high-pitched squeak coming from the rusty springs of an old bed, and it follows a specific pattern:

"Ha, ha, ha-haha. Hahaha-haha. Ha, ha, ha-haha."

I turn the corner and there he is: Wally, my roommate. He's slightly bent over, with his left hand on his left knee for support while he's laughing. He's decked out in his typical wardrobe: backwards black baseball cap, long-sleeved t-shirt and a pair of size 36 jeans hanging from his size 32 waist. His tiny eyes are squinting as he laughs his ass off over something hanging on the wall. Apparently he's the only one laughing at this. Everyone else looks pissed enough to be watching a Gallagher stand-up routine.

I take a few steps towards Wally before he turns to his side and sees me approaching. His machine gun-like cackling transforms into all-out howling once he catches me in his sites. Everyone else moves his or her glare from the wall to our general direction.

"What is it?"

"Did you see this yet?" Wally asks, gasping for air, taking only a second to squeeze out the question before he starts bursting out into more laughter.

"See what?"

"You serious? You haven't seen it yet?"

I push Wally aside and move closer towards the wall. I can't see what's on the wall too well; all I can see is a cork bulletin board with a bunch of scattered papers hastily stapled and push-pinned onto it. Usually this thing is masked with "help-wanted" flyers, or "roommate needed" ads, or those things that have all the little slips of paper cut into the bottom of it with a name and phone number you could take home with you. I try to ease my way through about four people who are reading something towards the bottom half of the board. Wally, who's full-on laughing has now subsided into minor chuckling while he catches his breath, is pushing on my back, forcing me closer to the board.

"This is fucking great! You gotta read this!" he snorts out through his giggling. I force myself between the four people who are making perturbed faces at me while I make my way to the center of attention. I finally catch the top half of what everyone is looking at. It reads in big, black, copier machine-print, "Have you seen this man?" I start to inch closer to the flyer, and under the top line there's a guy with bushy hair, big eyes, thick eyebrows and a narrow nose. Underneath him is a description:

Suspect is said to have dark-blonde hair, which is short and feels "bushy."

Suspect weighs between 190 to 200lbs., measures approx. 5'8 to 5'11.

He was last seen assaulting the victim behind Dill's Bar on Street Rd.

Suspect was reported wearing fraternity letters, blue jeans, light-colored sneakers and a black coat.

Suspect was later seen driving a dark-colored Chevy Caviler.

Wanted for questioning on the assault of Connie Ward.

"Dude! That's you!" Wally says before he starts giggling again.

"What're you talking about?"

"You kidding? The sketch even looks like you!" The crowd is hearing us. I'm starting to get more of the same looks I've been getting all morning.

"Okay, maybe it does a little. But except for that it's nothing like me. Well, he has the same kind of car and a black coat. And he's in a fraternity."

"...and the same hair cut and hair color. And he's, like, the same height and weight and everything! Hahaha! You're wanted for attempted rape! I gotta call Barry!"

Wally goes on about how funny this is. He's fucking sick in the head. I take another look at the giant flyer, easily a foot long and getting bigger. I guess I could see how it looks kind of like me. Maybe. I wonder if it'd be an admittance of guilt if I pulled the flyer down. The crowd is glaring at me more and more. Each face twists and turns as it gets an eyeful of the guy they think attacked poor Connie Ward.

The crowd starts to shift and churn. Some people leave. Others turn to the person next to them and whisper with their eyes fixed on me. I can physically feel how uneasy this small group of people is starting to act. I'm sweating and squirming where I stand. I can feel a cool breeze inside the back of my pants as my ass sweats and drips down the back of my thighs. I spin my head and look at the people around me. My arms and hands shake with paranoia. The only things this crowd is missing are torches and pitchforks. My stomach feels like it's boiling a little more each time I look at these people. I start to slowly walk backwards, wiping sweat from off my wet forehead. Everything goes silent and slow. I can still see Wally laughing, but I can't hear him. Every step I take away from the mob makes me feel like they're taking two more towards me. Everything slurs to a stop as two words flat on hit the front of my brain and immediately drip out of my mouth in a mutter:

"Oh, fuck…"

Renegade!

"Hehehe…nice." Barry says as he sinks into the broken couch. He's holding the "wanted" flyer in one and a cigarette dripping out of the fingers of the other.

"Don't laugh!" I yell. If they weren't so distracted by the wanted poster, they'd probably laugh at the shitty attempt of intimidation laced through my voice.

"I don't know. I thought it was pretty damn funny when I saw it," Jay interjects as he throws his backpack to the ground. "You're a wanted man."

"It doesn't look like me."

"Dude, it flat out describes you perfectly. It's got the weight, height and dress code down," says Barry, who has only stopped laughing five minutes ago. "It's even got your car on there." He shakes his head with a smile as he takes a deep drag of his cigarette. Wally is sitting in the kitchen, still laughing at the whole situation. Actually, now I think he's just laughing at the flyer itself. He's been doodling over the sketch for the past 20 minutes, drawing fake mustaches and shit.

"You should turn yourself in for the reward," Wally suggests subtly.

"I don't think there is a reward," I say going towards the easy chair and brushing off a collection of old trash and newspaper before I plop down into it. "Okay," I say, "let me ask you guys this: Did you immediately think this was supposed to be me when you saw it?"

"Yeah," says Barry.

"Yeah," says Jay.

"Yup," says Wally, who's now burning yellow, singed holes through the eyes of the police sketch with his cigarette.

"Dammit! The hell am I supposed to do?" I ask. "If you guys thought it was me, everyone else on campus is going to think so too."

"I don't see what the big deal is," Barry says nonchalantly. He hands me a lighter after seeing me with a cigarette in my mouth and fumbling through my pockets for a match. "Just go to the Public Safety office and state your case. You didn't do it, right?" I don't even answer him. I just look at him with tired, glazed eyes. After a second, when he's not expecting it, I fling his lighter back at him and nail him clear on side of the head. I rule.

"Ahh! Dick!" he says as he flinches back.

"You're right though," I mention as I lean forward, resting my elbows on my knees. "They have to change it once I tell them it wasn't me. I got an alibi and everything."

"And what would that be?" Jay asks. He always tries to add sarcasm to everything. At least I hope that's a sarcastic question.

"I dunno. What night did it happen?" I receive blank stares from everyone. Barry dropped the flyer a minute ago, and doesn't show any signs of picking it up. I exhale a cloud of smoke and reach forward, while the rest of the room remains silent. "February 1st? That was a week ago! I don't remember what I was doing then!"

"Hehe…you were probably in your bed, not having sex," Jay spits out as he heads for the stairs.

"Fuck you, you short piece of shit! I got fleas in my ass bigger than you!" I can feel the tension in my head swelling.

"The first was a Tuesday. You were probably at Dill's for karaoke." Barry says, stroking his fingers through dark hair on the side of his head.

"Oh yeah, that'll go over well. I'll just go tell them that

this sketch couldn't be me because I was at the scene of the friggin' crime when it happened! Yeah, that'll sound real fucking great!"

"Well," Wally's voice echoes quietly from the kitchen, "if you go there, you should wear like metal pants or something."

"Why?"

"They may try to cut your dick off for evidence."

"What?!" Barry exclaims.

"The hell are you talking about?" adds Jay.

"It happened to a buddy of mine back home after he was accused of rape. Swear to God," Wally says, continually doodling on the flyer. "That's why I came here to go to school. I had to get the fuck out of Jersey. Weird shit happens in Jersey."

I'm at a loss for words. Wally gets up from the kitchen table, not saying a word after giving us his twisted, little parable and stampedes full speed up the steps to our bedroom. Barry is still sitting on the broken couch, in all his overweight glory, quiet as the farm. I tilt my head back and blow smoke into the air. The humor behind the whole thing has finally subsided, giving me time to think this through and digest it. Now that all the joking and dicking around is done, I realize just how serious this is. I realize there's a good chance I'll never get laid in Berkshire University again. I have almost a year and a half left before I graduate. Granted, my sex life is about as active as a one-legged runner, but the idea of being strictly banned from any possibility of sex is, well, scary. My eyes roll and wander around the ceiling. Directly above me, two flies are chasing one another, gliding four feet above my head, swirling in a figure 8 motion. They latch on to the wall and freeze there next to one another, before the one pounces the other. That's when the fact hits me hardest: even the flies in my house are getting laid more than I am.

The house is now totally quiet except for Barry, who is releasing slow, quiet burps every few seconds. Moments of calm like this are rare in this area. There's always something loud and obnoxious going on around me. My life feels like it's constantly pressed up against the subwoofer planted in the trunk of an I-ROC. These rare moments of tranquility are so foreign to my body; my temples still pulse to a hard, fast tempo for the first few moments of this time. But once everything adjusts, these times become an intangible form of perfection. I get a feeling in the back of my head, as if some heavy, fluid mass is being drained out through a faucet. The only things I can equate it to are those brief moments of freedom between classes. That small slip of time where you forget your previous problems right before your remember the future ones. It's one of those self-nurturing moments where it feels like your head is sealed in bubble wrap and locked in a room full of pillows. The quiet, peaceful moment lasts only 12 seconds, before Wally's stereo starts filling the suburbs with the rhythmic, rhyming difficulties of being a black guy raised in Compton. It's funny how the only people who listen to hardcore rap music anymore are skinny white kids.

*   *   *

The sun burns and blinds my eyes as I step out the back door of the house to get into my car. It's only 1:45. I have nothing to do until 5, when we go to Happy Hour. Today, I'm a little more shaky and anxious to get down there—today I've got me a sort of-date with Hot Liberal Arts Chick, or Katie, as her parents seem bent on calling her. But until then, I've got to get out of this hole. I feel so battered right now. Not in a physical way, in a mental way. I feel like my brain has been bench-pressing an anvil for the past three hours. Barry and the others sitting there while they wax re-tarded is also starting to take a toll on my stress levels. On top of that, I don't feel like hearing Wally blow his ghetto-blasting stereo for the next three hours. And I know if I stay here any longer I'm going to have to hear Jay going into a sermon about how he's the only one who cleans. To hell with all that. I'm getting out of Apocalypse-Land here and I'm putting this "assault and attempted rape" nightmare to an end. I swear to God, if those fucking jackasses in public safety give me as hard of a time about this as they give for other issues, such as parking tickets, I'm going to stab someone in the eye.

It feels warmer outside than it does inside. Of course, that's because I have the benefit of the sun outside. It's probably about 32 degrees out here, as opposed to what feels like about 25 degrees inside. We have absolutely no heat in the bottom half of the place. Sitting in the living room like we were for a prolonged period of time is a rarity.

My jacket is starting to smell. I wear this thing day in and day out. It's always too cold to take it off, even when I'm inside. Sometimes I even sleep in it. I want to take it to get it dry-cleaned or something, but I'm broke. Not only that, but if someone gets wind of me doing that, they may think I'm trying to clean off some evidence or something.

Is this really that good of an idea? To head down to public safety? They obviously have some form of the wanted poster down there. They might get suspicious when they see me and try to pull something. Shit. This is a conundrum.

When it comes down to it, I'm essentially putting my life and reputation in the hands of the mentally inept Berkshire University Public Safety Department. On the one hand, if I go there, I run the risk of being formally accused of assaulting and attempting to rape Connie, which would really suck. On the other hand, if I don't go, I'll be continually considered as Connie's attacker until public safety comes after me for questioning anyway. Then again, their department consists primarily of locals and townies that are, among many other things, dumb as dick. There's a good possibility that they may literally be too dumb to understand what I'm trying to say. If I go in there and make up some kind of lie, saying I find the sign offensive or something, they might buy it. Or not. Whatever.

We're on the corner of the street, so we only have a

neighbor on one side. One set of neighbors, and we've had them pissed at us since the second week of the Fall semester. I don't know for sure what they're pissed about. It might be from the time Wally got drunk and mooned them for 20 minutes on a Sunday morning. It might be from that one time Jay and I got drunk and threw empty cans at their windows to see if they'd bum us cigarettes. It might've been from the time Barry mentioned, when he puked and fell asleep in the flatbed of Fat's truck. I don't know. For whatever reason, they hate us and aptly refer to us as the "stupid fraternity guys."

I think there are four guys that live there. I only recognize the fat one that we saw this morning; the other three are interchangeable. The fat one is just that: fat. It's not a simple baby-fat affliction. No, this kid is, like, "medically challenged" fat. He's one of those guys that are so fat that he can be perfectly comfortable in a short-sleeved shirt while he's outside in early February, as is the case now. He's standing there, with his short sleeves rolled up, working a hibachi that has about three burgers on it. He's probably pretending that he's sharing them with his roommates, but I know the truth. Even though they hate us, I still try to be friendly with them. I don't think they appreciate it much.

"Hey," I say as I casually nod my head towards him. He doesn't give a vocal response; he just kind of gives a half-assed nod back. So much for killing them with kindness.

Out of habit, my eyes direct themselves towards Jill's place, about five houses down. I casually walk my way until I realize a little speck of a person in the distance walking off the front porch. I look a little harder and realize it is Jill, with her long, jet-black hair flowing in the gusty wind behind her as she walks towards her car parked along the curb. At the first second of recognition, my stomach drops, hits my balls and bounces back boiling. The nerves and butterflies pair up and do a waltz in my gut as I slow my pace. I don't want her to see me. I don't want to get caught in an awkward conversation. And, of course, I don't want her to tell me how scared she got when she saw a certain "wanted" poster.

I freeze in my steps. I can't think of anything. My head goes blank and my ears deafen quickly after that. I can't talk to her. Not now. If I can see her, she can see me. Living up to her "let's just be friends" creed, she's going to want to talk to me. I can't do that. I fumble for a solution that my brain won't give me. And then it comes: the most unlikely of advice, unlocked from my subconscious and thrown onto a mental table for the grabbing. It's easily the worst solution my petty, feeble brain has ever devised. I mutter it aloud to myself:

"Talk to the fat kid."

I jerk my face to the left and see him standing where I left him. He pulls a long spatula from off of the doorknob it was hanging. He's transfixed on the meat while he flips each patty over. I quickly pace in Burger Boy's direction, concocting some kind of gibberish to pass off as small talk.

"Hey, buddy! How's it going?"

"S'up." We stand there, a foot and a half apart, staring each other dead in the eye. I have a grin so fake and dirty that you could probably pick the pieces of shit out of my teeth. He stands there, jaw firm, lips straight, silently expecting a follow-up question.

"Whatcha makin'?"

"Burgers."

"I see." This is going nowhere, but that's okay. I just need to do this long enough to avoid Jill while she's packing.

"You need something?" he asks. I'm surprised. There's not quite as much hostility in his voice as I expected.

"Well...uhhh..." Secretly, in my mind, I stammer on words, trying to develop a sentence that would make this awkwardness go a little smoother. "We've been living next to each other for a little over a semester now, and I don't think we ever met or exchanged names or anything like that." He raises an eyebrow. It's not in the confused way, though. It's more like the kind of eyebrow raise you'd expect while he's thinking about how much of a joke I am. "Anyway, my name's Kal."

"Steve."

"Nice to meet you, Steve."

"Yup."

I peer down the road to see if Jill's still outside. It looks like she's going home for the weekend, as usual. I used to hate that about her when we were together.

"You guys should come over sometime. Hang out with me and my roommates."

"I don't think so."

"Why not?"

"Because you or one of your frat buddies puked in the back of my truck, then slept in it for six hours."

"Heh…yeah…" How the hell am I supposed to talk my way out of that? "Well, you know how crazy things can get on a weekend."

"It was a Sunday night! The bars aren't even open then!" Crap. Fucking Barry. "I wouldn't even mind so much if he came over and apologized, or at least offered to clean it up, or something."

"Umm…sorry?"

"Forget it, man. I'm over it." The kid continues into some kind of "forgive and forget" speech. I'm making it look like I'm paying attention, but I constantly let my eyes dance over in Jill's direction. She slams her trunk hastily and speeds herself over to the driver's side door. She pulls off, and I've gently avoided one awkward situation by diving into a different one. This sucks. "…that's why I always just say 'Shit happens,' know what I mean?"

"Oh sure. Gotta be forgiving and stuff." Okay, now I've got to think of a way to get out of this.

"I'm done out here," he says. Hmm. That was easy enough. "It's my lunch…I mean, 'our' lunchtime. These are for my roommates, too." Yeah, sure it is, Louie Anderson. He loads each patty onto a clean ceramic plate that'd last six minutes in our house.

"Take care," I say. He just waves his arm into the air, not

even turning to look at me while he enters the house.

For a second, I almost forget why I'm outside, but then I remember I was going to talk to the mutants in the public safety office. I feel rinsed with dread. It's not the kind of dread you have when you're worried about something, like when you dread seeing your ex because you don't want to get into meaningless small talk with her. No, this is a different kind of dread—the lethargic "I don't want to go to work" kind of dread. I turn around and face my car. It's looking mighty good right now. Then again, I'm still feeling a walk right about now.

"Hey, stupid! Get off my yard!" Fat Steve yells from his upstairs window. To hell with it—I'm driving.

It's a cliché, but you really can tell someone's personality by taking a ride in his or her car. Mine's a cluttered mess. The floor of the passenger and back areas are carpeted with handouts from classes I had two years ago. A pile of clean, folded laundry has held shotgun for the past two weeks. The back is packed with empty soda bottles, two ice scrapers, a paintbrush, an old toothbrush, a back pack with no zipper, roughly 100 empty cigarette packs and various pieces of clutter I can't even recognize. My car, my personality. This is why I'm a friggin' screw-up trapped in the dirty chunk of permafrost that's been dubbed "Berkshire University."

My car takes some time to warm up. Hasn't been used since I came back from home two weeks ago. The clock reads 2:00. I have nothing but time. The fact sinks in that I just went to great lengths to avoid a small conversation with a girl I once had relations with, just because I don't feel adequate enough. I stare through a dirty, crusted windshield, and all I can hear is that 16-year-old version of me coming out to play.

"You're a coward, a fucking coward!" he says. It's not my fault. I was a rebound for her. I was her boyfriend for the time her and Fernando were separated. I'm better than that. I don't have to feel obligated to talk to her.

"But you feel obligated to think about her, coward. You

and her happened months ago. Quit pussying around and get over it!" Little 16-year-old Kalvin L. Gray. Deep down, I know that I'm crazy, and I am letting my psychotic feelings manifest in a comfortable form. In this case, it's the voice of a younger me screaming profanities at screwed-up, present-day me. Makes me wonder—will they take the form of present-day me when they're yelling at screwed-up, future me? This odd loop of future Kals crossing paths with past and present Kals fills and swarms the mind. I think about all this but not in detail. In fact, it doesn't even feel like I'm thinking about it all. It's almost like this concept is someone standing at the door that refuses to come in. I couldn't think if I tried. I feel blank. Empty. Deserted.

I feel a constant gust of warm air blowing in my face and rising into my nostrils. My eyes feel dry and scratched from the fake warm air coming out of the vents and that's when it hits me. I don't realize what's been going on until I look at the clock, now reading 2:06. Shit. The Stare. Another six minutes of my life, gone. Wasted. Burned up by thoughts that never happened.

Bound to Happen

"Amanda is different from Janelle. Janelle is different from Ryan. Ryan is different from Patrick. Patrick is different from Amanda. They may be different, but they are united by one thing: friendship."

This is what the Multicultural Club tries to pass off as a public service announcement. Who asked them to do such a thing is beyond me. If I was going to try to spruce up Berkshire with a spiffy array of cheap paper and shoddy Photoshop work, I don't think I'd turn to the Multicultural Club for help. Why don't they just get President Luther, the illustrious leader of our school, to set up some kind of campaign? I, for one, would feel more motivated to enlighten myself on the benefits of diversity if it came from a poster of the man the Pennsylvania State System of Higher Education pays ungodly amounts of money to act as the silent figurehead of the campus. But that's just me.

Berkshire University's Public Safety office is filled with tons of these little posters and flyers. The wall is layered with sheets upon sheets of posters from every little nonsense shit group that has formed on campus over the years: the Future Atheist Club, the Leaders of America Club, the Leaders of Campus Club, the Interpretive Dance Club, Future Republicans Club, the Anti-Republican Club, the Anime Club, the Hang Gliding Club, the Rastafarian Club, the Fight Racism Club—the list goes on.

I'm trying to read all these signs for amusement while I wait in a long-ass line of Berkshire students who've decided to file grievances towards one party or another with the public safety office. It's down to one person in front of me. I want to step closer to the signs, but I'll be damned if I lose my spot now. My cell phone reads 2:45. Goddamn, this ate a lot of my day.

One last person in front of me. That's it. But, because I'm already having an awesome day, I'm going to just go ahead and assume that this person is going to waste everyone's time by complaining about something that nobody has a relevant solution to. It's some weasely looking guy—most likely a freshman—and whatever he's bitching about, he's doing it in a hushed, nasal voice. Fine. All the better for me. I don't really want to hear his problems; I just want him to hurry up. I don't have anywhere special to be for almost two hours, but that doesn't mean I want to waste them here.

My eyes drift around the room. Directly next to the dozens of club posters hangs a cork bulletin board with the word "B.U. Blotter" stapled along the top in blue, construction paper cutout letters. The printing is too small to see from here, but my guess is that it's just a bunch of police reports from all sorts of incidents. I try making one of them out, but I can't. Instead, my eyes are pulled towards a poster of a very familiar face: mine.

"Oh, what the fuck?!" I exclaim.

"HEY!" A shrill, blood-thickening screech rips through my ears and tears my attention behind me. Gone is the hushed, nasal freshman. Here now stands an old lady—the sole public safety worker behind the desk this afternoon. Apparently, it's my turn. "We don't use that language in this office!"

"I'm sorry, I was…"

"Now, I want you to repeat what you said, but replace that word with something more acceptable."

"What?"

"Come now! Be a gentleman! You wouldn't want to leave

my virgin ears in this condition, would you?" The old lady, a quintessential member of the indomitable force that makes up our public safety office, is staring at me with a smile that resembles cracked ice more than a grin. She has inch-thick glasses balanced on her nose, and one of those tacky, bead-like necklace things that swoops around her neck and connects to her glasses. And as for her "virgin ears," some-thing tells me she lost all forms of her virginity about 40 years ago in an incident that involved a clambake and her father's best friend.

"Now make quick with it. Correct yourself," she insists.

"What the...crap?" I don't think I can think of a suitable, family-friendly version of the word "fuck."

"Much better!" Her face and neck shakes and hangs more like a wet, brown paper bag than wrinkled flesh. "Now what can I help you with?"

"It's about that 'wanted' sign that's been hung up around campus," I say in my most humble voice, nodding in the direction of the poster on the blotter.

"Oh, can you believe it? That poor girl..."

"Yeah..." I say in a voice that wouldn't at all imply that I was humoring her, "but, like I was saying, is there any way you could maybe replace it with a sign that doesn't have a sketch on it?"

"Why would we need to do that?" Her icy, cracked smile straightens out and snaps shut. Her brow sinks with suspicion.

"Well, the thing is, there's a whole shitload..."

"HEY! What did we just talk about?"

"Sorry! Sorry...I mean crapload! There's a whole *crapload* of people who think this looks just like me."

"And?" she shoots from her straight lips as she crosses her arms.

"And?!" I yell. "And it's not supposed to look like me!"

"And why's that?"

"Because it's not me!"

"Well, how do I know it's not you?" Christ. I knew this

41

was going to happen. I just fucking knew it. This was a bad idea. "Maybe it is supposed to look like you."

"Excuse me?" She sits there, staring through my eyes. "Look, I know you're just trying to do your job, but I'm not the guy you're looking for." She pulls a copy of the flyer from a file cabinet underneath her desk.

"Looks a lot like you. Sounds a lot like you," she says while staring at the flyer, spread out neatly in front of her, flat on the desk. She doesn't even look at me while she says this stuff.

"But it's not me. It's just a case of mistaken identity. I'm worried that if nobody does anything about this, or catches the real guy, that everyone on campus is going to show up on my doorstep with pitchforks and torches and little effigies of me burning on a stick or something."

"Well, maybe you should have thought of that before you attacked that poor girl," she says without flinching.

"Are you fucking retarded?! I. Didn't. Do. It!" Uh-oh. He eyes flare with rage. The little jagged pieces of shrapnel she calls teeth hang out of her mouth and overbite her lower lip.

"That's it...I warned you twice about cursing..." she says with a low-volume voice as she stands. "Ice Pick!" Her scream is so loud that my head buzzes.

"Ice Pick?" I mutter to myself. "What's that mean?"

"There a problem, Donna?"

I turn to the left, where the voice came from, and I see a twiggy, little wreck of a man, standing 5'6 under the doorway that leads to the back section of the building. Atop his stick of a body rests a giant, spherical head. The guy's built like a lollipop. I know this little man. His name is Robert Anne Hughes—another one of the little darlings from my fraternity. We call him "Spaz," mainly because he is just that: a complete spaz. Then again, what guy wouldn't be, after growing up looking the way he does and having a girl's middle name?

"Spaz?" I ask, draining any traces of confusion from my

voice. "What the hell are you doing here?"

"Ah'm here ta wreck your day, Kal," he says with his backwoods twang. "Now you heard the lady. Git out."

"And why is she calling you 'Ice Pick'?"

"That's what they call me 'round here since I started interning," he says as he holds his belt tight with both hands.

"I see… and how's that going for you?"

"Was nice an' relaxin' b'fore you had to come and make my day, punk."

"You're kidding right?" Spaz is my friend. I like Spaz. I sympathize with the fact that he likes to act like a big man since he probably developed some kind of Napoleon Complex from being the skinny little guy that got picked on his entire life. I try to treat him like I'd like my friends to treat me, but it'll be a frosty day in hell before I let him kick me out of here for cursing.

"Kal, ya have two choices. You kin leave like Ah tell ya, or you kin learn why they call me 'Ice Pick,'" he says as he cocks his fists around his head like an old-time Irish boxer. "Ah hope you're plannin' on takin' option number two, 'cuz I'm about half ready to kick some ass." Oh Christ. I look around the room. Donna, the evil, vile public safety worker who possesses the "virgin ears" that started this mess is eyeing me up, looking for a reaction. The six people who were standing in line behind me look less interested in this situation, and more interested in settling whatever business they have here.

"Okay, Spaz, there's not going to be any fight or anything. Just calm down," I request.

"Yeah, that's right," he says, as he drops his fists and sticks his chest out like a proud rooster. "Didn't think ya wanted any of this." He takes a few short steps in my direction before grabbing my arm. "You're gittin' outta here b'fore ya disturb any more of these nice people." The kid weighs about $1.20, tops. He's not dragging me anywhere. But, considering that I just edged the public safety department a little closer to assuming I'm an attempted rapist, I should just cut my losses.

"At least let go of my arm."

"No kin do, Kal. We're required to remove all hostiles with necessary force"

"Whatever." Donna's eyes follow us as we leave the building. She nods while exhibiting this really disturbing look of satisfaction on her face. Ugh. Everyone else just stares in arbitrary directions, apparently not interested in anything that just happened.

As we approach the door, Spaz picks up his leg and thrusts it into the door, swinging it wide open. He had his left hand free and could've opened it the conventional way, but that would have made way too much sense.

"Was that really necessary?"

"Ya goddamn right it was."

He pulls me outside a few feet before he lets go. A gust of frozen air wraps around me and immediately blushes my face. The icy wind wakes up my brain, making me all the more aware that yes, I actually did just get kicked out of a building for cursing at an old lady. My mental focus is broken by Spaz's awkward interpretation of the English language.

"Y'know, ya really lucky that ya have a tight alibi or you'd be in a jailhouse by now," he says in his usual, condescending manner.

"What? How do you guys know about my alibi? That's the reason I came down here to begin with." He has a point that I didn't even think of yet. If everyone, including public safety, thinks that I'm the attacker, how come nobody has tried to make any arrests yet? They haven't even questioned me about it. They may not be doctor material, but even our public safety department has to at least know to question a suspect.

"Someone vouched fer ya this morning."

"Who?"

"I can't tell ya! It's confidential!"

"Ah, c'mon! Was it you?"

44

"How the fuck could it've been me? I wasn't wit you that night."

"At least tell me what they said."

"Not much. They just proved that you were inside Dill's at the time o' the incident, then left." That's weird. *I* can't even remember what I was doing then.

"Can you at least give me a hint about who it is? Please?" Spaz isn't completely heartless. I'm hoping to prove that right now by pulling at his heartstrings. "I really need to talk to this person. Make sure that they're telling the truth. Even if they're trying to help, it could still hurt me if they say the wrong thing." Spaz just looks at me. He's got these dopey, big eyes that display themselves above his tiny, tight lips. I think this is what passes for a sympathetic look.

"Y'know, I shouldn't tell you anythin' after what you just did to Donna," he says. I don't know why he's trying to rationalize his decision to not tell me. He has to realize that if he doesn't tell me who this informant is, I'm just going to get drunk and give him a swirly tonight. "Okay," he finally agrees, "but this is all Ah'm tellin' ya: It was a girl."

*   *   *

A girl. A girl came and gave them an alibi for me. Not only gave them my alibi, but proved it, too. There could've been a ton of girls at Dill's that night. Any one of them could have seen me there. But how many of them actually know me?

Okay. So it's obviously someone who I know. That much is clear. Nobody would go out of her way like this for a stranger. Furthermore, it must be a friend. Nobody would be motivated enough to do this unless they had my best interests in mind. But here's the tricky part: Who was I with that night?

I head to the South Side. That's how everyone refers to this area of campus. Public Safety and all of the administration buildings lie in the dead center of campus, along the main drive of town, which is redundantly named Street Road. The cafeteria, student center and all of the class buildings nest within the northern half of campus. The dorms sit throughout the south half—the South Side, as students call it. The name probably came about in the 90s, when it was fashionable for rich, suburban white kids to sport their Cross Colours hoodies and sip on St. Ides. One of those kids, who probably acted like a disenfranchised minority in order to rebel against his proper WASP roots, most likely came up with the phrase "South Side" while trying to "toughen up his street cred."

What girls do I know that could've done this? I can only come up with two names: Molly and Lana. They put up with me and the other guys—probably the only girls I know who do so willingly.

The two of them room together here in Mackey Hall, my old dorm. I'm tempted to say something really lame and cliché like, "this place brings back memories," and force out a hearty chuckle, but my higher brain functions prevent me from stooping so low. There's a short flight of cracked cement steps leading to the front porch and the double-doored entrance. It's impossible to walk up the stairs to the porch without stepping on a single cigarette butt or piece of trash or cracked glass. This place is almost as much of a shit-hole as my place. The only advantage this place had was heat—nice, functional heat. God, I miss that.

The callbox unleashes a hiss of static as it waits for me to dial a number. 3156. That's the number to their room. It's easy to remember since it's my mom's birthday.

"Hello?" says the feminine voice crackling out of the box.

"Lana?" The two of them don't sound anything alike, but for the life of me, I can't pick out one person's voice from another when it's over the phone. I think my ears are just permanently damaged from all of the diarrhea that flows from people's mouths and finds its way to the inner workings of my ears.

"Yeah. Kal, is that you?"

"Yeah. Come down and let me in. I wanna talk to you two."

"K. Hold on."

I wait a minute or two before Lana makes her way downstairs and out the door. She's sporting sweats and dark hair holstered into a ponytail. She doesn't have class on Fridays. Lucky bitch. I'd stab an orphan in the eye for a schedule like that.

"Must be nice to lounge around all day and not have to worry about 10,000 people thinking you're a violent, attempted rapist," I say as a greeting to Lana. She's probably one of my best friends. Then how come, no matter how hard I try not to, I always end up releasing my problems and aggravations on her?

"Yeah. That's a nice picture they have of you. I think I have that in a frame somewhere."

"Maybe you should've mentioned that to public safety when you went down to seal my alibi this morning."

"What?"

"Eh...I'll fill you in about it in a minute. Is Molly up there, too? I want to talk to both of you about the same thing, and I don't feel like repeating myself."

"Yep. Come in."

This place doesn't look much different than I remember. Immediately when you walk in, there's a lobby and a reception desk, which is manned by a staff of resident students. The girl working now looks very familiar, with her curly, yellow hair and eyes that could replace the headlights on a Mack truck. The glaring, friendly expression she wore on her face when I came in twists right away at her first sight of me. Her eyes turn small and dark as they peer through me and fixate on the wall behind me. I turn around and see about six of the wanted posters hanging on a bulletin board.

"I bet you regret talking to her Wednesday night," Lana says while we walk through the lobby towards the hallway.

"Why? What did I say?"

"You don't remember?" she asks. I stare at her. I'm sure

my face is giving off an expression that tells her that I obviously have no capacity to remember something from two nights ago. "Oh, Kalvin...c'mon, are you serious?"

I shrug.

"Jeez..."

"Are you mad at me?"

"No," she says as she turns her face from me. "I just wish you'd be more careful. Why do you always feel like you need to go out and get completely bombed every night?

"It's not every night. I usually take off on Sunday and Monday nights. And I stayed in last night, too."

"Why? Because you got drunk and passed out in the afternoon?"

"What? Are you my fuckin' wife now?"

We're silent for the rest of the short walk down the hall. The low lighting and light-blue cinder-block walls make the place look particularly cold, practically sterile. The overcast sky seeps in through the windows at the far end of the hallway and bounces off the walls, making everything look that much dimmer, almost damp. I feel like I'm touring the insides of a giant raindrop.

We walk past about six doors on each side of the hallway. Each door is decorated with scraps of construction paper shaped like snowflakes, jackets and wool caps; each one has the name of the room's tenant on it. Tacky.

When we reach Lana and Molly's room, the door is already open, and a sharp ray of light is streaking out of the room and into the hall. I walk in first, pushing the door all the way open. Molly is sitting on the futon, watching TV.

"Hey Kalvin," she says in a chipper voice without even turning her head away. "Don't forget to wipe your feet!" I look down, and sure enough there's a big "Welcome" mat on the floor.

"Why'd you guys get this?" I ask as I stomp my feet all over its clean, purple lettering.

"Why not?" Molly responds.

"Okay. Fair enough," I say as I take a few steps in the

room. There's a stack of empty milk crates in the corner that I decide to sit on. I look at the wall adjacent to me and see a poster of empty shot glasses entitled "What I Really Did in College." I'm speechless. 16-year-old Kal is probably really pissed right about now.

"Okay, so what were you saying outside about public safety?" Lana says as she sits on the floor Native American-style.

"This is going to either make complete sense, or it will make none at all," I start to bring up the topic, but then I stop. I notice in Molly's folded arms sits a chunk of fur, maybe about a foot long. It's moving, squeaking and just being an all-around distraction. "Okay, what the fuck it that?"

"This is Thor."

"The Norse God of Lighting?"

"What? No! My guinea pig, idiot," she says, dumbfounded and annoyed. I don't know. I thought it was pretty funny.

"Why do you have that here? I thought they don't let you keep pets in the dorms."

"They don't," answers Lana.

"That's why he's staying at *your* place," says Molly, with a big, shit-eating smile.

"The hell he is!"

"Barry already said it's okay," says Molly.

"Fucking Barry…" drips out of my mouth as I face the ground and shake my head.

"Hey!" interrupts Lana, trying to pull me back to reality. "What were you saying about public safety?"

"I don't feel like explaining all this, so I'm just going to come out and ask: Did either of you go to Public Safety and tell them what I was doing the night Connie Ward got roughed up?"

"Nope," says Molly, stroking Thor's head with her middle and index fingers.

"No, why?"

"I saw Spaz, and he said a girl came in and proved I

wasn't the guy who attacked Connie. I figured it was one of you since you two are probably the only girls I was with that night." The two of them look at each other shrugging and shaking their heads. "So it wasn't you guys?"

"Don't you remember who you were with that night?" Molly asks, squinting with confusion. She glares at me like it's hard to believe that anyone could get so drunk that they don't remember anything the next day.

"Nope. Wild night. Don't remember a thing," I say, still facing the floor. I don't have to look up to realize that Lana is shaking her head with disappointment and disbelief. "You guys were there. Do either of you remember seeing me talking to any girls in particular?"

"We didn't go out that night," Lana says. "Remember?" I shrug and shake my head at her—it's easier than answering with a "no" and admitting that I'm wrong.

"Why not?" I ask.

"Because it was a Tuesday night! Some of us have classes to go to!" Lana says in a bold voice. It's not quite a yelling voice, but it's louder than she usually gets. This is about as close to yelling as she gets when she's angry with me. "That didn't stop you from bringing the party to us, though."

"What do you mean?" I ask. Molly stands up and drops Thor into a glass aquarium filled with thin wood chips and sawdust. She then goes over to the phone sitting on a small table next to the futon and pushes a series of buttons. "Ahhh, shit…" I mumble. "Did I call you guys again?"

"You should leave your cell at home if you're going out," Molly says as she pushes one last button on the phone, enabling it to go on speaker. A fizzy static comes through and a prompt for the voicemail comes next. Molly accesses the saved message archive and sits down with a giggle.

The next thing I hear is my own voice, blurred and guttural.

"Hey…HEY! It's me! Pick up, pick up, pick up! Where are you guys? This is the Admiral speaking, and I command you to answer the phone! Don't you eyeball me, sailor! Answer the fucking phone!" My voice goes silent for a second, and all you hear is my nose exhaling into the receiver.

"Ahhh...gotta love the Admiral," Molly says as she laughs. Lana once again shakes her head. The Admiral is my liquored-up alter ego. I don't know why, but I start calling myself the Admiral when I'm hammered. I've been trying to do something about that.

The heavy breathing on the phone continues.

"Did I fall asleep here or something?" I ask. "Cuz it's not like I'm the first person to ever pass out on the phone."

"Shhhh. You're going to start talking again," Molly says.

"Hey! I gave these broads my number. They said I was freakin' awesome! Then I told them to ride the Admiral's shit! They shot me down! They shot me down HARD! Man, I fuckin' rule."

My voice starts to slur a bit. Molly stands back up and shuts off the machine. She's still laughing and smiling. Lana is looking quite the opposite.

"It pretty much goes on like that for five more minutes," Molly says. "At one point, you start yelling at Wally. It sounds like you throw an ashtray at him or something."

It's quiet for a minute after that. I'm kind of embarrassed. Noise from a TV nobody is watching takes center stage. Finally, Molly decides to shake things up with conventional chitchat. "You going to Happy Hour, Kal?"

"Yeah. I probably shouldn't after hearing that, but yeah, I'm going."

"Yeah, so are we," she admits. "Actually, you need to go now. We need to clean up and get ready."

"Well then," I say as a clap my hands, "I guess I'll see you two in a little bit." I stand up slowly with a sigh and a grunt. I head towards the door and give them a wave.

"Stop!" Molly yells.

"What?"

"You're forgetting someone," she says, waving her arm over Thor's glass aquarium, as if she were a poor man's Vanna White.

"No way. I'll have no part in this."

"C'mon," Molly whines. "You have to! We can't keep him here any longer. Please? It's the least you could do to make it up to me."

"For what?!"

"For all the calls 'The Admiral' has been making, not to mention the ones he probably will make this weekend."

I look over at Lana, who nods. "She's right, Kal. You owe us." She agrees with Molly, but when I look at her eyes, I know she means something else. She knows I treat her like shit. She can't be happy with that. No person could. When she looked me in the eyes and says that I owe her, she means for being a sub-par friend. She means I need to do this one favor to not only make up for the phone calls and antics, but to make it up to her for forcing her to watch me deteriorate into a sloshed mess. And when you stack up all those facts, it's hard to say no.

I hate my fucking life.

*   *   *

This thing fucking stinks. It's too heavy. Fuck. We're being nice enough by letting her keep this rat at our place, least she could do is bring it there herself. Barry can be such a friggin' pushover sometimes. He should drive his ass down here and pick this up. Of course, he doesn't pick up his phone when I call to tell him that. Ass.

They have some of the South Side gated-off for construction. That means I have to take the long way back to my car, which I'm now happy I brought. All I hear are my out-of-shape lungs hacking and straining as I carry this thing, which has to weigh about 40 pounds. This little freak's squeaking doesn't help.

I sit on the closest bench and set the pig next to me. I light up a cigarette, which is usually part of the deep-thinking, self-loathing ritual I'm acting on right now. I've been having more of these little sit-downs lately. I'm almost

22 years old. I've got almost three semesters until I'm done with school, which at that point I'll be 23. 23 years old and I'll just be coming out of the oven. What am I going to be doing with myself? Am I still going to be drunk five nights a week? Am I still going to be getting kicked out of places for cursing at old ladies? Still getting dirty looks for fighting argumentative fat chicks over donuts?

Will I at least be on track to getting settled into a "normal" life, free of stupid, petty conversations and inner dialogue over how I've let others down? All I can think about lately is the last time I went home. I woke up on a Sunday morning and sat down to a fresh box of Apple Jacks. I opened the brand new box and shoved my fist in deep to the bottom. There was a free dinosaur figure in each box, and all I wanted was the T-Rex. I let my hand swirl and pester around those dry, scratchy little Os until I could finally feel the plastic bag holding the free toy. I pulled my hand out with the toy in tow, little pieces of Apple Jacks falling and bouncing off the tabletop like hunks of flavored moon rock falling to Earth. I tore into the plastic, fingers crossed for a T-Rex.

"Aw, dammit!" I yelled in a fit. My mom, who was sitting across from me the whole time, who saw me probe an innocent box for a cheap plastic dinosaur, just looked up at me. "I already have the brontosaurus," I explained to her.

Without notice, my mom stood up from the table, shook her head and said one thing:

"When I was your age, I was already married and had a kid."

She walked away without explaining any more. One sentence and she blew my brain open. With that one remark, she shredded into my core and sliced it to ribbons. That one instance has become a metaphor for my life lately.

I try not to think about it too often. It seriously hurts to think about. I like living the way I am, but does that make it right? Is there some other path I could be walking that I'm not?

"Hey Kal!" Oh shit. I know that voice. Oh, God. Please tell me this isn't happening. I'm freezing up here. I don't want to do this. Not now. Okay. Deep breath.

"Hey Jill," She stands a few feet in front of me, slowly edging closer. Her almond-shaped, emerald eyes make immediate contact with mine. Long, dark hair flows straight from under a knit cap and stops just above her shoulders. Her small nose and the tiny freckles it carries wrinkle a little as she opens her mouth with a smile, exposing shiny pearl teeth on the inside and little dimples on the outside. She's dressed like any other 21-year-old girl: a navy-colored long-sleeve turtleneck peaking out of a form-fitting vest that shares its orange-sherbet color with her cap. Tight, worn denim hangs from her hips and dangle over brown boots, completing the ensemble. "What's that?"

"This?" I ask, trying to hide my shivers of fear by casually glancing at Thor's tank. "This is a guinea pig."

"Do I even want to know?" she giggles slightly.

"Probably not." She smirks a little. "So...how's it going?"

"Good, good," she answers. "What're you doing out here in the cold?"

"Nothing. I was about to ask you the same thing," Good. Just play on the defensive. Let her pick up that vibe. If she sees I'm being short with her, I'll be set.

"I just came from the library. I've got a mock lesson plan due Monday," she says with a polite smile. She never went home. Damn. My hands are shaking, sweaty. I feel beads of sweat drop from my armpits and streaming down along my ribs. "What're you doing here?"

"Nothing. Nothing really. Just...nothing, I guess." I say with a dumb smile.

"You came out here for nothing?"

"Well, not just nothing. I'm actually doing something, right?" That makes no sense.

"Okay..." She looks around her, as if she's now avoiding eye contact with me. There are so many things I want to bring up right now, so many things I want to say. I want to

54

talk about her, and us and how we should get together to-night and roast Fernando on a pike. But none of that comes out. "So, I heard you and Lisa had it out today."

"Who?"

"Lisa? My friend, Lisa? You have class with her, right?"

"Ummm...do I?"

"Yeah. You got into a fight over donuts, or something?" Does she mean the fat chick from my Advanced Communications class that verbally castrated me over a donut?

"Oh! *that* Lisa. You're friends with her?"

"Um, yeah. You met her, like, 20 times while we were dating. You passed out on her couch once. You don't remember?"

"How could I remember if I was passed out?"

"Well, it's not a big deal. She said you guys straightened it out." I've got nothing to say here. I don't want this to turn into useless small talk, but that really seems like my only option.

"So...you staying up this weekend?" This'll probably be the most intelligent thing I say to her today.

"Yeah, actually. Me and Fernando have our anniversary this weekend."

"Anniversary, huh?" I say, dropping my eyes to the ground. "Cool. I didn't know you guys were together for a whole year." Bitch. I can't believe she'd deliberately act like me and her didn't date a few months ago.

"Well, technically we weren't. But me and him aren't counting that little gap we had a couple months ago..."

"Of course not," I say, raising my voice. "Apparently nothing really major or anything happened then, right?" She makes a face, squinting her eyes and twisting her mouth. Her face telling me she's taken back a little; she wasn't expecting me to show any spine. I can see in her eyes she's feeling nervous. She knows she's offended me, and she's picking up on my anger.

"You know what I meant," she finally explains.

"Of course I do. I mean, after all, I was just a rebound for you after the first time he cheated on you."

"What?"

"Or did we date after the second time he cheated on you? I only talked you through the first time. I have no idea who the rebound was for the first time. But, yeah, I was definitely the rebound for the second time." I pretend that I don't sound completely pathetic.

"Kal...!"

"Even though you didn't say that at the time when you were dumping me. I think the excuse you used at the time was 'we're moving too fast,' or something like that."

"You're not being fair, Kal..."

"Yeah, I know. You also said something like that when we broke up, didn't you? Something like 'this isn't fair: I care about you so much, but I just can't date you.'"

"But I do care about you! That's why I said I still wanted to be friends!"

"Yeah, because nobody's ever said that during a break up," Checkmate! I have no idea where all this came from. It's like that anniversary comment sliced open a vein and splashed out everything that I wanted to say but shouldn't. Oddly enough, this might actually be the best I've felt around her since the break up.

"Listen," she commands, "you can sit here and feel like shit for yourself, or you can believe me. I don't say things I don't mean." As I watch her eyes swell up, I start to wonder if maybe I'm making a mistake here.

She walks a few steps away from me, like she was leaving, then turns around. Tears spread across her cheeks like veins.

"You know, I really do care for you, and I did back then. I meant it when I said I wanted to be friends. Don't act like I just abandoned you for someone else. You're the one who doesn't answer or return my phone calls. You're the one who never walks 50 feet down the street to visit, and you're the one who makes your fucking roommates answer the door when I come over and tell me you're in the shower or you're sleeping or whatever when I can hear you in the other room.

So don't you dare even try to act like I'm the bitch here! You're the one who made things this way, not me!"

Wow. I did not see that coming.

Suddenly my edge in this debate disappears quicker than Ralph Macchio's career. Her face is soaked and dripping like a sponge. Her eyes are so red and swollen that they look like they could fall out any second.

"Yeah, well which part of caring about me entails dumping me for your ex and lying about it later?" Her dimples disappear into her sharp, flat cheeks and her eyes fill with malice as she shakes her head numbly. I know what her response is before she even says it.

"Go to hell, asshole," she says as she turns around and power walks away from me.

"Jill!" I yell, "Hold on! That's not what I meant to say!" She keeps her stride. Her only response is a middle finger.

I look around to see if anyone was around for that little spar we just had. This is one of those occasions where you don't realize you were actually in a yelling match until you notice that noiseless void where said yelling once was. Luckily, I think the only person who heard us was little Thor, who has his nose pushed to the glass while he stares at me with black, condescending eyes. He probably thinks I'm an asshole now, too. But who cares? I wasn't asking him.

5

Down in the Hole

Across America, bells are going off. Sirens are blaring. Time clocks click and tick with millions of timecard swipes sliding in unison. Cars are bottlenecking out of crammed parking lots, radios are blaring, and people yell and honk their horns in a battle for attention. It's 5:00 p.m. on Friday. The one moment of the week when Berkshire moves in sync with the rest of the country and actually feels almost like it belongs on a map. This second means more than just quitting time for a large hunk of Americans; it means it's time to let go of the monkey that's been clawing and shitting on their backs for the last week. 5:00 p.m. on Friday doesn't just mark the end of the workweek. No, it also means the beginning of the happiest time of the weekend: Happy Hour.

A bunch of the guys and I always start off our weekend at the aptly named Happy Hour Pub in downtown Berkshire. It's one of the nicest bars in town, even though it's a complete dump by normal standards. The good part about going there is that we usually monopolize the joint. I don't know if it's because we overstay our welcome by coming at 5:00 and leaving at 9:00 before coming back at 11:00, or if it's because we get so obnoxiously drunk that our conversations usually just degrade to us yelling "penis" to one another. Whatever the reason, we're usually the only ones there. Tonight is going to be different though. There are usually a few girls that grace the bar with their presence, but I never noticed Katie being one of them. And even if she usually is, I'm a bit taken back that she's coming into the lion's den like this just to meet with me. Whatever her reason is, I'm going to find it out tonight. I just hope I don't have some weird slip and call her "Jill" accidentally. I've had that argument on my mind for the last hour.

It's actually 4:45. I'm a little early. I thought it'd take longer for me to find a parking spot than it did. The tricky part about driving here is that I need to find a parking spot that's going to be safe enough to leave my car for the night. Berkshire has a big thing with towing cars at a moment's notice, whether they're legally parked or not. In fact, I'm pretty sure that parking tickets make up a good portion of the yearly revenue the town pulls in. This town is really shady like that. The locals of the town hate the university. They feel that if they nickel and dime the students out of a few grand in parking debts during their tenure here, it may drive off students permanently. It's come close to working on me a few times. This year alone, I've gotten a total of 12 parking tickets, averaging about $20 a pop. My car's been towed twice, at my expense of course, which came to $150 each, including the impound fees. $540 total for this year so far, and I've still got three and a half months left. I swear I'm going to transfer every single time I shell over a buck to this town. I've come close to going through with it, too. I've even looked at other state schools in the area—IUP, Bloomsburg, Kutztown, Lock Haven—the problem is, all of them are just like Berkshire. They're shitty little universities which happen to be the focal points of shitty little towns that are built upon the loathing bite it takes at the hand that feeds it, because lets face it: these towns would be nothing if they didn't have the revenue they pull in from the students who come and camp out for four to eight years at a time. But, I guess that's just Pennsylvania for you. What else would you expect from one of the only states that outlaw the privatization of liquor stores?

This topic swims around in my head every time I walk from my car to the pub. Today is no different. I get so caught up in the process that I don't notice the lights of the pub aren't on yet, which is a bit unusual. The only sign of life in that direction is coming from one person: a tall kid with spiky hair pinched between two giant ears on a head that's rested upon a body that hasn't been to the gym in four months. His name is Donny Dutchetski—another one of my fraternity brothers. We call him "Dutch," because it's impossible to say his last name without sounding like you're puking. He's pacing in circles in front of the entrance before he catches me in his peripherals, stopping dead to face me with irritation.

"Can you fucking believe this?" he asks, passing that off as a greeting.

"What's up?"

"They're not fucking open yet," he says, tugging on the doorknob and grunting with each pull.

"It's almost 5:00, right?"

"Yeah. Which means they should be open now. Owner's probably coked up or something. That's probably why he's late."

"I don't know what to tell you," I say, playing it cool and leaning against the wall. "Where's your roommate?"

"Doug?" he asks. "He had to hit MAC and buy cigarettes. He'll be here soon," he assures me. "Where's the rest of your clan?"

"Barry and Wally probably went to get something to eat first. Last I saw Jay was 20 minutes ago. He was cleaning his car." We're silent for a moment. Dutch finally stops tugging on the door and faces me again.

"What about Spaz?"

"Right now, I wouldn't be surprised if Spaz was running around town pretending he was Eric Estrada."

"What's that supposed to mean?" he asks.

"He gave me a hard time today at Public Safety over the whole Connie Ward thing."

"Fuck him!" Dutch says. "Insecure little fuck..." He's quiet for a moment before changing topics. "What're you doing tonight?" he asks.

"I don't know. I'd like to start drinking, but that doesn't look like it's happening unless we get in here."

"No, I mean later tonight. After we're done here."

"I don't know," I want to tell him about the plan I have orchestrated in my head. About how I'm hoping Katie shows up, and I can buy her a drink. How I intend to knock her on her ass with amazement once I pull out all the witty shit I've been coming up with in my head since this morning. I'm tempted to tell him how I fantasize that it'll only take a couple hours to talk her into coming to my place so we can talk. I want to mention how I have this master plan to hook up with her, and then pull away and act like I'm not interested in sex so that maybe she'll want to come over again tomorrow. But I don't, because I'm a big pussy, and I know that none of this will work out the way I want it to. The last thing I want is to have to hear the snaps and gloats from my friends about how my big plan with the Hot Liberal Arts Chick never came to be.

"I'm thinking we should try going to Dill's instead of coming back here. There's no cover tonight," he suggests.

"Actually, I think I might call it an early night."

"Why? What the hell are you talking about? It's Friday! You don't make Friday an early night!"

"I don't know. I think I might be drinking too much—or at least drinking too much at one time. I keep blacking out and calling myself the Admiral."

"So? What's wrong with the Admiral? I love the Admiral! We only have, like, 11 weekends left before we're out of here. Quit being a fag." I can understand where Dutch is coming from. The thing is, by "before we're out of here," he means, before *he* is out of here. Him, Barry and Spaz are out of here come May. The other two are taking it okay. Dutch, on the other hand, has been acting like he's been diagnosed with AIDS. To his credit, he's been living every night like it's his last. I even think he has a "things to do before I graduate" list.

We stand there quietly respecting each other's boundaries. He doesn't argue against my empty attempt to control myself; I don't argue against his current "live life by the barrelful" philosophy. An awkward silence comes in the form of soft, chilled wind blowing across us. I decide that one awkward moment deserves another.

"I ran into Jill today."

"Yeah? How'd that go?"

"It didn't. We yelled a lot. She left and flipped me the bird. Good time. You would've loved it."

"What'd you argue about?"

"I don't know, something about her and Don Quixote's anniversary," I say.

"Hmmm…" Dutch moans as he goes into thought. He looks like he's about to share some insight before we hear the pops of a loud muffler chattering from the other side of the street. A shit-green Neon missing its hubcaps makes its way parallel to the curb. Out comes the man of the hour: Mitch Chicano, resident coke-fiend and owner of the Happy Hour Pub. He steps out and does a quick lap around to the other side of his car to make sure the passenger side doors are locked, before he turns around and checks the driver's side locks.

"About fucking time," Dutch says as he claps and rubs his hands together, generating just enough heat to keep his hands from numbing. "What were you saying?"

"Ah, fuck it. Let's go drink."

*   *   *

"Public enemy number one!" Doug yells, in a voice that's loud for his normal, mumbled style of talking. He's hiding his young, yet receding hairline under an old Cubs cap. His loose, frumpy designer jeans drag against the floor as he walks towards the table where Dutch and I are already seated. He already looks glazed over and sloshed, but he always looks like that whether he's drunk or not.

"Shut up," I burp out. "I don't wanna talk about it."

"It's funny though," Dutch mentions, gripping a pint glass in one hand with his pitcher rested next to the other. "I never would've thought you'd be a rapist."

"I'm not."

"Yeah," Doug comments, "he's just an attempted rapist."

"That sucks," Dutch says. "You can't even rape a girl right."

"That's sick."

"Well, seriously!" Dutch exclaims. "How hard can it be? You already got her pinned down! Are you that bad at fucking?"

"Shut up!" I growl. "It's bad enough I've got my face everywhere on campus. I don't need someone going to public safety and telling everyone that I was joking about it with my friends."

"Nobody's even going to recognize you from that poster," Dutch reassures me. "Quit being such a puss."

"The hell are you talking about? People have been staring at me since they started piling in here!"

We sit silently amongst ourselves, despite the screeching music and the clattering conversations in the background that's clouding around us. Doug and Dutch casually glare around to see if anyone is staring.

"I don't see anyone staring. You're just being retarded," Dutch says.

"I see one girl staring over here, but I think she's checking me out," Doug says, nodding across the bar. For a second, I hope it is Katie standing in waiting and hoping I'd come up to her. It's not—it's just some mediocre-looking blonde.

"She probably digs me," Doug casually chirps out, pulling his glass to his mouth.

"Digs you?" Dutch asks.

"Yeah," Doug reassures Dutch. "She's a girl—of course she digs me."

"Huh..." Dutch says, pondering out loud. "Too bad for

her that you're gay."

"You're calling me gay?" Doug asks. "You, of all people?"

"Yeah," Dutch replies.

"Well, I just think it's funny that the guy who spent the better part of this morning watching *Pretty Woman* thinks I'm gay..."

"I told you," Dutch yells. "I thought she'd be naked in it..."

"What?" I ask, reluctantly interjecting.

"She's a hooker right? I thought she'd be all slutty and naked and stuff." Dutch's eyes flicker and his jaw drops. Insecurity washes over his face as he tries to defend himself.

"Yup," Doug says. "You're full-blown gay."

This is the regular conversation that takes place between Dutch and Doug on a daily basis. The two alleged heterosexuals live together, but spend the better part of each day trying to convince each other that the other is gay. I've developed a six sense for phasing out their constant accusations at one another.

6:00—no Katie. I'm not surprised. It's hard to expect any kind of good luck today. Probably for the better. The bar is surprisingly packed tonight. Barry and Wally got here around 5:20, and by then the place was halfway crowded. It's doubled since then. I was hoping it wouldn't be like this. I don't want it to be too crowded when Katie comes. I don't want our first real conversation to be yelled over 50 drunks and a remix version of "Back 'Dat Ass Up."

I look at my pitcher—almost empty. I listen in on the ping-pong match of a conversation that's developing at my table:

"...that's why you should make out with him: because you're gay," I hear Dutch yell, the conversation as empty as my pitcher.

I stand up, stretch my legs a bit and look around. Barry and Wally are sitting at the bar, with their asses facing in the direction of our booth. Spaz is standing about a foot away from them. Barry and Wally are laughing at something, but I don't know what. At least I didn't until I heard one of them yell "Ice Pick" with a king-sized chuckle.

Down at the far end of the bar sit Molly and Lana. They usually sit at a table with some girls they know from their social work classes or something along those lines. Lana looks at me, smiles and waves, then turns her attention to a yellow-haired girl across from her.

The bar is dimly lit—the kind of dim I thought you could only get with candlelight. A good-looking brunette is zipping back and forth from one end to another, serving as the sole bartender. I can't help but stare as her large, puffy breasts bounce with each hurried step. The actual bar is scarcely populated; most of the crowd is lingering in the back half, near the dance floor and the pool table. A gray cloud of cigarette smoke hangs over the entire room like thick humidity on a muggy summer day.

I nod at Barry and the others when I approach an empty spot on the bar. I don't hear the popping sound of plastic hitting wood when I drop my empty pitcher on the bar. This is probably the worst part about going to a bar. I absolutely hate waiting for anything, let alone booze. I'm very impatient. That, and because waiting gives me time to think, which is the last thing I need lately. I play with all of the petty expectations I have in my head about Katie as if they were action figures. I work each possible scenario that pops into my head to the full extent of my imagination:

Scenario #1: Katie is a no-show. That one sucks.

Scenario #2: Katie shows up, and without a word grabs my junk. We slam our lips together, everyone cheers and Queen's "We are the Champions" rings triumphantly throughout the bar over the echo of 50 people chanting my name. Unlikely.

Scenario #3: Katie walks in, makes immediate contact with me, and says she took her time getting ready because she wanted to look good for me, and says it loud enough for all my friends hear. Maybe, maybe not.

I'm going with Scenario #4: She shows up and talks to me. I've learned it's harder to get disappointed if you don't set high expectations for yourself.

I look at my cell phone. 6:20. Nothing. Worse still, I can't even get my pitcher filled. Christ.

6:30...

I light up a cigarette. Five smokes left in the pack. Got a full one in the car if I need it. Still no Katie, still no beer. It's really hard to blow smoke rings. A lot of people say the trick is to use your tongue. Others say you can only do it by curling your upper lip downwards. I try both. Nothing. Barry grabs Wally's attention as he points and laughs at me. I feel something wet on my hand. My eyes roll down. I'm drooling. Dammit.

6:45...

My head feels lighter as the weight of a full pitcher eases my world. I sit down with Dutch and Doug in the booth.

"Why would you pick Brad Pitt, when you can just pick, like, a porn star or something?!" Dutch yells.

"Because, if I picked to hang out with a porn star, I only get to fuck her. If I hang out with Brad Pitt, I could sleep with lots of different girls because they'd see me with him and want to sleep with me on principle," Doug desperately explains to deaf ears.

"So if you could hang out with anyone in the world, it'd be Brad Pitt?" Dutch asks in his normal, criticizing voice. "You're a homo."

"It wouldn't work anyway," I add. "The girls wouldn't give a shit about you. They'd just go straight for him."

"Yeah, but that's all I need. He's just a launching pad for me to work my way into talking to them," Doug argues.

"But they wouldn't talk to you! They'd talk to him, and say stuff like 'Hey, why are you hanging out with that guy who looks like a scarecrow with a heroin problem?'" Dutch yells, practically standing up.

"Dude," Doug says, preparing his defense, "there's, like, a whole sub-culture of hot girls just waiting to fuck the underlings of A-list celebrities."

The door to the bar opens. The pale glow of street lights peeks in behind a silhouetted figure. It's only Jay. Damn.

7:00...

The bathroom looks like a swamp. A slimy mix of toilet water and piss glazes the floor. A bathroom like this can only work in a bar, where people are just that desperate to piss. The guy standing at the urinal next to me teeters and sways while he pisses.

"Hey," he says to me in a slurred, dragged-out tone. "Aren't you that dude who raped that chick?"

7:30...

The crowd's thinned out a lot. It's down to me, the rest of the speds in my fraternity and a few other people. Lana and Molly are gone. I didn't say goodbye, and I'll catch shit for that later. Most of the crowd probably went home to eat dinner or get showers or to do something normal people do. Us? We just sit here, most of us on our second or third pitchers. We'll be here for probably another hour and a half or so, maybe longer. Katie, on the other hand, will not be. It's awfully hard to stay somewhere all night if you've never showed up.

All the guys in the booth are pretty wound up. Dutch, now joined by Barry and Wally, took a break from calling everyone gay so that he could focus on telling Doug how hot his mom is. I sit here, nice and quiet and slurred. I drank too much, too slow. If I drank a little faster, I'd be about as hyper as these guys. But no, I wanted to be sober for Katie, the little skank who stood me up. She's probably sitting in her room, drinking wine coolers with a bunch of friends and talking about how she almost met up with some guy from class before she found out he tried to raped Connie Ward. I'm a fucking idiot. She had absolutely no reason to meet me.

67

None whatsoever. Son of a bitch. I'm drunk. Slow, dumb drunk. Fuck. My eyes don't feel like they work. My eyes suck. So do my eyebrows. Doug's got cool eyebrows. His are normal looking, normal sized. They match his brown hair and thin face. Mine are bushy as shit. Little pieces of them hang over my eyes. No wonder she wouldn't show up. I got bushy, rapist eyebrows.

"Dude, you have no idea what I'd do to your mom if I was alone with her," Dutch says.

"Is she really that hot?" Barry asks.

"Dude, you have no idea," Dutch explains. "And his step-mom is even hotter."

"Yeah, my step-mom is pretty hot," Doug says nonchalantly as he pulls the pint glass up to his mouth. Dutch and Barry drop their jaws, taken aback by Doug's attraction to his step-mom. Wally just giggles like a creep. I'm distracted. I don't want to be here anymore. I don't feel myself. I should be chiming in about fucking the maternal figures in Doug's life too, but I'm not. I'm just flicking my half-full pitcher on the side with my index finger, watching beer swim up and down, back and forth on each side. I glance at the door every three seconds. She's not coming.

8:15...

Wally is dancing. That's how you can tell he's been doing shots; he only dances when he's been drinking liquor. He does this weird dance where his arms stay still along his sides, but his shoulders jerk forward, in a weird pattern: left, left, right, right. His knees rack back and forth, creating some weird swaying motion. My head sways and swims, looking in one direction of the bar to the other and back again. No Katie yet. All I see is Barry on my far left and Dutch on my far right.

"Penis!" yells Barry.

"Penis!" replies Dutch.

"Penis!" Barry yells a little louder.

"Penis!" replies Dutch even louder. The pretty girl serving drinks behind the bar shakes her head, dejected by the fact that retards like us are her bread and butter.

This is the Penis Game. It's a lot like that game "Chicken." Basically, two or more people take turns yelling the word "penis" in a crowded place, yelling it a little louder each time. The point is to see which person is willing to embarrass themselves more by yelling "penis" in a crowded room, making themselves look like a complete asshole. The person who chickens out first and stops yelling is the loser. It's a depressing fact to realize that the penis game is the only thing my friends and I have contributed to the Berkshire Community.

I feel myself sobering a bit, so I call the bartender over. Four shots of rum, all for me and me alone. One shot is for my life being ruined by a poster. Number 2 is for the fight I got into with Jill. The third is for Katie not showing up. And the last one? Well, I'm sure something else shitty is going to happen today.

Jay is standing next to me. He's drunk as hell. He's not doing much, just kind of swaying and giggling.

"Hey. Hey!" he yells, trying to get my attention. "What're those for?"

"Me."

"Gimme one."

"One of these?" I ask.

"Yeah."

"Fuck yourself."

"Fuck me? Fuck me?" he asks. "No, no, no, sir. Fuck you." He shuts up for about 10 seconds before he tries again. "Gimme one."

"No."

"I gave you a ride to class."

"I scraped your windshield."

"Touché," he says, giving up. He puts one hand on the bar to stop himself from swaying so much. I stare down at the four shots I just bought. They all look the same, but I'm sure there's some particular order I should drink them in.

"Eeny, meeny, miny, moe…" I spit out, finger dangling numbly over each glass.

"Whoa…" Jay says, dragging out the last part of the word. "She's fucking hot."

I turn around to the front door. Katie. She showed. And just in time to watch me do four shots. She walks across the room, slowly. Her hair is deep brown, hanging above her shoulders. She's sporting a green tank top, filled up with plump tits that jiggle slightly with each step. She's got a suit coat on over it, and a pair of tight jeans that might as well have been painted on her. She's dressed like an actress making her first appearance on Letterman. She looks friggin' hot. Just plain hot.

Moments like this only happen in movies. She walks slowly across the room—practically in slow motion. Either she's somehow managed to control the flow of time in order to move that slowly, or I'm really fucked up.

Her big, brown boots clap along the linoleum like a drum beat. She tosses her hair back with her left hand while waving at me with the right. I feel like I'm in a beer commercial. A really, really hot beer commercial. I finally regain enough control over myself to take some of the excitement out of my eyes and close my mouth just as she approaches me. I can't move. She's a foot away from me, staring me in the eyes as my lower lip hangs outward. She looks at me, smiles, and then looks at the two shots I'm holding in my hands.

"Read my mind!" she says, pulling the full shot glass from my left hand. Rum flows over the top rim and spills on my hand as it shakes when she grabs it. "What are we toasting to?" Think of something funny, think of something funny, think of something funny. "I got it," she says, beating me to a good punch line that I'd probably never come up with. "How about we toast to me being late and you still being here?" She grins with a closed mouth and a tilted head, looking at me as she raises her glass. I follow, and we let the shots burn and swivel down our throats.

"I kinda thought you weren't coming," I say, starting off

the first of what I hope are many conversations we share tonight.

"Yeah, sorry about that. My ex-boyfriend called up giving me some big sob story about this and that." Ex-boyfriend? This sounds good. "Hey, are those two yours, too?" she asks, shaking her index finger back and forth as she points at the other two shots.

"Hey!" Jay says, sloshing over towards us. "How come she gets one?"

"So, ex-boyfriend?" I ask, doing my best to shun Jay's drunken ramblings while hiding my own. "You guys break up recently, or…"

"Nah. Like, four months ago, I think. We dated for about two years," she explains. "Then he decided to cheat on me about a million times. Told him to fuck off." She grabs the other shot, tilts her head back and throws it down her throat. She's got a confidence in her voice that I can only dream about.

"I see…" I don't know what to say. I mean seriously, how do I respond to that? It's not like I can say "Awesome! I'm glad you had a falling out with some asshole! Now that means I have open opportunity to fuck you! Let's dance!"

"I'm sorry, I don't want to make things awkward by starting the night off with the history of my life," she says, turning to me. "So how you doing tonight?"

"Pretty good…pretty good. Been a long day." She sits on the bar stool next to me and rests her back against the bar. She tilts her head and sways her hair when she turns to face me. We both pause for a bit. She smells unbelievable, like peaches and vanilla tossed around in a bed of dried flowers.

"I'm glad you met me here. Anytime I ask a guy to meet me, I always get a little worried if he will."

"So this is a regular thing for you?" I am a whore in her mind.

"Nah, not a regular thing," she says with a smile that shines through her voice. "But seriously, I'm glad you came." This is surreal. I don't need to know why she wanted to meet

71

me—hearing that was worth the whole trip.

"PENIS!" yells Dutch, who somehow snuck up on us. Katie backs her head up with a flinch as he yells, knocked back by bad breath. I notice Jay hasn't gone anywhere. He's standing with his eyes closed. I wonder if she can see the horror in my face right now.

"Do you mind if we go to that booth over there and talk?" Katie asks, pointing at an empty booth far from where we're standing. "I actually have something kind of important to talk to you about."

*   *   *

I'm glad Katie has her back to me right now. Really glad. And I'm even happier that she's leaning over the bar, giving me a good shot of her ass. She said she wanted to get us something to drink. I'm not stopping her. My head feels like it's filled with thick honey. My mind feels swashed and mashed up. I'm kinda drunk, kinda tired and just generally dumb—a bad mix. Hope Katie isn't buying us shots.

"Here we go. Four more shots. Two each." Dammit. She has all four shot glasses clasped tight between both thumbs and all her fingers before she puts them on the table. "This isn't going to be too much for you, is it?"

"Nah. I'm kosher." Confused. Gone is flirty, teasing Katie from this morning. Here now is confident, badass Katie. I'm loving it and feeling intimidated all at the same time. She slides two shot glasses over to me, leaving a trail of liquor drops behind each glass. "So what's the occasion?" I ask, picking up a glass, pinching it between my middle finger and thumb.

"I don't know. I picked last time. Your turn this time."

"How about we drink to a good time?"

"Not very original."

"Heh. Creativity's never been my thing." Drinks go down, bottoms go up. She slams her glass down, like a biker's bitch in a dirty roadhouse bar.

"So what time did you and your friends get here?" she asks, looking around. She eyes Dutch, Barry and Jay doing a shot. Wally continues dancing as if he was the lone queen of the disco. "Looks like you guys have been here for a while."

"Yep. Since 5:00."

"I see," she says, bringing her attention back to the table. Her eyes float a little before they anchor on my half-empty pitcher. "That your third one?" she asks, with a tap on the side, making the beer swim a little.

"Yeah. Good guess."

"It wasn't a guess."

"How'd you know then? Do I look that drunk?"

"No. I can just tell, considering how long you've been here and how drunk your friends are." She reaches towards my pint glass and drags it across the table. "You don't mind, do you?" I shake my head.

"Anything else you can 'just tell'?"

"I can figure out lots of stuff by just looking at you." She pulls my glass to her lips. Her eyelids drop slightly, seductively covering half of each eye as she drinks my beer.

"And why's that?"

"Let's just say I've got an eye for detail." Her hand guides the pint glass onto the table before she fills it from the pitcher. "If that makes any sense."

"Uh-huh." My mind sways back and forth. She seems different. Then again, I don't have much to base it on since this is my first real conversation with her.

"I don't want to talk about me though. I want to talk about you," she says. It's a random comment, one I don't see coming. "But first," she stops to raise her shot glass, "I want to give you a second chance to make up for that first toast you made."

"Hmmm. Well, let's drink to having some good, clean fun." Hopefully she won't realize that I just said the same thing I said with the last shot, only in different words. I throw the shot down my mouth. The taste is like sweet cough syrup mixed with cleanser. My face twists when I swallow.

73

"That's funny. I hear 'good, clean fun' hasn't really been your thing lately," she whispers quickly before knocking off the shot. "Especially when it comes to girls you meet at the bar." The statement jars me a little. Warm phlegm clogs my throat and sinuses. Coughing follows and my lungs run out of air.

"You okay?" she asks. Breathe, breathe! Don't lose it! Don't look like a pussy! Deep breathes. I cough a few more times, holding my chest in one hand. I throw out my other hand, palm facing her, hoping she realizes it means, "I'm fine."

"Excuse me?" I choke out. Breathe, breathe, breathe.

"The whole Connie Ward thing." She's leaning on her arm and covering her mouth; I can't tell if she's straight lipped or smiling.

"Whoa, hold up! Where's this coming from?!" A wave of sobriety washes over my eyes and brain. Nerves fly from my stomach to the base of my skull and back. My legs go numb, my testicles shrivel and the brow on my head sharpens.

She quietly ignores my question.

"You always wear that jacket. I've never seen you without it," she mentions casually, moving her hand from her mouth and combing it through her hair. "You're always wearing a pair of jeans with that lovely black jacket. It's almost like a uniform." We exchange nasty glares. Hers is filled with arrogance; mine's soaking with rage. She opens her mouth some more. "From what I hear, the guy seen at the crime was wearing the same thing."

"I'm sure you didn't come here just to tell me some rumors you've heard," I say. My fists form under the table as I finally remember how to breathe. Venom and acid boils in my gut. My mind twists Katie's face. No longer does it view her as a tight, little sex kitten. Instead, it sees a viper coiling around my leg, readying to lunge into my left nut and pull away the flesh. "You obviously got something to say, so say it already and we can leave and get on with our lives."

"I don't have anything to say," she says, "I'm just telling

you what I saw from the wanted poster."

"So what?" I ask. "You're supposed to be a cop now, or something?"

"No, just a concerned girl looking for the truth."

"Why?"

"Because it makes me feel a little uneasy being a girl and knowing there's some rapist on the streets," she says, crossing her arms.

"Right..." I say. "Because all girls worried about being raped dress like that and set up meetings with the alleged rapist at the bar." Crap. That probably wasn't the best thing to say.

We both lean back, wide-eyed and stunned. Neither of us expected assertiveness to come from my lips. Music, noise and conversations chatter around us, but we're silent. Both of our eyes dart around the room, occasionally meeting to look at each other head on. Each time they meet, I practically feel shock waves of emotion shaking between us. Awkwardness, hostility, irritation, guilt; they send out a void that engulfs us.

"Listen," I say, breaking the silence, "as tacky as it sounds, this was fun while it lasted. Seriously. But we should probably just cut our losses here and leave before one of us says something we'll regret." She's silent. Her eyes are pointing down, fixated on the table. She doesn't even have the decency to look me in the eye after she just accused me. I wait for her. I tell myself she'll say something, even if it does turn out hostile. But she doesn't. She sits there. My mind warps her image again. Gone is the flesh- and testicle-hungry viper. Here now is a little puppy, upset after her master hit her with a newspaper for chewing on some old shoes.

I give her about a minute total to say something. I light a cigarette and try to calm myself before looking at her again. Nothing. To hell with this. She's the one who came at me. I didn't do this. I shouldn't feel guilty. She took a swing at me, and I defended myself. End of story. There's not a court in the country that'd convict me. She's not my responsibility, and if she was for any reason, she allowed me to relinquish that duty when she went on the offensive. Not my problem.

"Yeah, well..." I say, expecting her to chime in. She doesn't. "I guess I'll see you Monday, then."

I stand up. She lifts her view from the table and refocuses on me. I glance at her, make brief eye contact and put my cigarette in my mouth. She watches me grab my glass and pitcher. With a puff of smoke from my mouth and a nod in her direction, I turn around and rejoin my friends.

"Hey...hey!" Dutch is staring towards me—not at me, towards me. "Who's that chick?" Like he'll remember if I tell him.

"Some girl from class."

"Dude," Barry interjects, "I'd plug her."

"Yeah. That's hot. Give it to her," says Dutch, leaning his long, tall back against the bar with both elbows supporting his weight. Doug hears the conversation and stumbles up. He holds his glass at chest level with a cigarette at the same height in the opposite hand.

"So..." Doug says, forcing his way up against the bar. "You fucking that or what?" I shrug and shake my head. It's when Doug asks that seemingly rhetorical question that I get nailed with piles of revelation. What if I could have fucked her tonight? What if I just blew any further opportunity to sleep with her? What if she was just fucking around with me, and I just completely bitched out? For all I know, she could have been busting my balls. And instead of playing it cool like the guy she may have thought she was meeting, I acted like a sniveling, awkward, 14-year-old girl who cries when her friends decide to go out and experience their first hand-jobs instead of spending the night watching *Grease* with her. She may have been talking like that to look for dick, and all I gave her was pussy.

Maybe it's not too late. Maybe I still have a chance to show her that this cigarette butt hanging off my pelvis is actually a dick. I turn, ready for a second at-bat. It takes a few seconds before I realize she's not sitting there anymore.

A deep breath calms me. Closing my eyes while I do it helps delay the regret. I feel someone's breath ricocheting off my face. The eyelids open and there she is. She's literally an inch from my face.

"Next time when you're talking to somebody and say, 'You obviously got something to say, so say it already,' make sure you actually stick around to hear what the person has to say." Her eyes stay locked on me; her hand reaches for my coat. She pries open the left half and slips something into the inside pocket just before making a quick twist and several fast paces towards the door.

"So…" Doug says after a few moments of dreadful silence, "you fucking that or what?"

I take several steps towards the door, before I wander outside. It's dark, but the streetlights provide a bright haven from the night. The air is cold, but dry and mellow. The few deep breaths of cold air speeding through my nose and lungs alter my perception and wake my brain up some. I swear I can feel my blood carrying the cold oxygen through each inch of my body. My rapidly increasing heartbeat gets lost among the constant nerves and acids shuffling through my stomach as I reach for the inside pocket of my jacket. It's a crumpled piece of paper, probably ripped from a pocket-sized memo pad. Her soft, feminine handwriting is shown off in big loops and wide lettering scribbled in blue ink.

"I'm sorry and I believe you," it starts. "I don't like saying I'm sorry. Let me cool off. Find me tonight so we can give this a second chance."

Second chance? Second chance for what?

Wet Dreams May Come

"Nocturnal blue balls." That's what I call them. Those dreams that you wake up really excited about because everything seems so real, so genuine. You can remember every taste, smell and touch; sometimes you can even remember things in the dream better than you can remember things from your real life. Nocturnal blue balls. I say "blue balls" because usually these dreams make you very excited and leave you excitable when you wake up, only to realize that none of it ever did or will happen. The blue balls guys experience while they're awake come from an unfulfilled desire to ejaculate after a girl relentlessly teases his cock. Are dreams really that different? Guys can ejaculate from their dreams; is it so hard to believe they can get worked up and let down by them as well? That actually might be the reason for morning wood, now that I think about it.

This dream—the one that left me as giddy as a fat stoner in a Taco Bell—didn't directly have anything to do with sex. It had to do with girls, just not me having sex with any of them. Actually, it only revolved around one girl: Jill.

The reason this dream gave me nocturnal blue balls is because it didn't seem like a dream at all. Most dreams leave me feeling like I'm watching TV; even if I'm involved in the dream, ultimately I still feel like a spectator. This one was different—so vivid and lush, without any strange pretense leading me towards suspicions of a phony existence.

It started with Jill and I sitting on my bed. We were both doing homework; she was reading some textbook, and I was looking over notes from class. She put her book down on her Indian-style folded legs, looked up and smiled. A brain could never forge a smile like that in a dream; it could only mimic it from memory. She asked me a bunch of questions to make small talk: how was your day, what was class like, what do you want to do this weekend—tiny questions that seem so insignificant coming from someone other than that person you so utterly and truly care about. We set our books down and got into bed. She kissed me on the cheek and said, "We should go to the beach this weekend," and I agreed before I woke up. It's kind of strange how when I fell asleep in my dream, I woke up in real life.

Wake-up time. "Life beckons," as they say in the beer commercials. My mind gives my heart a good seven seconds to enjoy the blissful fact that Jill and I are scheduled for the beach this weekend before I come around completely, realizing it was a dream. The baby blue sky and an unusually bright sun serve a brand new twist on what I'm used to with conventional wake-up routines. This is all well and good until I realize I'm waking up outside.

Of course, it's not just the sun and sky that tell me I'm outside. It's the frosty inch of snow burning into the backside of my body that does that. I lay snow-angel style for a good minute—that's how long it takes for my nerve endings to wake up, apparently. The upper half of my body jets upward like it was spring-loaded. The shining sun casts a deep reflection on the unblemished snow, feeding excessive amounts of blinding, white light into my eyes. It works its way into my already-pounding brain. It takes me a few seconds to realize I'm on my front lawn.

Well, this is as good a time as any to figure out how I got here. I remember my incident with Katie at Happy Hour. I remember doing some shots and going for pizza. I remember pissing in an ally. I remember going to Dill's, and it was packed. I remember being sweaty, but I couldn't take off my jacket because I had nowhere to put it. I don't remember finding Katie. I remember pissing in a different ally after last call. I think I was in a car at one point.

The more I think, the more it feels like I'm twirling a screwdriver through my temples. Car doors crash shut nearby, and I swear I see the sound waves as they come from the doors and fly through my eardrums. The back of my neck feels like it has been run through with an icicle. My spinal column feels like a long, bony freeze-pop. A couple twists should work the kinks out of a night of sleeping without a pillow. The door slams at the house next to ours and big, fat Steve comes jiggling out, his body pouring off the front porch towards the car. Along the curb is a blue Mustang. A tiny blond woman in a form-fitting overcoat and black pants comes from one side, a man consisting of broad shoulders and a lean torso comes out the other. The two of them greet Steve at once with a group hug.

I can't help but watch this as I rub the icy burns out of my neck. I'm assuming they're his parents. At least that's the best I can tell from here. Their conversation translates over the short distance between us as a mere mumble. They begin towards Steve's place, but all stop in unison. Steve stares at me, his smile turning upside-down at my sight. His parents cock their heads and raise their eyebrows like a set of lobotomized puppies when they see the stupid-looking drunk sitting in the snow. Suddenly, instinct takes over and my mouth goes into autopilot.

"Whoa," I say, "your parents are really thin."

They grumble a bit to themselves. Steve circles behind them and quickly rushes them into the house. Shit! What did I just say?

"Wait! I meant that as a compliment!" Dammit! That destroys any progress my empty shell of a conversation developed with him yesterday. Not like it matters. Barry's probably passed out in Steve's flatbed again anyway.

My house is a shit hole, but I can't really think of a time when it's not. Actually, it doesn't look much different than

80

when I left it yesterday: broken plates, smashed glass shards, crumpled papers, indiscernible trash. There was a time where I could be confident that I'd come home to a different shit hole each day of the week. There was a time when Barry and Wally used the house as a canvas and flung trash across the room with the artistic intent of an impressionist painter. Those times are gone. Now, we're all just lazy contributors to a slop hole that somehow stays colder than the temperature outside. Things change. I hate change. Change is a melancholy bastard who takes his boredom out on happy souls like me by taking people away from them and removing them from happy situations. Sometimes I wish I could personify "change" just so I could feel the delight of bludgeoning it bloody with my fists.

"S'up, party boy?" asks Jay, coasting out of the kitchen area, drying a glass with a moldy rag. "How you feeling?"

"Cold."

He chuckles a little after I answer. "Yeah," he says between his tiny laughs, "that was pretty funny."

"You saw me?"

"Oh, yeah." He looks down at the glass in his hand, grinning as he continually polishes it.

"How long did you know I was out there?"

"Few hours. Saw you when I woke up." The glass is dry as sandpaper, but he keeps rubbing.

"Why didn't you wake me?"

"I tried. Didn't you feel the snowballs?"

"Ass…" I mumble, heading up the stairs. I need to get changed, I need to get warm and I need to get a decent nap.

The short hallway at the top of the stairs is hallowed ground; all of us make an effort to keep that area livable, as per an unspoken agreement. The top feels like a haven. Fresh heat is delivered from below, where a space heater has been snuggled into a hole in the fake-wood paneling. My frost-ridden knees buckle when the heat makes contact. I shiver my hand around the doorknob and slowly creep into my room. Wally is on his bed, wrapped in blankets and con-

cealed by the low lighting of the room. The curtains and
black trash bags over the window turn the room into a cave.
The only light is the gentle glare and flicker of the small TV.
Bats live in brighter conditions.

"Yo," Wally says. I return the greeting by waving a limp
arm up and down in his general direction. Blank silence follows. The low volume of the TV isn't enough to cut through
it. "Where you been?"

"Front yard."

"Nice," he says. The smile he forms is almost encourag-
ing.

"What'd you do last night?" I ask.

"Drink."

"Where?"

"Bunch of places."

"Oh."

"It was alright."

"Cool."

"Yeah...I hooked up with some chick."

"She hot?"

"She was alright. Wouldn't give me her number though."

"That sucks," I say.

"She'd only give me her email."

"That's kind of weird..."

"What's on your shirt?" he asks.

"What?"

"Right there." It looks like he's pointing at my dick before
I realize he's looking at the bottom ridge of my shirt. "Those
your business cards?"

"No..." I crack my neck to the side while I look down.
Four of them, all stapled to my shirt. "The hell...?"

I tear one from the bottom. I'm sure not to pull the staple
out at a weird angle—I like this shirt too much to shred it
because some asshole (probably me) decided to put these on
my shirt instead of in my pocket. The card is crinkled and a
little wet.

"'Katie Lynn Moore, Assistant Editor,'" I read out loud,

"Berkshire Courier; Campus Newspaper.' Katie?"

"Who's that?"

"Some girl from last night."

"You fuck her?"

"I don't think so. It'd be cool if I did."

"Yeah," he says.

"Yeah."

*　　　*　　　*

At the risk of sounding like a character from a John Hughes movie, I hate coming to school on a Saturday. I know I don't have to go to class, I know I don't have to actually do anything at all. Just being here though makes me feel like I'm wasting time. This is time that could be spent in bed, resting up for the next occasion where I'm actually required to be here. I could spend this time doing one of any number of things: playing Playstation, watching DVDs, drinking, watching whatever crap MTV is repeating for the fifth time this week, searching for free Internet porn—tons of things. But instead, I'm obeying soggy, crumpled business cards.

I pull one of the cards out of my coat pocket. On the back of each of the cards was written "See me in the office by 5 p.m. and I'll make everything all better!!" Two exclamation points used to make a smiley face followed. At the bottom is written, "XOXOXO, Katie" I don't understand how "XO" became interchangeable with the phrase "hugs and kisses." Whatever. Maybe I should be excited that she implied giving me hugs and kisses. Maybe I shouldn't. The address on the front of the card says that the newspaper office is in room 205 of the Student Center. I didn't even realize they kept the Student Center unlocked on weekends, and I wish I still didn't know. Now that I do, it's only a matter of time before I come in here all drunk and stuff.

The building feels completely hollow. Not a soul in here other than my own. I can hear each breath I take echo through the vacant halls. The wet soles of my sneakers squeak with each step and leave a trail of dirty, wet footprints. The sky outside has been filling with clouds. The lights in here seem so much brighter in contrast with the stale, gray, overcast view outside.

I enter the first stairwell I see. The door slams behind me and sends an echo upwards. The long florescent lights hum and buzz rapidly as I walk by them, climbing each concrete step one by one. I hear the sky opening up and releasing thunder. Eerie how it was so bright and sunny all day until I got here. I wonder if that's a sign. Maybe I'm right and this whole thing with Katie is too good to be true. Maybe this is a sign telling me that shit is going to come down if I actually show up for this little "rendezvous." Flat sheets of cold rain start pattering against the outside of the cinderblock walls. I get to a long window on the platform between the first and second floor. Rain splashes against it so fast that you can barely see anything outside, like water against a windshield in an automated car wash. The climate control machines pick up all the humidity and moisture in the air and release a crisp draft throughout the building. My skin shrivels and pops goose bumps when the breeze hits me.

Outside the stairwell on the second floor, I hear chattering coming from down the hall. There's a visitor's lounge. The TV is on and tuned onto some crappy Saturday afternoon movie—the kind that'd be perfect to watch from my bed as I'm drifting in and out of sleep on this soaking-wet Saturday.

The hallway narrows down to half the width as I go deeper into the guts of the building. Sharp corners and checkered tiles make the walk feel so much more confining. Several doors, shut and locked for the weekend, line the walls and make me feel even more trapped. Further down the hall, the lights are turned off; the only thing keeping it protected from the dark are the small amounts of gray light peeking in through the windows. More closed doors run along the hallway. Where the hell is room 205?

A thin veil of light reveals itself from around yet another corner turn. The low rumble of casual chitchat carries down the hall. This has to be the place. It's the only occupied part of the building. The back, bottom part of my skull feels like it's swelling, almost like someone is pumping up a balloon back there. I don't want to do this. This is ridiculous. Why would this turn out to be any different than last night?

My back rests along the wall. This was a waste of a trip. Katie is obviously after something. That's the only clear reason for her to be so forward about sitting down with me. I didn't know she worked for the paper. She started questioning me about Connie's attack. Maybe she's trying to interview me. Maybe talking to her could help clear myself publicly. Then again, what if she's incriminating me? What if she's got the nuts and confidence to think that she'll actually ooze a confession from me? That'd make sense. That'd explain why she wanted to meet me yesterday at Happy Hour, when she knew I'd be wrecked. Whatever her plan is, I shouldn't go in.

Okay.

That's settled then.

I'm turning around and leaving so I can run like a fairy to my car so I don't get too wet.

Okay, but then again—what if talking to her now sets off a series of events that'll ultimately lead to me sleeping with her. That'd be so sweet.

"Excuse me?" A nasal voice travels down the hall. A short, dorky-looking kid with red hair and freckles walks towards me. He's not obese, but he definitely likes his pizza and it shows. "Can I help you?" asks the redheaded dork.

"Umm…" I wait for a second and stare at him while my brain formulates an answer. "I don't know. Maybe." That's all he needs to know.

"Wait…you're Kalvin aren't you?" Okay…little weird. "C'mon! We've been waiting for you all day!" he screeches, pushing me from behind. He nudges me until I move on my own, around the corner and into the halfway-open office door. "Everybody," the redheaded dork announces, "The Admiral has arrived!"

Three other people are in the room. A tall, skinny guy with a goatee and a vest—probably their resident piece of *GQ* Euro-trash; a chubby, Goth chick—most likely their photographer (fat Goth chicks love photography); and finally, the voluptuous Katie, sitting at a desk pushed back into the left corner of the room.

They clap. The only one not clapping is Katie, who stands at her desk, looking in my direction with half a smile while she shuffles stuff around her desk, as if she's too busy to be paying attention.

I can't think of anything nice to say, and I don't want to humor them by asking what the hell is going on, so I keep my mouth shut and take in this very unusual, very disturbing sight. The room has six cubicles set in the dead center of the room, and a desk in both of the back corners. Each desk and cubicle is decorated with little trinkets intended to personalize the area. Along the walls are maps and bulletin boards, as well as various posters. One poster has some generic college band posing like pissed-off pretty boys. Another features John Lennon. A third one has a list comparing women to beer. I'm basically in a giant dorm room. The only difference between this and typical dorm room decor is the giant message, "If you have time to read this, you don't have enough work to do!" Not terribly witty people working here.

Katie continues to organize herself. Meanwhile, the other three people in the room are staring at me, smiling. They expect me to say something. I don't like being the center of attention. I'm content with just being in the background, left alone to myself to carry on with my own business. I don't like situations like these. I don't like the fact that these people have nothing better to do than put me under their microscope for whatever goal they're trying to accomplish. I don't like being shoved into someone's spotlight.

"Well," starts *GQ* Euro-trash, probably in an attempt to break the silence, "you clean up very well!" He glares up and down, taking in eyefuls of my appearance. "You look nothing like the corpse you resembled yesterday." His voice is bold enough, but has an almost feminine frailty. There's not any kind of stereotypical lisp in the voice, but it's definitely easy enough to assume that someone like him, with a silk voice to match his shirt, is most likely gay.

"Yesterday?" I ask.

"Yeah, at Dill's," he says, as if it were common sense.

"We were at Dill's together?"

"You don't remember?"

"Honestly, I don't think I've ever met you guys before in my life." I say. "Sorry, I don't mean to be rude or anything, but I think I'd remember hanging out with you guys." Well, I've succeeded in mildly offending them. Perfect. That gives me an out.

"We gave you a ride back to your place after last call. We all crammed in Lola's car," he says, subtly pointing his head in the chubby Goth chick's direction. "That doesn't sound familiar?" adds the *GQ* Euro-trash, raising an eyebrow. I think he thinks I'm lying. "Well, you were fucking wasted last night," he adds. "I'm surprised you're even able to move today." He folds his arms and leans back against his desk. "Fucking frat boys. Make all the jokes and stereotypes you want, one thing's for sure—you guys can drink."

"Yeah," I say, trying to cloak my pride. "It's not necessarily a good thing." I dart my eyes around the room; everyone is still staring at me. "So...I guess I told all of you about The Admiral last night?" They look at each other and snicker.

"My God! That was *so* funny!" chubby Goth chick says, giggling. "That's got to be *the* funniest thing I've heard in a *long* time."

"You must not get out much," I say, sparing any false courtesy.

Goth chick starts blowing out laughter like it was puke. "You're *so* funny!" she squeals. "I definitely got to introduce you to my roommate. She is so crazy! You guys would definitely get along. One time we went to the mall and stopped in this German place to get some bratwurst and she's Jewish, right, so she started saying all this crazy shit like 'You killed my ancestors!' and stuff like 'My people didn't die in your holocaust just so you can sell your kraut food here!' My God, you had to be there. She is *so* crazy!"

"That's not funny, Lola" says *GQ* Euro-trash. "That's just stupid."

"Fuck you, Hal!" chubby Goth chick screams, turning around to face him.

"Here," says redheaded dork, sneaking up from behind me, poking at my arm with a cup. "We got you some coffee. It's kind of cold, though." I'm speechless as I take the cup from him. "We thought you'd get here earlier."

"So," Katie says, finally getting involved, "did you think about my offer at all, Kal?" This is a new, third side of Katie—the no-nonsense worker who cuts straight to business. I don't think I'll like this side as much.

"Offer?"

"Yeah. The one I mentioned last night? In the car? Before we dropped you off?"

"You got to open your ears now and then, dear," GQ Euro-trash—Hal—says to Katie while keeping his eyes set on me. "He just said he doesn't remember our talk last night."

"Really?" she asks, squinting.

"Yup," I say without looking at her. I take a sip from the icy, stale coffee. Tastes like cold antifreeze—at least I'm assuming it does. I never drank antifreeze.

"Okay," she says, after taking a deep breath. "Let's go for a walk." She pulls the cup out of my hand and trashes it. "I'll get you some fresh coffee," she says, booking down the hall.

"You really don't need to buy me any coffee." I say, power-walking to keep up with her.

"Yeah, I do. Have you looked at yourself yet today?"

"I don't look that bad, do I?" I ask. "I got a shower and changed before I got here. Granted, I haven't shaved in four days, but I can't look that bad."

"Actually, you kinda do," she says.

"But that guy in there said I 'cleaned up good.'"

"Yeah, well, Hal will fuck anything that sweats and has a functional dick." I don't say anything; I just up my walking pace to keep with hers. "Hal's gay, in case you didn't know."

"I do now. Listen, I really don't want any coffee." She stops on a dime and looks at me straight-faced. "Instead, would you mind coming out outside with me while I have a cigarette?"

"Fine," she says. "This way." We walk down an empty stairwell until we reach an emergency exit at the bottom. Katie pushes into the door and walks out with a strange sense of urgency. No alarms go off—she must use this door often.

Immediately outside the door is a long green awning. Thick rain drops against it as I light up my cigarette. Katie lights one, too.

"I didn't know you smoked." I'm so shitty when it comes to small talk.

"Don't you want to know why I stapled those cards to you last night? Don't you want to know what we talked about last night or why I wanted to talk to you today?" I take a deep breath, and I lift my head as I exhale. When she flat out says it like that, I start to wonder if I really do want to know. I get negative memories from our short spat yesterday and feel my stomach tremble with nerves. Reluctantly, I nod.

"Okay. Why?"

"Alright," she starts, straightening out her back and shoulders. "I'll boil this down as much as I can to make this as simple for you as possible. What if I told you I had a way not only to prove that you're innocent, but also to restore your reputation to a much higher status than it was before this whole thing started?"

Foreign Affairs

"So that's it? You just have to work for the school paper and all your problems are gone?" Barry asks cynically. He's coddling Thor, our evil new "pet," who sits there and squeaks while trying to struggle out of the old t-shirt wrapped around him.

"They want me to help them write a story about what happened when my face showed up on the poster, and then some follow up," I say, blowing smoke into a straight, puffy line in front of me.

"What kind of follow up?" he asks. The devil pet continues to squeak in his hands. Barry moves his index finger back and forth, towards and away from Thor, who's trying to bite.

"That's where it gets tricky. They want me to find out who really did it."

"That's stupid," interjects Jay, who's using a snow shovel to force all the garbage into the corner at the bottom of the stairs.

"That's what I said. But Katie said she has a bunch of 'leads' to follow, or whatever," I tremble when I say the word "leads." I feel like a complete phony, a hack. I feel like some tool that's been watching to many movies and has a glamorized view of how the media works.

"What kind of leads?" asks Barry.

"I dunno. I didn't feel like asking," I say, acting only half-interested as I sink deeper into the broken couch. Truth is,

I'm very interested. I really wanted to get started on this right away, but Katie didn't feel like it. Better to act laid back and uninterested than admit that I got shot down for a journalistic play date.

"How the hell do you plan on solving some crime the police can't solve?"

"I don't know. Dumb luck?" He brings up a good point. I don't care how good of an "investigative journalist" Katie thinks she is, we don't have the means necessary to do something like this. But damn, I'd really like to have sex with Katie. Damn.

"Do you at least know anything about reporting or anything like that?"

"Nope. I know dick about it. I've got no clue."

"Well, good luck with all that," says Barry, closing the conversation. Jay continues shoveling trash into the corner, removing any broken plates and glass he sees. I can hear Wally scampering around upstairs.

"What are you doing, Jay?" He keeps his head facing the ground as he continues shoveling, in a zombie-like trance.

"Cleaning," he finally answers. Wally's pitter-pattering upstairs gets more rapid.

"What time do you want to go tonight?" Barry asks, referring to us going out drinking.

"I don't care. I'd start now, but it's only 6."

"So?"

"I'm trying to be a little more…disciplined."

"Dutch said you were talking about that yesterday," Barry says, lighting a cigarette. Jay continues on as if we're not around.

"Yeah. It's not a big deal. I still want to go out and all. I just don't think I should do it until nighttime."

"Dude, it's dark out," he says nodding towards the window. "It doesn't get anymore 'nighttime' than this. Besides," he adds, "these two are already shit-faced. We have to play 'catch-up.'"

"Ready!" Jay yells up the steps. I hear Wally's footsteps

pattering faster. No, wait—not footsteps—banging. It's a soft banging, like someone is hitting the ground. The stained carpet muffles each thump.

The banging increases, becoming faster and more rapid. I hear Wally's voice matching each bump, making a noise with his voice as if he was mimicking machine gun fire. That's when he crashes into the pile of trash Jay collected in the corner. He wasn't cleaning at all—he was creating a landing pad. Wally rolls off the plastic sled he came down in and tries to stand up, shaking with traces of disorientation as he holds his dick.

"Ahhhh…my nuts!" he screams before his voice turns to soft mumble. "My sweet, precious nuts…" Wally whispers out of his mouth as he leans against the wall, trembling with pain.

On the other side of the house, the door creaks open. An unfamiliar voice calls in.

"Hello? Anyone here?" There's something different about the voice. It's a male voice, but it almost sounds like there's some small remainder of a foreign accent creeping out of each syllable.

"Back here," Barry yells, facing the back kitchen area, anxious to see who he just invited into our home. His mouth floats open, like he regrets inviting this person in without any kind of visual confirmation.

"Dude, why'd you invite him in?" Wally says in a drunk, panic-stricken whisper. "What if it's a vampire?! They can't come in unless you invite them! You just fucking killed us all!" I think he's joking, but I can never tell anymore.

We all keep our eyes latched towards the back kitchen area. The three seconds it takes for this person to come in lasts forever. Well, it does for me, anyway, because I've got a bad feeling about this. And then I see why: Fernando—Jill's Fernando. And for whatever reason, he's decided to walk into my house. First, he takes my girl and now he comes into my house. Got to give it to the guy—he's got bowling balls hanging between his legs to do something like this.

He walks a few steps into the living room and stops. He takes a deep breath and pumps up his chest. I can only imagine what this scene must look like to somebody who doesn't know us. I'm sitting on a broken couch; Barry's nursing a rodent. Jay is leaning proudly against his snow shovel, and Wally is climbing out of a pile of trash while cupping his denim-covered testicles. He's probably saying something to himself like, "How could Jill date this retard?" or "How drunk was Jill to slum down this far." Dickhead.

"Kalvin, right?" he looks at me, finally breaking the silence. His smirk is clear as day on his tan face.

"Yeah, I'm Kalvin." I want to punch this kid in the side of his freakin' head right now.

"Nice place," he says as he kicks around some small pieces of trash with his sandal-clad foot. Yeah, he's one of those idiots who thinks sandals serve as perfectly normal apparel during the winter. He keeps his hands in the pockets of his official Berkshire Tennis Team windbreaker as he wanders slowly across our living room. He's got a smirk as he explores the area. He knows he's better than me. He might as well declare "Checkmate."

"Who the fuck are you?" Barry asks.

"My name's Fernando," he states with his back to us. He's staring at our most recent fraternity composite picture. "Me and Kal—can I call you Kal?—me and Kal kind of shared a girl for a little while."

"Ugh…at the same time?" Jay asks, disgusted.

"Awww…Christ…" Barry says, equally as disturbed.

"Nah, nothing like that," Fernando says as he turns around. I keep my lips straight and my eyes focused. I don't know what to expect. "Truth be told, Kal actually stole my girlfriend from me many, many months ago," he says staring at the ground.

"Who's that?" asks Barry.

"Jill. I'm sure you guys probably met her at least once."

My housemates look at me as if I tried to explain advanced chemistry.

"Oh, but don't worry," says Fernando, "I got her back." There's not enough manure in this country to feed a shit-eating grin as big as the one that opens on his face.

My nerves are bubbling out of control while my hands shake and sweat. I think I'm hiding it pretty well though. Fernando is captain of the tennis team. If he were here to start a fight or something, he'd have brought a chess-set variety of lackeys in little white shorts and windbreakers. But no, he chose to come alone.

"Jill's doing fine, by the way," he says. "Thought I'd save you the trouble of asking." I stare at him silently. I don't know what else I can do. "And she doesn't know I'm here, so you don't have to worry about that, either."

My friends stare at me the same way they've been since this started. It's like I can hear the monologue in their heads. It's like I can hear them pondering whatever my reasons are that are stopping me from saying anything to this 6-foot pile of mongoloid. I can feel Fernando asking himself the same thing in his head.

"Okay…" The word pops out while I exhale. I pause to grab my smokes. I light one up, hoping it makes me look more intimidating, more badass. "So why are you here?"

He takes his hand out of his pocket and rubs his chin while he releases a small chuckle. "Thank God you finally asked. I was starting to feel a little awkward." He looks down at me, smiles slightly. "Mind going for a walk?"

Shit. Maybe he did come here for a fight. If he has me alone, he doesn't have to worry about my friends getting my back. Maybe Jill got so pissed off after our fight that she went home and said I hit her or something. Nah, that's pretty unlikely, she's not the type to do that. But why would he want to fight me? Maybe he doesn't. I got to calm down. I don't want this shithead to know that he's gotten the best of me again.

"Well?" he asks. I jerk my head, snapping myself out of a short trance.

"Fine," I reply. "Just make it quick. I've got things to do."

94

I want to do and say anything I can to make him feel small. I want him to feel like he's an insignificant part of my weekend. I want him to feel less significant than the run-off dripping down a hooker's thigh.

My housemates don't say or do anything to convince me against going alone with Fernando. They give me some more looks, but at this point their looks are so twisted and perplexed that I can't discern the thoughts and meanings behind them. I stand up and straighten my jacket. A subtle nod towards the door lets him know I'm ready to go.

The door slams behind us. We walk along the back parking alley that runs along all the houses on Cohen Street. It's wet and windy from the rainstorm that slammed the town a little earlier today. The damp wind somehow penetrates my sneakers, frosting my socks and toes. Fernando paces slowly next to me, as if we were two old friends on a reminiscent walk down a trail of memories.

"Aren't you going to ask why I wanted to talk to you?" he says.

"Actually," I reply, "I'm more tempted to ask how you're able to stay so calm." He looks at me and cocks his head with confusion. "It must be a little weird, y'know, sharing small talk with the guy who got with your girlfriend after you dicked her over."

"Heh…" he forces out a short laugh. "Actually, it's not weird at all," he mentions with a small smile. "It's hard to feel weird around the guy who fucked my girlfriend when I know that guy's bubbling with anger and jealousy right now, driving himself crazy wondering when the last time I fucked her was." He looks straight ahead, as if I'm not here. "And it was about an hour and a half before I came to your place, by the way."

I don't tell him I'm boiling with rage. "What do you want?"

"Well now! I'm glad you asked!" Sarcastic asshole. We both take about five slow steps forward before he says anything else. "What's the best way to put this?" he asks to himself, pressing the fingertips from each hand together in front of his chest. "I guess I should just be blunt: you and Jill don't need to be talking to each other anymore."

"She must be relieved, huh?" I snort sarcastically with a laugh. "Knowing she doesn't have to make anymore hard, social decisions since you're making them for her."

"She told me about your talk yesterday."

"And?"

"She says it got pretty heated," he stops dead. His arrogant smile drops as he turns to face me. "Normally, I wouldn't worry about something like that, but it seems like there's a lot of rumors going around lately about what happens when you get angry at women." He bends slightly sideways to look behind me. He nods, implying I should turn around and look. The big, green community bulletin board is 40 feet behind me, covered with tattered versions of my wanted poster.

"I don't care if you are worried. As long as she's not, there's no problem."

"You act like you're still a part of her life." His brow dips down in the middle, sharpening his eyes, which are already full of gleeful arrogance. "But you're not! So get over it!" I stare at him, trying to look as menacing as I can, hoping that he feels threatened somehow and shuts up. He doesn't. Instead, he rubs it in—he rubs it in deep. "Let's see what you've got going for you." He lifts his hand and starts counting on his fingers. "You live in a shit-shack, your excuse for 'friends' is a group of retards who drink with each other because nobody else is pathetic enough to do so, and, as of late, you're a prime suspect in a student's attempted rape." The marrow in my bones feel like it's shaking fast enough to vibrate my skin off. "See, and right there is the piece you're missing. You sit around your place, drunk as shit, probably blaming me for taking her from you. But the thing is, she had a lot more reasons to leave you other than me." My hands hide in my jacket pockets, closed in tight, shaky fists. My mouth and tongue are dry; my mind stutters with anger.

96

"Yeah. I guess I can't compete with the captain of a team full of guys in tight, little shorts who initiate new players by making them eat a pizza covered with their own jizz." I can't think of anything intelligent to say in my defense, so I resort to attacking his reputation. If there's one thing I've learned in the past couple days, it's how painful a shot to the rep can be.

"That is a goddamn rumor, and you know it, asshole!"

We stand staring at each other. The arrogant, jovial front he was laying on until now is gone. He stands in front of me, his brow heavily forcing over his rage-filled eyes. The same tense glare reflects off me and back towards his direction. Thunder crashes in the background, just like a movie. If there was going to be a fight, it'd be now. We're unarmed, and we have nobody here to pull us out of danger. Invisible emotions flick back and forth between us. A void of negative energy grows in the space between our eyes. The only thing preventing a fight is a cushion made only with the few short seconds it takes for one of us to take our courage, form it into a fist and fire it like a cannon at the other person.

"Jill doesn't want to talk to you anymore. She may not have the nuts to say it, but I do. Stay the hell away from her, or I'll fucking bleed you." In typical, amateur hardass fashion, he glares at me for another few seconds before he walks away.

"Bleed me?!" I deliberately wait until he walks a few feet away before I open my mouth. "What are you? A fucking medieval doctor? They still do that shit in El Salvador, or wherever the fuck you're from?!" He says nothing. Prick.

Big, Busty Justice

Are tight jeans out? I mean for guys—are they out of style? I thought they were. I thought guys who wore tight jeans were supposed to be either hicks or gay. Fernando had tight jeans on the other night when he decided to threaten me. I bet he's gay. I think he's European. A lot of European guys are gay. Then again, the straight ones usually act kind of fruity, but it helps them get women. Maybe that's the appeal. Maybe Jill likes him because he has that gay, European flair. Then again, I guess I shouldn't really be thinking about how gay some guy is when I'm the one commenting on his jeans.

It's been four days since Katie "propositioned" me about doing this article for the paper. She's been busy chasing leads, however the hell you do that. I've just been drunk and watching the Game Show Network. When I compare the two, it kind of puts things into a strange new perspective. Makes me realize that, yeah, I lead a pretty asinine life.

Lana's mad at me. She hung up on me every time I called in the past two days. Molly probably told her about how I passed out and woke up sitting against the dumpster outside of Dill's on Sunday morning. I got really drunk and followed some creepy-looking guy and an awkward, mildly unattractive girl after they left. The guy looked a little like me, or at least I thought he did at the time. I thought maybe he was the rapist. I thought I could catch him in the act. Turned out to be crap. A car full of people came and picked them up. I got bummed, leaned against the dumpster, lit a cigarette. I woke up in the morning to a Mennonite nudging me awake by sticking his foot into my ribs. Could've happened to anyone.

Katie, on the other hand, made some progress. She was not only able to find the Public Safety officer on the Connie Ward case; she also booked an interview with him, which leads us to this not-so-enjoyable moment. I don't know what I'm doing when it comes to interviewing. I didn't want to come. I shouldn't have come. I look at my watch to confirm that. It's 4:30 p.m. I'm missing *Saved By the Bell* reruns.

"So how much time is Berkshire's Public Safety force devoting to this case?" Katie looks and sounds like a pro. At least I'm assuming she does—I don't know what a pro sounds like. She sits with her back straight and her legs crossed. On her lap rests a memo pad, and on that rests her arms, crossed at the wrists. I told her before we came here that I'm letting her do all the talking. I don't want another incident like the last one I had in this office. I'm fine with just sitting here with my feet on the desk and relaxing.

"Well, miss, we've devoted about as much time as we kin to this case. Sir?" he says, turning to me, "Please remove ya feet from mah desk."

"Fuck you."

"Kal!" Katie's alarmed. She shouldn't be.

"Don't worry about it. I know this guy. He isn't going to do anything." Little does she know the person sitting across from us is none other than little Robert Anne Hughes— Spaz. Or, as he's known in these parts, "Ice Pick."

"Kal, Ah don't wanna to hafta make an example outta ya like Ah did last time ya came here."

"Like to see you do that. You don't got your wrinkly, old reception lady to give you any back-up muscle this time."

"Kal?!" Katie looks at me, her soft, full eyes curving downwards above an opened-lipped frown, begging for my subordination. I grumble and put my feet down.

99

"Yeah, that's right, bitch. Ya betta listen to me. Ah'm the law in this room."

The room is quiet for a second. Katie looks down at her notes. I can tell her mind is trying to digest what just happened. She has no idea what it's like. Spaz and I just have a natural rapport. When it comes to acting like asses, we're the pros.

"If you don't mind sharing, how much time is 'as much time as you can'?" She asks after collecting herself. Her eyes refocus on Spaz. She's totally composed. Before we came here, she called me and told me that we'd be meeting with Spaz. Once she found out I knew him, she asked if there was anything we could do to persuade him to loosen his lips. I told her there was nothing I could do, but I did tell her that a little cleavage may go a long way in this case. I didn't think it'd really make a difference; I just wanted to see if she'd do it. And here she is, wearing a tube-top in the middle of the winter. God bless America.

"Well, that depends. We kin only do so much with what we have," Spaz says, leaning back and resting his head into his folded hands behind it, just like a lazy southern sheriff. His eyes are focused on Katie's rack. Mine are too. She doesn't notice me, but she definitely can tell that Spaz is interested. She gingerly glides her fingernail along the inside curves of her full, plump cleavage. It may seem a bit obvious, but I don't think Spaz cares. She's definitely greased his wheels. This is why you should never trust a smart woman. Smart women will do anything and everything to get what they need or want. There is nothing in this world more dangerous than a smart, ambitious woman.

"But can't you just request to put more men on the case? Aren't you afraid that this may not be a one-time thing?" She seems genuinely concerned and rightfully so.

"Don't look at me. Ah'm just an intern." Spaz admits.

"Wait, what?!" Her mildly flirty façade disappears.

"Now, I can understand your distress, Katie…" Spaz begins spouting the textbook reaction to her outrage. She doesn't let him get too far into it.

"You're damn right I'm distressed!" Her tone blows Spaz back a few notches. "I mean…ugh! Can you believe this?" she asks, turning to me. All I can do is shrug because yeah, I do believe it.

Katie starts scribbling feverishly on her note pad. She's angry as she writes. I can hear the page scraping under the pen as she digs it into the pad. Spaz looks at me and shrugs. He doesn't have enough experience with women to know exactly how to deal with what's happening in front of him. Not like I'm an expert or anything. I'm getting sleepy. All I can do is stare at the tape recorder Katie put on the desk in between Spaz and I. I point my sleepy eyes at it, watching each cog spin the tape around inside. I'm bored.

"Kal, start asking him your questions," she says without even looking up.

"What questions?"

"You didn't prepare any questions for this?" She jerks her head up and stares at me while she waits for an answer.

"I didn't know I had to."

"Do you even know what an interview is?"

"You didn't say anything about questions!"

"What the hell?" she exclaims. "Did you think I was going to do all the work?"

"No…" I say softly, "I just thought I was more like a consultant or something…"

"You don't have any questions at all?" she asks, forcing herself to calm down.

"Okay, hold on…give me a second…" I say, trying to fumble through questions in my head. "So…" I begin. Spaz is gawking at Katie's rack with greasy, glazed-over eyes. He's enjoying the opportunity he has to stare since Katie is focusing on her notes. "Who was the girl that filed that report with you?"

"What report?" Spaz asks. His attention doesn't shake away from her chest.

"The one you told me about last week. You said a girl

101

came in and gave a report that proved I was innocent." Katie's head darts up and faces me.

"Ah know what report you mean," he finally takes his eyes off the boobs and squints them at me. "But Ah thought me and you had an agreement that we'd both forget it exists."

"Wait…" Katie interrupts, "someone filed a report about this?"

"Ah'm not at liberty to disclose that, miss."

"Quit acting like a real cop and tell me the truth!" she demands. "Is there a report?"

He looks at me as if I did something wrong. "Yeah, there's a report."

"Well, can we see it?"

"Nope."

"Why not?" Katie asks. She looks at me, as if I could do something about this. "It's a matter of public concern…isn't there some kind of rule or law or something saying that you have to share them?"

"Shouldn't you know that stuff yourself?" I ask.

"No…why?" Her voice gives off an innocence I didn't think existed inside of her.

"I just thought you'd have some concept of the Shield Laws in this state, you know, being assistant editor of a newspaper, and all."

"Shut up. Journalism's only my minor."

"Hey, Ah'm just an intern." Spaz rejoins the conversation. "Even if there is, Ah don't have clearance for that."

"Clearance? Spaz, this is a Public Safety office for a mid-sized state college. You're not in the fucking CIA here. Isn't it just sitting in a filing cabinet or something?" I ask.

"And lose my internship? Fuck that. Ah'm about half ready to deck ya for just sayin' that."

I shrug at Katie. She points her stare downwards and starts thinking. It's quiet. Spaz leans back and relaxes in his chair. In his mind, this is some sort of competition or game, and he just called "checkmate." Let him think that way. I feel light bulbs blowing up in my head as I come up with a plan. I grab Katie's arm and pull her towards me.

"Dump 'em out," I whisper in her ear. Spaz tilts his head sideways like a confused puppy.

"What?" she replies.

"He's been staring at your rack all day," I explain. "I know him. Trust me on this one."

"No!" Her face twists. "I'm not doing that!"

"Hey! Before we came here, you asked if there was anything we could do to loosen him up if we needed to. And what did I say?"

"Yeah, but this is different than just showing some cleavage!"

"No, it's not! You're still just showing cleavage…just a little more of it."

"I'm not doing it!"

"Whatever," I say. She doesn't sound like she's fighting too hard. She probably wants to show off her tits—most girls do. There's a reason why every girl has a closet full of tight sweaters and low-cut shirts. All girls instinctively want to be naked and sexual. It's written into their DNA. It's a survival thing. Women want to put on a sexy appearance so that men think they're appealing. In turn, men are attracted to them and have sex with them (or die trying). Because of this, the human reproductive cycle stays full and complete.

"No! Not 'whatever'! I'm not doing it!" I shrug at her, acting uninterested in her rack. Reverse psychology. "I'm not going to flash my boobs to a stranger!" And this is where the roadblock is. The thing stopping girls like Katie from acting upon their liberal, bare-chested nature is a simple matter of programming. Katie, while I'm sure she instinctively wants to take her shirt off, she has to deal with the cleanly, ethical upbringing that most girls in our society are accustomed to. Right now, her conscience is waging an uneven battle upon her shoulders. On the right are her angelic mother and father, both of whom are doing a poor job of reinforcing the values of prudence and chastity they've laid on her since she was born. On the left is big, bad me, donning a red devil costume complete with pointy tale and pitchfork. Her mind is trying to side with her parents and all the good they've instilled in her. But her very body and soul are taking sides with me, a dark liberator with the key to free her natural, lusty instincts from the man-made limits and mores of our society.

"If you feel uncomfortable with it, then fine. No big deal." More reverse psychology.

"I don't feel uncomfortable! I just don't want to do it!" Our whispers have evolved into a full-volume conversation. Spaz ping-pongs his eyes back and forth to focus on whoever's talking.

"Okay, I get it!" My hands are sweaty, my fingers are crossed. Everyone in this room knows that she wants to set the twins free. Just have to push her some more. "You're the one running this show. Do what you think is right."

She bites her lower lips and sets her eyes down towards her chest, almost like she was asking her breasts for permission. This is it. This is where it happens. She pulls away from me and runs her hand through her hair, rubbing her head. She rolls her eyes several times. She's definitely going through the pros and cons in her head. Spaz' fingers lie flat on his desk and twitch. He knows what's going on. It's like he has some kind of "pervert sense" that picks up on this stuff.

"Don't look," Katie says to me. She's staring straight ahead.

"Why not?"

"Because I don't want you to."

"C'mon!"

"Hey! I'm doing this whole thing to help you out! Just do what I ask, okay?"

Katie arches her back. With both hands, she flings her hair back from the shoulders it rested on. She slowly cups each breast in her tube top, gently moving and squeezing each one.

"Kal!" She catches me staring. "Turn around!"

Christ. Spaz is going to be rubbing this in for a week. I don't even think the kids seen a tit before in person, and now he gets to see hers. Meanwhile, I'm stuck here with only a vague imaginary picture drawn out in my head. I can't even jerk off to that. Story of my life.

"Yea...that's it. That's the stuff," Spaz says in what may be the single creepiest voice I've ever heard. It sounds like a cross between the Crypt Keeper and Barney Fife choking on someone's piss. "Okay," he says, seconds later. Katie taps me on the back to let me know that I can turn around and stop torturing myself over how busty and beautiful her tits are. "I can't give it to you now," Spaz says. "I'll bring it by your place later, Kal."

"Thanks..." Katie says, suddenly showing a new, chipper mood. She doesn't have a trace of regret in her voice. This is just another testament to my ever-expanding wisdom when it comes to the innately slutty instincts of the fairer of our species. "We'll be in touch, sweetie." Gone is Katie, the dedicated journalist. Back for the first time in several days is flirty, seductive Katie. I missed her.

I hold open the door and let her out in front of me. "I'm impressed," I state. "I could've bugged him for months and never gotten him to fold like you did. That must be a hell of a rack."

"Heh...wouldn't you like to know?" she teases.

"Still," I say, trying to forget how pissed I am that I couldn't see her goods, "I'm surprised things worked out the way they did."

"Stick with me for a while, Kal, and you'll learn one thing."

"And what's that?"

"I always—*always*—find a way to get what I want. No matter what."

It's like I said: There is nothing in this world more dangerous than a smart, ambitious woman.

Quiet Conflicts

I always forget about how sleazy the cafeteria at Berkshire really is. Along with the shit-colored walls, the chipped floor tiles and the large portion of inbred America that serves as the operating staff, our cafeteria is one of those places that makes you feel more slimy leaving than you did before you came. A constant stink floats in the air and hangs in your nostrils long after you've exited the building. Most of the time, the smell resembles rotting cabbage, but sometimes it smells more like burning condoms. I can't enter this place without feeling like I've been glazed with some kind of translucent film.

"What're those?" Lana asks as I'm sitting down with a fistful of crumpled paper in one hand and a cup of tea in the other.

"Wanted posters."

"Wanted posters?" Her eyebrow rises. "Of you?"

"Yup," I say. "I'm getting rid of any I see."

"Won't that kind of look like an admittance of guilt?"

"Fuck it. I'm tired of people giving me weird looks."

"Does that really happen?"

"See for yourself," I say, twirling my index finger in a circular motion, gesturing around the room. The few people that are here and awake glare at me. In their mind, they're looking at a wanted felon. Dumbasses.

"Aren't you eating?" Lana asks me, changing the subject.

"Nah." I stare into the ripples waving around inside the cup of tea in front of me.

"You should at least drink some milk or juice—something with some kind of substance to it."

"Nah," I say again. "Tea's fine."

"You don't like coffee?"

"Nope."

"I thought all college kids drank coffee."

"That's just what Hollywood wants you to think."

"Funny." She's not at all amused. Who could be at 7:06 a.m.? "I'm surprised you came."

"Why?"

"It's early. Shouldn't you just be leaving from the bar?"

"That's why I wanted to talk to you," I say. This is the first time Lana has agreed to speak to me since Sunday morning. I haven't been able to get her to tell me why. But from what I can tell, it probably has something to do with her thinking I have some kind of drinking problem. "Are you mad at me?"

"Not anymore." She dices a hunk of scrambled eggs with her fork.

"But you were?"

"Not really."

"Okay…"

Lana isn't the confrontational type. She's more the quiet, loathing type. I could slaughter her family before her eyes and she'd still find a way to keep her anger silent. She's just not the type to get verbally angry. She will, however, use the "cold shoulder" routine with the timing and accuracy of a surgeon. She's got this magic in her eyes that makes her silence pierce through my heart like a couple of 9-mm hollow points.

"I just…" she starts and stops her sentence with those two words before dropping her face into her cupped hands. She rubs her forehead, drops her hands limp onto the tabletop and releases a heavy sigh before continuing. "I wish you could see things through my eyes right now…"

"What do you mean?"

"To you, this seems fun and all. And I know you're supposed to have fun in college and do all the crazy things you can't do after you graduate. But still," she says, her expression growing more depressed, "it's hard not to get a little worried when I see you passing out in random places and getting so drunk that you can't remember the night before."

"But didn't you just say that this is the time when I should be enjoying that kind of thing? The time I should be able to enjoy being totally irresponsible? All I'm doing is living things up while I can."

"I don't get so worried about how drunk you get or how often you do it," she begins. "I'm worried about why."

I look away from her. She can't tell that I'm a little moved by this topic if she can't see my eyes.

"You really have nothing to worry about. I'm fine."

"Typical Kalvin L. Gray answer," she says. I can't tell if she's trying to be smug or not. "Don't you at least want to know why I think you're doing this?" I'm quiet. I let her use my silence as a response. "I think you've got a lot of emotional stuff to work out."

"It's okay. You can use the word 'issues.'"

"So there *is* something wrong?" Her face beams with sincere concern.

"No. I just said that because I thought it sounded better than 'emotional stuff.'" We're quiet. She's only trying to help, but I still shoved it in her face faster than she could swallow.

"It's weird seeing you this way anymore, Kal." I let my raised eyebrow tell her that I don't understand. "In some ways you weren't always like this, but in other ways, you were."

"I'm not following."

"I don't 100 percent know what I mean, either," she says, disrupting eye contact. "Okay, it's like this: the drinking has always been there, it's just that it was there in a different way, you know?"

"I'm not sure…"

"Okay. What I mean is, you've always been a binge drinker. Most guys in college are. But before, it used to seem more about the fun, party-like aspect with you."

"Okay…as opposed to…?"

"…as opposed to how it is now. It still seems like you drink for fun, but it also seems like there's something else there."

"Like what?"

"I don't know. It's like this really negative kind of vibe. I don't know—you can just tell that you're different about the whole thing, you know? It's almost like you're more aggressive about it. Like you're trying to attack yourself."

"By drinking?"

"Am I that far off?" The truth is, she's probably not. I don't pay much attention to the "vibe" I've been putting off lately—or at least I didn't before this "assault" thing started up. "Remember last year? When we first started becoming really close?"

"Yeah, I remember. What about it?"

"You always had this kind of smile. But it wasn't like a physical smile on your face. It was like an emotional smile. You always kind of put off this vibe like you were smiling on the inside. Even when you'd be pissed or upset, you still had that, I don't know, 'energy' about you. Even if you didn't smile with your mouth, you still did with your eyes." She's quiet for a moment, with her eyes focused on her plate below. She looks up and aligns her eyes with mine. "I know that sounds really cheesy, but do you know what I mean?"

"I think so." My fingers dig hard into the soft, fleshy area between my thighs and knees. Shivers shake through my body and cover my muscles like a blanket. It's a unique kind of shiver—somewhere between nervous, scared shivers and excited, anxious shakes. I like and dislike talking about my issues at the same time.

"You're not like that anymore. Not lately. You haven't been like that for a while," she says, looking back down towards the table, watching her thumbs twiddle over each other. "You haven't been like that for a few months."

"Shit happens," I tell her. "I'm still the same person I've always been. Things are just weird lately. I'll get over it, and things will go back to normal. No big deal." I don't know what it is about Lana that makes me act like I'm some kind of hardass. We both know that I don't think this cut and dry. I'm not the "no worries" type.

"You've always been able to talk to me, Kal. You're one of my best friends." Her voice shivers a little while she talks. "But lately, you just seem so quiet and...I don't know? 'Loathsome' I guess would be a good word. You always look like you're going to self-destruct." The shaking in her voice takes a cheap shot at my heartstrings. "I'm not the only one who's worried about you, either."

"Listen, people change. I'm no different." I feel a nervous energy inside me trying to shake it's way out through my pores. "I mean, seriously, maybe I have been acting differently, I don't know. I think I'm the same person I've always been, I'm just going through some different shit lately." She stares at me in silence that's cut only by the clanging of silverware and plastic chairs in the background.

"You know you can still talk to me, right?"

"Yeah," I say. "Of course I do."

"Then why don't you?"

"I don't know."

"So, there is something on your mind then?" she asks, trapping me.

"I don't know."

"You can talk to me."

"I know," I say, "and I appreciate it, I seriously do." With that, our mouths shut softly. She tries to help. Do I need help though? She remains quiet. I sip some of my tea. It's ice cold.

"You look upset," she says.

"Seriously, I'm fine," I tell her. "It's just been a long couple of days."

"Why?"

110

"I don't know. All kinds of reasons."

"Okay..." She dips her head low, avoiding further eye contact. She closes down because she feels I'm trying to close down.

"Listen, don't take it personally."

"Take what personally?"

"I'm just not, you know, like, good at talking about stuff, you know?"

"Okay. You used to be, but okay."

"I feel weird about talking about my problems lately."

"That's fine. I won't pry."

"But it's not because of you or anything," I say. "Seriously."

"Alright," she says. "You can talk to me though, if you change your mind."

"Thanks." She continues working on her food. Her eyes are still dripping down, staring at the tabletop. She feels offended—I can tell.

"What?" she asks. She can tell my lips are on the verge of pushing out a sentence.

"I don't know..." I say. "You ever wonder about just...everything?"

"Yeah," she says, her eyes pointed up as she gently nods. "Yeah, sometimes I do. You too?"

"Yep."

"What in particular?"

"You know, that's the funny thing," I begin. "I spend so much time thinking about this stuff, that anytime I try to actually think about it or solve it, I can't remember or focus enough on what I was worried about in the first place."

"Hmmm..." she hums. "That's different." Time flows by and we're both silent. She's made the last move, now it's my time to follow up. What have I done? I've talked and left myself slightly open and ready for exposure. The hard part is knowing what I have to do next.

"I don't like who I am," I say. "Is that normal?"

"I don't understand..."

111

"Okay, it's like this," I say, taking a deep breath and swallowing, knowing full and well that I'm getting into a tell-all confession. It's early, and I know I'm not running on all cylinders. I don't think I'll regret this now, but I will later. "I feel like this isn't who I'm supposed to be."

"Okay, well, who're you supposed to be?"

"That's the thing—I don't know. It just feels that everything I do, every choice I make, is only made because I made a wrong turn somewhere else."

"Like where?"

"I don't know…earlier in my life. I mean, look at me: I'm in college. Traditionally, when you graduate high school, you do one of three things: you get a job, join the military or go to another school. The problem is, when people go back to school, it's because they're learning what to do to become who they want to be."

"Okay…" she says, rubbing her chin while she takes mental notes.

"Like, if you're planning to be a doctor, you go to med school. If you're planning to be a priest, you go to seminary school. If you're planning to become an electrician, you go to trade school. I don't fit into that."

"Yeah, you do," she says. "You wouldn't be here if you didn't."

"But that's the thing. I'm not planning to be anything in particular. I'm not setting myself up for any kind of career or anything. I'm just here, in limbo, hanging out and drinking myself to the point where I call myself a different name and pass out somewhere awkward and uncomfortable."

"Alright, I'm not trying to be insensitive here or anything, Kal," she says, "but it's not like you're the only college kid who spends most of his time getting drunk and doing stupid things."

"I know, and you're completely right," I say, "but this is different than that. For me, the drinking and everything is almost like a side effect, you know?"

"So you drink because you're angry at who you are?"

"I think so, but not really. I mean, I always drank, even before I started thinking about this. I just don't like who I am generally, which includes the drinking problem. The difference between myself and every other drunk in Berkshire is that they are all moving towards something. Like, look at my roommates. They all drink as much as I do, but at least they know that they're okay with who they are and what's going on. They all got stuff to live up to; they all know what they want to do after school. For them, this is all just like a passing phase, a rite of passage."

"And it's not for you?"

"I don't know. To be honest with you, now that I'm talking about it, I don't even think that's the reason for things being the way they are lately. Sorry." We grow quiet. She stares at her food, her feelings of helplessness spreading across the table, hitting me hard enough to make me feel guilty.

"I wish I could help you out more," she says, sending my conscience into a maelstrom of anger and self-resentment. Her eyes are sad and carry a genuine sense of pity. Maybe she's right. Maybe I do have issues. Maybe I should talk about them.

"Promise you won't—I don't know—be weird if I tell you what's really been on my mind lately?"

"Of course."

"Jill."

"Your ex?"

"Yeah," Damn...this is going to hurt. I already regret opening my mouth.

"I kind of figured."

"You did?"

"Yeah," she says. "That's when you started acting like this. After you two broke up."

"You mean after she broke up with me."

"Yeah," she looks at me. "Are you okay about the whole thing?"

"Yeah, I think so." I say. "It's just awkward...the whole

feeling of being rejected and all by someone you care for."

"I know," she says. "Doesn't it kind of bother you when someone you care about has so much power over your life?"

"Yeah…"

"Listen," she says as she stands and collects her silverware in one action, "I'm sorry to stop in the middle of this, but I've got to go. I have a class to get to." My thumb and index finger rattle upon the tabletop. I don't know what to say. "I'd skip it if I could." Her eyes swell and turn red. "I'm really sorry," she says.

"I know. It's cool."

"You going out tonight?"

"I don't know," I say out of reflex. "Probably."

"I might, too," she says. "Let me know what you're doing. We can talk about this then?"

"Okay." She walks away from me, each step she takes reeks of low self-esteem. She feels like she's failed me. She takes it personally that I don't open up, but not because she thinks I don't trust her. She takes it personally because she feels like a bad friend. She doesn't know how to help me. It's a shame really, seeing as she's so sincere, so generous with her friendship. I thought she was pissed at me for being a drunk, but she's just concerned about me drowning myself in beer and depression.

The truth is, I'm not going to be willing to talk about this later. My brain feels exposed; my insides feel raw. I don't know if I could physically or mentally handle talking about it again. It's a shame. She's such a good friend, and I'm not. I wish I could talk about it more, I do. It just seems like this takes as much of a toll on her as it does on me—maybe more. I'd love to tell her that I feel this little spore inside of me that spreads, burns and eats away at me more and more by the hour. I wish I could have that kind of honesty.

The cafeteria slowly begins to fill with early birds. It's too easy to make a joke about them trying to get a worm from a place that no doubt serves some kind of worm-related meat. People gaze around the room like zombies when they first enter. They get their meal card swiped through a small machine that beeps as the card slides through. They gather themselves into lines and wait to be handed whatever slop they're willing to eat at this hour. They bounce between the mazes of tables like a pinball bouncing off of flippers. The whole thing makes me think and freezes my mind at the same time.

My legs feel numb. They're not used to being awake this early. My hands hide in my pockets under the table. My neck is stiff and my head doesn't move; my eyeballs feel like they're floating away from their sockets. I'm bored and I can't get up. I just sit here. My face is scruffy. Haven't shaved for a week. The hair on my chin isn't as soft as the hair covering the rest of my face. It feels weird when I rub it, like toothbrush bristles. Why don't I shave more often? It's not hard. Why don't most guys my age shave more often? Facial fuzz has somehow become a part of the college uniform, right up there with hooded sweatshirts and pre-ripped baseball caps from designer clothing stores. It hurts a little bit inside to realize that. It hurts a little bit inside to cave in to the fact that I've totally given up on trying to have any kind of individuality. I think I gave that up as a freshman. I thought most people didn't give up that dream till after they'd graduated.

I keep thinking about what Fernando said to me a few nights ago. How he said, in no certain terms, that I'm a sloppy drunk with nothing going for me, and that's why Jill left me.

Jill—thinking of her doesn't bring me anything good. Her name is like a knife cutting down the middle of my body leaving me in two separate, pain-riddled halves. One half aches at the very thought of her name. It aches after remembering the freckles on her cheeks and flavor of her lip gloss. The other half screams with a different pain. It's filled with all the anger and self-loathing that comes with one realization: I'm a huge, stereotypical, college-educated pussy. I sit here crying about a girl, in a fleece of stubble and greased hair that I wear like a nametag.

Sweat drips down my neck and my heavy lungs make it hard to breathe. My eyes finally move a little out of reflex. They feel dry. In the corner of my eye, a clock reads 8:00 a.m. The Stare strikes again.

10

Happy Birthday, Mr. President

Through dimming darkness,
And empty evenings void of light,
Like brilliant shining stars,
Our brown and gold colors shine ever bright.
Under powdered, white clouds,
And heaven-bearing skies
Our colors hold true,
And our flag proudly flies.
Oh, Berkshire University
Our pride runs long.
Your social grace and academic excellence,
Bound by glue, ever so strong.

I remember during the second semester of my freshman year, Berkshire had a contest in order to develop a new alma mater. From what I remember, participation in the contest was so low that they opened the contest up beyond student participation, and allowed members of the town to participate. Interest remained low, apparently, because looking at this alma mater, pressed and engraved on a solid bronze plaque, I see a thin plate of gold with the engraving: *Berkshire, The True—Created by Mrs. Ostman's 4th Grade class, Berkshire Elementary School, 2001.* Such a fine institution we have here.

I'm nervous. Waiting rooms make me uncomfortable. Shit…why did I get called here? Why does President Luther want to see me? What business do I have with the fucking president of the university? Does this have to do with Connie Ward? Is he going to expel me? *Can* he expel me? I didn't do anything…

"Just go and see what he has to say," Katie said to me earlier. I tried talking her into coming with me, but she said if she talked to Luther she'd probably say something she'd regret. "If he talks about Connie, just try to take mental notes. Chances are, he doesn't know any more about it than we do."

Easy for her to say; she's not in my shoes. It's really quiet in here. I can only hear the clock ticking and the secretary turning the pages of her romance novel every couple minutes. My appointment was for 2 p.m. It's 20 after. Why can't we just get this over with?

"Kalvin?" the secretary asks in her meek, elderly voice. "He'll see you now."

Maroon double doors lead into his office. The first thing I notice is how big his desk is. It's as big as my parents' dining room table. Two giant windows border the desk on both sides, blinding me enough to make me stumble my way in.

"Kalvin Gray!" he beams as he spins his chair towards me and stands up. "Dr. Al Luther. Good to meet you!" His wide smile hides his age. He looks about 40 when he has to be at least 50. He's as bald as a cancer patient. He Bics his head; you can tell from all the little stubs forming a horseshoe along his head. He reminds me of a bald Gene Hackman.

"Good to meet you, too," I say humbly, sitting in front of his desk. He didn't offer me a seat, but to hell with it—if I stand he'll see me shaking like a dead, wrinkled leaf.

"Don't call me 'Mr. Luther' or anything like that anymore," he says randomly. "I hate that."

"I…I didn't…"

"But you were about to!" He points at me and smiles.

"Well," he says while he reclines back in his leather chair, "you probably want me to tell you why I asked you here…"

"Yeah, I…"

"But before I tell you," he says interrupting me, "you need to try one of these!" A plate of brownies materializes in his hands out of nowhere. "It's my birthday, and my wife made me these cheesecake brownies. You have got to try one!"

"Happy Birthday," I say. "But, I'm really not…"

"C'mon! Take one!"

"No, really, I just…"

"Take one." His voice raises and loses all sense of humor. "They're cheesecake." What the hell is wrong with this guy? Did he ask me here to eat his wife's brownies? He watches with an open smile as I eat one. He looks at me like there's something funny about me eating it—oh, God—please tell me he didn't jerk off on these.

"They're good, huh?" I nod slowly while my mouth is full of fudge and cream cheese. "Guess what?" I hate when people ask that. I look up at him as I stop chewing, waiting for the punch line. "There's pot in that!"

"What?" Even though I know there's no pot, I play along by looking mortified. It's not hard to pretend, considering the last three minutes have felt like a nightmare.

"HA!" he throws his head back. "I'm just messing with you! You should've seen the look on your face! You looked all like, 'oh no! I just ate pot brownies!' HA!"

What the hell is wrong with this guy?!

I try to force out a fake laugh, but it literally hurts mentally to do so. Then, it hits me: now I know why Berkshire is such a mess of a school. Katie would've loved this little meeting. "Okay." he says with a sigh, finally finished with his laughing. "Want to know why I summoned you?"

"I think so…"

"I heard about your situation—looking very similar to the description given by Connie about her attacker."

"You did?"

"Yep," he says. "I also heard about how you're working along with the school newspaper to not only prove you're not the guy, but to also find out what really happened. Is that right?"

"Yeah..." I say. "But how'd you know?"

"Well, first off, Chip in the Communication department is a close friend of mine. We were fraternity brothers back at Ithaca. You're in a fraternity, aren't you?"

"Yeah...how'd you...?"

"I looked through your records. Which one are you in again?"

"T-H-E. Tau Eta Epsilon."

"THE? Your fraternity letters are THE?" What does this have to do with Connie Ward? What does Chip have to do with Connie Ward? "That's funny, but I digress," he says, breathing out and letting his beer belly plop out proudly. "Chip and I were getting a couple drinks at Toad Creek when he let it slip. And as for the newspaper thing, I found that out at a Student Government meeting when they were trying to allocate funds for something." Toad Creek. Classy place. My friends and I never go there because it costs more than $2 a beer.

"With all due respect," I say, keeping up my humble routine, "can I ask why I'm here?"

"What's your rush?" he asks, almost like he's accusing me of something. "Got a date? Got to go to work or something? Do you even have a job?"

"No..."

"You don't?"

"I work over the summer. Save up all money for the school year..."

"Like a squirrel hoarding nuts, huh?" A big, goofy smile splatters across his face.

"Yeah...I guess so..." I want to go home.

"Huh..." he says. "Well, I brought you here because I feel for you."

"Feel for me?"

"I feel for you, brother!" he says, reaching across his desk for a high-five. "C'mon! Meet me up here, buddy! High-five!"

This guy is on crack!

"Umm...thank you..."

"I know how it feels to be accused of something you didn't do," he says matter-of-factly.

"You don't think I did it?"

"Nah, I know you didn't."

"How?" I ask.

"I looked at your files, remember? You seem like a good shit."

"Thanks!" Finally, something good comes from this meeting.

"I got friends in high places. You need anything, remember Luther is there for you!" he says with a politician's smile. "I'm all about keeping my school safe!"

"Cool," I say as my small burst of enthusiasm dissipates.

"Well, that's about it," he says. "I just wanted to tell you I admire your little crusade and this office will do anything it can to help you with your cause."

"Thanks..." Random. This whole meeting can be summed by the word "random."

"Good Luck!" he says, shaking my hand. "Keep in touch!"

"Sure..." I say, walking out.

"Wait!" he belts out. "Take some brownies with you!" I grab a small handful from the pile. Nice guy—very nice of him to offer to help me. Still...it's almost 3:00. I missed *Charles in Charge* reruns for this?

11

Duh.

Katie, from our first real conversation at the bar, seemed like a genuinely smart girl. Not in just a book smart way, though. She also showed that her mind contains a lot of that common sense stuff that most people call "street smarts." But if she's so damn smart, how come she didn't think of this idea sooner? I mean, she's smart *and* she's a reporter—between those two facts, someone is bound to assume she would have had this idea earlier. It's so damn simple and obvious. There's only one answer as to why she didn't think of this until now—I'm rubbing off on her.

"Yeah, hi," she says into her candy-apple-red flip phone, "is Connie there? Yeah, Connie Ward." Of all the people we should ask about this thing, why not the victim? I thought of it at first, but hell, why would I want to do that? That'd go well—"Hi, I'm Kal. I resemble the guy who assaulted you. Do you think when you get out of the hospital you could help me show everyone at school that I didn't attack you?"

It's been quiet for more than a few seconds. Katie looks at me while she rolls her eyes; her head rocks back and forth from side to side in a tick-tock manner. She didn't know what to think about my meeting with Luther. Of course, I didn't tell her about everything that happened in there—particularly the brownie incident. I felt like crying after that.

My bedroom's a mess. Why the hell did I agree to do this at my place? I should've talked her into letting me go to her place. She's going to think I'm even more of a waste than she probably already does. It doesn't help that Wally is sitting Native American-style at his computer watching cripple-themed porn. At least he doesn't have 50 Cent blasting loud enough to rupture our ears.

"What's happening?" I ask.

"She's there. Her roommate is getting her," Katie whispers loudly. She looks like she's ready to say something else, but she's apparently cut off by whoever's on the other end of the phone. "Yeah...didn't you just say she was there?" Katie's face straightens into a ridged form. "And now she's not there? Okay...well I tried her cell, like, six times already, and she doesn't pick up." Katie looks at me and shrugs. Wally nods his head with a smile while he watches two guys in wheelchairs double-teaming some girl. "Yeah, well if she doesn't pick up 'cause she's at work, than why doesn't she ever call me when she's done? Or just return my messages at least?" Katie's voice picks up in volume and drops in tone. She's shedding the "polite reporter Katie" costume in exchange for her "anything to get the job done" costume. She's still shifting between all these personalities, but at least I'm getting used to them. "No. No," her voice softens back to normal. "Yeah, I know, I wasn't yelling at you. Sorry." Katie rolls her eyes at me again. "Well, can you tell her Katie called? Yeah, from the newspaper. Thanks."

"So now what?" I ask.

"I don't know. She's obviously avoiding us."

"Why?"

"If I knew, you wouldn't have to ask."

"Okay." I'm trying to hide the fact that I'm a little unhappy that this isn't the first time she tried calling Connie. I'm not surprised, just upset. I thought we were equal partners on this thing. "This isn't the first time you tried calling Connie?"

"What?" she asks. She may be hot, but she's a piss-poor liar. Her eyes are too clear to hide any secrets.

"Ha, ha, ha-haha. Hahaha-haha. Ha, ha, ha-haha."

Wally's cackling interrupts what may be a mildly important conversation.

"You said to that person that you called Connie six times already," I mention casually.

"Oh, yeah. I wanted to do it while you were around, but I couldn't get a hold of you."

"Why not? I always have my phone…"

"Oh, you picked up when I called," she says. "You were just drunk."

"Oh…"

"JAY!" Wally yells. "Get in here, retard!" Katie looks at him while he yells. I just stare at the ground, trying to think of a way to justify being drunk when I should've been helping work on this situation with Connie.

"Don't worry about it," she says reaching over and tapping my knee. "I obviously didn't have any luck anyway."

"JAY?!" Wally yells again.

"Ugh…" Jay says walking in, exchanging a grunt instead of a greeting. Katie looks at me with an expression that asks what's going on.

"Dude!" Wally yells. "Check it out! This dude pisses in the girls mouth then decks her!" he says, cackling some more.

"NICE!" Jay responds. Christ, kill me now, because I didn't have a hard enough time proving to Katie I wasn't a jackass. Seeing this probably doesn't score me any bonus points in her book.

"Well," Katie begins, "as much as I enjoy the irony of trying to solve a female abuse case while watching one on high-speed DSL, I think I should be going."

"Well," C'mon…give her a reason to stay. Give her a reason to get to know you better. Make sure she doesn't leave thinking this is all there is to Kalvin Gray. "Shouldn't we look into this some more?"

"Yeah, but I got to go. I got a lot to do tonight."

"Okay…" Ouch. What do I say to that?

"I'll talk to you about it in class tomorrow."

"Alright."

"It was nice meeting you two!" Katie smiles to Jay and Wally, who just return a wave without any words as she sees herself out.

"Yo, Kal, look at this..." Wally says.

"What?"

"This dude is getting a BJ from a chick with one of those voice box things," he says. I respond with a stare and a shake of my head. "You know...like the ones they give to people with cancer? The ones that make their voices sound like robots?"

"Christ..." I'll be amazed if she talks to me again. All I can do is let the look in my eyes scold Wally.

"What?" he asks. "I just wanted to watch some cripple porn..."

12

Rock the Kasbah

"Penis!" Barry's voice rings inside the half-crowded bar.

"Penis!" answers Wally.

Happy Hour. It's been two weeks now, and things haven't really changed. Spaz hasn't brought me that report yet, and Katie has been on my ass about it. I'm starting to wonder who's doing who a favor when it comes to this whole newspaper story.

"So how's my little baby?" Molly asks to me. She wakes me out of a small trance that very likely would've turned into The Stare.

"Who?"

"Thor."

"Oh...the pig."

"Yeah, the guinea pig," she replies, "how do you like living with him?"

"I don't."

Molly cocks her head sideways. "Why not?"

"He's a noisy piece of shit," I say. "He squeaks all fucking day. And it's not just little, small squeaks, either. It's like these giant, blood-curdling shrieks. He does it all fucking hours of the night, too. I hate that friggin' thing." I pause for a minute. Molly's head nudges backwards a little, flinching from what I just said. "Oh," I continue, "he also smells like the inner sanctums of my ass." I take a long gulp from my glass. Through the gold tint at the bottom, I see Lana on my left. I'm careful not to make myself look too "aggressive" while I'm drinking.

"Christ…" Molly says. She sounds a little disgusted. "What crawled up your ass?"

"Nothing. I just don't like that thing, and I don't want it in my house." I don't want to tell her that I get pissed at the very thought of her little critter. I don't know why, but that thing just annoys the hell out of me. On the good side, it definitely gives me something to focus on. I use that little shit as an emotional dartboard; all my anger, irritation and anguish get focused into little imaginary arrows that I fling at Thor through my eyes. I don't know why I hate it so much. I guess it's just an easy target.

"Maybe you should just sit down with him and talk," Lana suggests.

I turn to her. "Talk to him?"

"Yeah," says Molly, pulling my attention back towards her. "He's a really good listener." My silence states what I'm thinking better than words ever could. "Have you ever tried talking to him?"

"Once," I say, humoring them, "but it was more like me just yelling at it." I leave it at that. They don't need to know that by "yelling at it" I mean, "having a full-blown argument with it." They don't need to know that I came in drunk at 4 a.m. last night and started yelling at the guinea pig for no reason. They don't need to know that I got on all fours just to argue face-to-face with a mammal that doesn't have the ability to reason or talk. They don't need to know that I almost broke into tears while I was yelling at it. And they don't need me to tell them that all my yelling woke up Jay, who opened his bedroom door and punted me in the ass. He kicked me so hard that I flew forward and crashed my head halfway through the fake wood paneling on the wall. I think I blacked out after I fell to the ground. I woke up with pictures of dicks and phrases like "I love cock" written in blue marker across my face. All these things are minor details that the two of them don't need to know.

"Well, you should try actually talking to him. It always makes me feel better," Molly suggests, signifying that it's time for the conversation to change direction. I can feel where this is going. She's going to ask me if I've been feeling okay, just like Lana did the other day.

"That reminds me," Molly says. I look at Lana—she knows what's about to happen, too. "I've been meaning to ask you something lately…" She starts digging through her purse for her cigarettes. She continues talking while her attention is focused on her search. "You've been doing okay lately? You seem…I don't know? Kinda weird lately."

I pause and stare down at the tabletop. I can feel her eyes on me, waiting for an answer. This can go one of two ways: it can turn out like my conversation with Lana—which was a small disaster—or it could turn out worse. Molly probes when she thinks something's wrong. Her heart is in the right place, and with most of her friends I'm sure it's a welcomed gesture. I don't know if anything is wrong. If I tell her that and she thinks I'm lying, she'll keep probing—and there is nothing worse than searching and digging for something that isn't there.

She stares at me in quiet wait. But luckily, I hear a rescue signal in the background. The opening piano and harmonica of Billy Joel's "Piano Man" starts at a low volume and gets louder with each note. A smile beams across Molly's face.

"I love this song!" Of course she does. Everyone likes it; it's a good song. But college students, for whatever reason, have turned it into an anthem. I look around and watch expressions of excitement and satisfaction decorate the faces of almost everyone in the bar. The song lyrics start and everyone sings along. I could never understand why people in their early twenties all gather and unite around a song that seems like it's about a mid-life crisis.

Molly, Lana and almost everyone else in the bar sway and sing with smiles as they're "sharing a drink they call loneliness." I take baby steps backwards, slowly. No sudden movements. Ease out of here and they won't notice and I won't have to get into a discussion about my "issues."

There's one little section of the bar that isn't singing: the dark corner where my friends are. We always have a way of opening a negative void, even in the most positive of places.

"…yeah, you would think that, fag." Dutch tells Jay, who's shaking his head as I sit down.

"Yo," Doug says to me. I nod. The four of us are quiet as almost an entire bar continues to croon.

"So what's up?" Dutch asks, nodding in my direction.

"What do you mean?"

"What's going on tonight?"

"What the hell…?" I groan with a shrug. "Why is it always up to me to decide what's going on?"

"Who else is going to do it?" Dutch asks. This is a regular problem for us. We all want to do something, but nobody wants to take any responsibility. I guess in some ways that could be used as an ass-backwards metaphor for our generation.

"I don't know…" I say. "Ask Doug." And naturally, the three of us look at Doug.

"Well…" Doug says as he exhales, "I don't know what to tell you, boys. We got a whole lot of nothing here."

The problem here is the slight guilt I feel while I'm lying to these guys. I'm actually going to a party tonight with Katie. Right there is enough reason for me not to tell the guys what I'm doing tonight. The party is at Hal's, the gay Eurotrash guy who works with her at the paper. If there's nothing but gay men around, I'll have Katie all to myself.

"Hello, sirs," Barry says. He walks up to the edge of our table and knocks twice against it, as if to let us know he was there. "Young miss," he says looking at Dutch and making a hat-tipping gesture. "What are we doing tonight?"

"I dunno," Dutch says, "that's what I was just asking fuckwit over here." He points at me.

"It's almost 9. We should figure out what we're doing soon," recommends Jay. Shit. Katie said she'd meet me out front at 9.

"Hey!" Wally walks over to our table from the bathroom, zipping up his fly. "What're we doing tonight?"

"Jesus Christ…can we have one fucking Friday where this doesn't happen?" Dutch asks.

"Why don't we just go home, get a keg, then go to the bar again," suggests Jay.

"You got money for that, be my guest," says Barry.

"Beer distributor's closed anyway," adds Doug. A small debate begins. I tune it out, just by habit. I hear bits and pieces, people being called "fags" and "douchebags" and things of that nature. There's no background noise. Time stops outside of our table. I continually look at my cell: 9 o'clock on the nose. Hope Katie doesn't feel ambitious enough to come looking for me in here.

"…Christ! How is it we're all in a fraternity and we have to worry about finding a party to go to?" I hear Barry yell.

"Because we only have 10 active guys, and we're the shittiest frat on campus," Doug replies.

Is there such a thing as a happy place? People always talk about finding their "happy place" when they're in stressful situations. I don't know where my happy place is. I don't know if I have a happy place. I have a frustrated place. I have a mental playground that's in a state of demolition and clearing in order to build a new Wal-Mart. That's about it. Doesn't do me much good in situations like this. Is that where the little 16-year-old version of me hangs out? For the first time, I can almost envision him, or me, or whoever he is. He stands there—disappointed, of course—tapping his foot, arms crossed and yelling at me. He's angry and confused, like all 16-year-olds. And like all 16-year-olds, he takes comfort in the fact that after high school, everything will start to add up and make sense. He's happy thinking that once he's in college, all the pieces of the puzzle will finally clip together and form a vivid picture of the individual he strived so long to become. Right now though, he's pissed. He looks at my friends and I and realizes we can't get our shit tog-ether. With that, he comes to the realization that if I can't figure out something as simple as where we're going to drink tonight, what hope is there? I'm supposed to have it together by now; be thinking with a solid mind and making smart decisions and whatnot. He realizes that if I can't pull myself straight about something so trivial, how am I supposed to pull myself together for a real decision? How am I supposed to be the adult he wants to become?

"You're a confused mess," he says to me in a voice that only I can hear. "You can't figure out where to drink let alone what the fuck to do with your life! I want to be a biologist! How the hell am I going to do that if I'm stuck turning into a motionless, confused piece of shit like you?" After hearing him, I'm starting to think I may have been more intelligent when I was 16. More assertive, too. But I don't ever remember wanting to become a biologist, which is weird…

"Dude, I think he's staring at your junk," I hear Dutch say. His voice sounds distant. Reality washes over me like rain on a windshield. 16-year-old Kal and the demolished playground fade away like a dream. That's when I realize that I've again fallen victim to The Stare. Only this time, things are a little creepier. This time, when I "wake up," I realize that I'm staring at Barry's crotch.

"Don't just stare at it—eat it," Barry says in his best child molester voice. He starts giggling. "I got that from a movie."

"No kidding…" I say. Everything's quiet again. I look around and notice Jay and Doug are gone. "Where'd everyone else go?"

"To get beer and shit…" Dutch says. Damn, I must've really been out of it this time. I should get myself checked out.

"Holy shit! What time is it?" I look at my cell—9:15. Crap.

"Got somewhere to go?" Barry asks. Right as he finishes his sentence, I see Katie walk in through the door, knowing I'd still be here. Christ, I'm predictable.

She walks through the bar in the same slow, sexy way she did last time. The few heads left in the place turn towards her. She spots me almost immediately and doesn't waste any time.

"Aw, Jesus, Kal! Are you hammered?" she asks. She made me promise I wouldn't get shit-faced until after we got to the party.

"Calm down. I'm not that drunk," I say. Who am I kidding? I'm shit-faced.

"I am," says Wally. Nobody asked him.

Typical "awkward" silence fills and disturbs the area like a fart in an elevator. Katie puts on a polite smile and puts her hands in the pockets of her tight, brown leather jacket. She looks around the table and soaks in what I'm sure is an impressive sight.

"Hi," she says in a voice almost as perky as her fine, tanned breasts. "I'm Katie." She waves. Everyone waits for me to make some form of introduction.

"Okay," I begin, "That's Dutch. That's Wally. That's Barry. They're all drunk."

"Oh," she says. "Nice to meet you guys." Things stay quiet.

"Holy shit!" Dutch screams. His eyes flare and light up. "*You're* Katie?"

"Yeah…" she says in a confused, almost scared, voice.

"Shit!" Dutch slaps the table and shows his teeth with a slack-jawed smile. "You're the chick who showed Spaz your titties!"

"Nice!" yells Barry.

Katie's naturally tan face turns pale. Her jaw hanging low enough to catch a knuckleball. "I had a good reason," she says, defending herself in a low voice. Everyone at the table is quiet. Barry, Wally and Dutch stare at her with all the nonchalance of a fire alarm.

"Ready to go?" I ask, trying to save her.

"Where the fuck you going?" Dutch asks.

"A friend of mine is having a party," Katie answers before I have the time to come up with a lie.

"You lying little shit…" Dutch says. "You weren't even

going to tell us, were you?"

"Well, it's not like it's private or anything," Katie interjects. "You guys can come, if you want…"

"Nah," I say, "they wouldn't want to go."

"The hell we wouldn't!" Dutch says as the others stay silent, observing Katie's rack. "So there's going to be broads and shit at this party, right?"

"Yeah, I mean, I would think so…" Poor Katie. She never saw us coming.

"Dude, you're not going to want to go…"

"Yeah, that's great, Wonderfag," Dutch says, keeping his focus on Katie. "So what're these guys charging for a cup?"

"I don't know, to be honest," Katie says. There's a look of uneasiness in her eyes, but her shiny lips form a cocky smile that holds up her normally confident front.

"So, wait a sec…" Barry chimes in. "You showed Spaz your boobs why?" Expressions of subtle shock are painted across Katie's face.

"Hold on a minute," maybe I can change the subject enough to save Katie's pride. "If we're all going, we're going to need to find another ride. We're not all fitting in one car."

"Well," Katie starts, "we could probably all fit in my car if we tried and…"

"NO!" I yell. "We'll just walk and meet you there." I'm not taking any chances. I need some time to "brief" them on what kind of party this is going to be.

"That'll work. You know where it is, right?"

"Yup!" My phoniest grin is armed and aimed right at her.

"So wait," Wally says, "how come Spaz got to see your titties?"

*   *   *

"Goddamn, it's cold!" Dutch whines. He's wired with a kind of drunken energy that could only be generated from the desperation of knowing his time as a college student is quickly coming to a close. "What the hell did you make us

133

walk for?"

"Yeah, seriously," Barry chimes in, bundling himself tight in his jacket. "I think I just felt one of my nuts freeze up and crack."

"It's not too much further," I say. I've been keeping myself quiet for most of the walk. I'm debating if I should try to talk these guys into acting a little less like themselves. I love my friends, I do. I'm just nervous about putting them and Katie in the same room, especially when drinking is involved. I'm like a different person with Katie than I am with these guys. I can't list the differences, but they're there, I can feel them. Then again, Katie, of all people, should understand what it's like having more than one personality. It's like I'm with someone else every time she talks.

"There going to be a lot of girls at this place, Kal?" Wally asks with a touch of innocence in his voice.

"I don't know. I'd assume so."

"Well, your little 'Lois Lane' is going to be there. She got any friends or roommates?" Barry asks.

"Hmm," I say, "that's a good question."

"What do you mean?"

"I don't think I've ever seen her with any friends. Well, other than the people at the newspaper."

"She's hot," Wally says. "Hot girls always have hot friends."

"Except for the hot girls who realize that they're the hot girls," suggests Dutch.

"What do you mean?"

"She might be one of those chicks that likes being the good-looking one in her group. So she hangs out with ugly chicks just to make sure she's got one-up on them," says Dutch.

"Hot by comparison," Barry adds.

"I've seen it a million fucking times," says Dutch. "They're the ones you've got to watch out for."

"Why?" I ask.

"Because they're the ones who refuse to fuck guys like us.

They think just 'cause they're the hot commodity they can be picky and choosy with the guys they go home with." Dutch takes the lead as we walk. It's almost as if he's becoming some sort of sage, passing on his college wisdom before he leaves. "The good thing about girls like that are their friends. Their friends are going to feel like such shit around the hot girl, they'll blow anyone for an ego boost."

"He's right," Barry says. "They may look like Lilith Fair rejects, but even you could probably bring one of them home." He nods towards Wally as he talks.

"Fuck that. I'm not banging any fat, ugly chicks again," Wally says. "That was only a four-time deal."

"Yeah, well it's good to see you've got life figured out to a 't', Dutch" I say.

"Stick with me, man. I know my shit." Dutch smiles. "All you got to do is make them feel better about themselves."

"Yeah? And then what?" I ask.

"What do you mean?"

"What do you do when you've made them feel so good about themselves that you fuck them and then they keep calling you for the next week?"

"You don't pick up your fucking phone, dude," Dutch answers. "Dumbass..."

"But you don't need to worry about that!" Barry comments. "Because you're going to try to fuck Katie."

"Yeah," I say. "Easier said then done."

"That supposed to be a pun?" Barry asks. "Cuz she looks pretty easy."

"Nah, I don't think she's the one-night stand type."

"Then make her the one-night stand type!" Wally interjects, his breath turning to smoke in the icy winter air. "Just get her really drunk and do stuff to her!" Wally says, as if he were re-instilling me with some kind of common know-ledge. "She doesn't have to know about it."

"Oh yeah," I say, "because I really need that kind of karma right now."

"Ohhhh...that's right..." Barry remembers. "You already raped one girl this semester."

"Shut the fuck up..." I mutter in a low, tired voice.

"Nah," Dutch says, "That was just attempted rape. He can't even rape a girl right."

"You already used that joke, Dutch...okay," I announce, turning to face my friends. "This is the place."

"Fuckin' A..." Dutch complains. "Took long enough."

"I wanna lay down some ground rules."

"The hell you talking about?" Barry asks.

"He's embarrassed of us and wants us to behave," Dutch suggests to the others. "That's why he wasn't going to bring us!"

"I'm not embarrassed of you," I reassure them. "I just wanted to remind you guys that I am trying to make a good impression here..."

"What've we ever done to embarrass you?" Barry asks, half-drunk, half-irritated. I'm quiet for a second, not admitting anything.

"Okay..." I say, pointing a finger at Barry. "No puking unless it's in a toilet or trashcan."

"Fine," Barry agrees reluctantly. "Anything else?"

"No mooning people! No matter how much they deserve it!"

"Dammit..." Barry whispers in anger.

"No discussing child sex, crippled sex, robot sex, animal sex or anything else that'd make a dark man blush," I say, looking to Wally.

"What about dark-man sex?" Wally asks. "A dark man wouldn't blush about dark-man sex."

"And absolutely," I say as I approach Dutch, index finger extended towards him, "positively no exposing of your balls tonight! Your balls stay in the pants, not on a counter top or on the keg or on anyone's forehead. Do you understand me?"

Dutch is quiet; his brow is heavy as he stares at me with serious eyes. His glare is voided and empty of any indication of what he's thinking.

"Fuck you," he finally says in a simple, straight-on voice. "My balls go where they want. I have no control over them." This is his way of complying.

"Fine," I say with a deep sigh. "Let's go in…"

"If my balls want to go on someone's forehead, they go there themselves. They don't ask me or anything…they just go…" Dutch says as we walk up the shallow concrete steps. "I'm just their vessel."

A wall of cigarette smoke greets us as we go through the front door. There's a giant ceiling light that has red plastic wrap covering it. The whole room is a dim mix of red and orange. The four of us stand still for a moment. We don't know what to do or expect.

"Oh, fuck no!" Dutch yells.

"What?" Barry asks.

"What the fuck is that?" Dutch points straight ahead to where two guys are kissing. "Ugh…no…Ahhhh!" Dutch squeals like a bitch as I turn to the left to see what he's looking at: two more guys hooking up, only one of these guys has his hand down the other's pants. It looks like he's going to town, too.

"Uh-oh!" says a little blonde-haired guy in a wife beater. "Somebody brought some breeders!"

"Dude, what the fuck is a breeder?" asks Barry.

"What the fuck is this place, dude?" Dutch says in a panicked whisper.

"I don't know," I respond.

The room is wallpapered with guys. There are a few random girls sprinkled throughout the room, but it's hard to pick them out from the guys. Not a good sign.

"Hey," Wally says, "I thought gay dudes were supposed to get a lot of poon."

"Dude, what the hell are you talking about?" Barry asks, his face scrunched up the same way a newborn's is right before they cry.

"I thought gay dudes were supposed to have, like, groupies and stuff," Wally explains. "You know, like girls to go shopping with and shit."

"He's right!" Dutch exclaims. He sounds like he's going to cry. "Where are all the girls?"

"I don't know, dude. I've been here as long as you have." I bob my head up and down, trying to look over the 20 or so people in the room. I can't see Katie. People are going up and down the stairs in the back. She seems like the type who would spend her time in the less-occupied, upstairs area during a party. The type who would hang out and be the laid-back, cool girl. At least most of her personalities seem that way.

The initial shock looks like it wore off with Barry and Wally. Wally slowly bumbles and nods his head with the techno bumping in the background. Barry is lighting a cigarette and soaking in the surroundings. Dutch, on the other hand, is jittery and antsy. He's taping his feet and making quick, jerked movements with his arms and neck, and just looking generally uneasy, like he has to piss.

"Yep," Dutch says to himself. "I'm getting the fuck out of here."

"What?" I ask. "Why?"

"Why?" he asks back, squinting his eyes. "Because I don't feel like sitting around watching two dudes argue about who's going hog-wild in which guy's ass!"

"Yeah," says Barry. "I'm not really feeling this place."

"What's wrong with it?" I ask. The cold, silent stares they give me for an answer are something I'll never forget. "Okay, a room full of guys cock-teasing each other *is* a little weird. But can we jut stay for a little bit?"

"Why?" Dutch whines.

"I just need to do this thing with Katie, then we'll leave and get shit-faced. I promise."

"Hey, if you want to sit here and play *Oz* with a roomful of ass-hungry, butt-fuckers, be my guest. But I wanna go some place where I don't have to worry about what'll happen if I bend down to tie my shoe laces!"

"What do you care anyway?" Barry asks. "You didn't

want us to come in the first place." And he's right. But at the first sight of the guy-on-guy action that's going on, I don't want to be stuck here alone while I look for Katie. They might think I'm fresh meat or something.

"Beep, beep! The Admirals here!" comes an interrupting voice from behind before I can answer Barry's question. It's Hal. He's well dressed in a strange, rugged kind of fashion. I would assume he was straight if Katie didn't already tell me otherwise. "How's the night finding you, Kal?"

"Hey, Hal."

"You've brought friends…" he evaluates the guys from head to toe.

"Yeah, is that cool? Katie said it'd be cool."

"No problem at all!" Hal begins. A flamboyant smile splashes onto his face. "Let's get you boys drunk!" Barry and Wally don't say anything. I think they're just happy to drink. Dutch is the only one bothered.

Hal's drunk. I can tell because his breath is enough to give me a hangover. He aims his left shoulder in our direction and squeezes between Dutch and I, wrapping his arms around both of us. "Keg's this way," he says, pulling us closer with each arm, wrapping around us tighter as he steps forward. It feels like we're being dragged along by an octopus that has been swimming in stale booze and Nautica cologne. "Kal, introduce me to your friends." he demands.

"Right…" I say. "Well, this is Barry and Wally behind us." I try to turn around and point at them, using that as a physical excuse to worm out of Hal's awkward grip, but his arm wraps tighter when I struggle. "And that's Dutch." Dutch is frozen with what I can only assume is some kind of fear. His shoulders are raised with his head partially tucked between them. His arms are still and hanging close to his body, kind of like a T-Rex. He's cringing with each step, as if he's going to catch a dose of gay from direct contact with Hal.

Hal finally lets go of us once we reach the back kitchen area of the place. The bright, white light bounces off of the unusually clean, white tile flooring. The room is filled with a handful of guys who're just lingering. It kind of reminds me of a high school locker room. Dutch physically closes up once Hal releases us. His arms tightly cross and fold in front of him. He shakes with all the mental security of rape victim.

"Is Katie here?" I ask.

"Yeah, somewhere," Hal replies, handing out a plastic cup to each of us. "Don't worry about paying, guys."

"I wasn't…" Dutch says under his breath.

"So where is she?" I hope that doesn't sound too desperate.

"Whoa, buddy!" Hal says. "Give the girl a chance to liquor up before you try jumping inside of her."

"No, we just got to talk about some things," I say.

"Right. And the real reason you're working on this story for the paper is because of your blooming interest in journalism."

"He's got you pegged," Barry says nonchalantly as he fills his cup.

"Nah, I'm really not interested in her like that."

"Sure you're not," Hal says. "You should at least admit it."

"Seriously," says Dutch, breaking out of his disgust to chime in for a moment. "Quit being such a faggot about it." Hal and about three other guys in the room whip eyes in his direction. "Wow…" Dutch says. His cup is trembling within his hand. "Awkward."

*   *   *

"Oh my God!" she exclaims. "You guys are crazy!" Lola, the chubby Goth chick who works with Katie and Hal on the newspaper is one of those people that are missing the ability to notice when people aren't interested in talking to her. I feel bad for people like this for about three minutes, but then they just piss me off beyond all limits of compassion.

"Yup. We're a handful," I say, shifting my weight from

side to side, making sure my eyes don't meet with hers. My eyes are too busy looking for Katie. I don't see her down here, but I can't get upstairs to look for her until Fatty Labelle shuts up and moves.

"You going to look for this broad or what?" Dutch asks, walking up to me out of nowhere. Barry is right next to him.

"Yeah, I want to get out of here soon," Barry says. "I'm getting a weird *Crying Game* vibe from this dude who's standing by the bathroom checking everyone out."

"HA!" Lola bursts out with a single, loud laugh. "You guys totally remind me of my friends!"

"I bet," I say. Barry raises an eyebrow, confused by what the hell this round little woman is saying. I just shake my head and lift my hand, letting him know he's better off not thinking about it.

"I brought them to the last party Hal had. They got all drunk and went nuts!" She stands in place, jiggling with a chuckle, expecting us to ask her what was so damn crazy about when she brought her "crazy friends" over. She goes on without us saying anything. "My one friend, Mindy, started dancing on the table and shaking her ass and saying all this stuff like, 'Yeah, does this make you straight, Queer Eye?'" It's not hard to keep a straight face during these shitty, little anecdotes. I observe Lola. Her face is so chunky that it forces her eyes to squint. "That's not even the half of it! After that, she started going around calling all the guys here 'Queer Eye!' Get it?" She looks at me, expecting me to laugh and smack my knee. Ain't going to happen. "Get it? 'Queer Eye?' Like that show about the gay guys?"

"What the fuck are you talking about?!" Dutch bursts, once again showing the full girth of his patience. "I mean, seriously. Do you think any of us give a shit about your retarded friends?"

"Ew!" she responds. "Nobody asked you!" She slowly creeps her stout little body towards Dutch. "You don't talk to me like that! You don't even know me!"

"Thank God I don't! I think the people I know need to fit

141

inside some kind of weight limit," Dutch says. Barry breaks out, blatantly laughing in her face.

"Go fuck yourself, you big-eared freak," she screeches, walking away, sashaying her chubby ass back and forth in each direction.

"Yeah, walk it off, Odd Job!" Dutch yells at her. "And make sure you walk off a couple of those McGriddles you put away this morning while you're at it!"

"Hmm," Barry observes. "A James Bond reference?"

"Yeah," Dutch responds. "It felt right."

"Good one."

"Yo," I say, interrupting, "where's Wally?"

"Do I keep dibs on him now?" Dutch asks. "Am I his keeper? Do you see my name and number on the tags hanging around his collar?" He pauses long enough to observe my silent stare. "The answer is no. No, I am not his keeper. So why do you ask me?"

"Right," I say. I'm really shitty with comebacks. "I'm going upstairs to find Katie and see if she'll meet me somewhere else. Go find him and get ready to leave." I say while I turn around in the opposite direction.

It takes me a few steps towards the stairs to realize I've seen something like this before. I think it was in every high school/college movie ever made. Each step in the staircase is about three feet wide, but there is only about eight inches of space to walk since each side of the stairs is littered with people, forming a tight corridor in the middle. For some reason, the staircase at a college party serves as some kind of social pyramid. The better-looking people with more to talk about stand towards the top. It's kind of like they're keeping an eye on the lesser members of the party, keeping check, making sure that they still belong at the top of the steps above the rest. That's the funny thing about real life. In the movies, no matter how old the students are, students are always bullying and picking on the social bottom-dwellers. You don't see that in real life. Nobody bullies anybody "just because" after they turn 17. Instead, they just form these weird, subconscious, physical manifestations of a social hierarchy. It's kind of strange and funny to see in person.

It's hard but possible to nudge my way through the party's social elite that guards the upstairs area with blank stares and quiet acknowledgements. The chattering and small talk rolling off each inebriated set of lips muzzle the music rising from downstairs. A small handful of people have decided to bring the party up into the upstairs hallway. They line the walls like a trail of breadcrumbs leading into one of the rooms at the far end.

The room at the end of the hall has about 10 people in it. Most of them are crushed onto the same couch that leans against the back wall, under a large window without curtains. The room carries a weird mix of smells: old booze, pot, dirt and, strangely enough, some kind of spray paint smell I can't really figure out. There's a banner barely hanging off the back wall. It says "Congratulations, Class of 2002," with the "Cl" in "Class" botched out with marker. The banner's covered with about a million different tags, many of which are names and assorted messages. All of them spilled along the banner in every imaginable color, forming a sloppy weave of names and graffiti that almost totally covers most of the original print.

Katie is leaning against the windowsill, practically sitting on it. She's sandwiched between two dudes—and I'm not just saying "dude" as a generic term for a guy. No, these are actual living, breathing "dudes." Everyone knows the type. It's the guy with longish-shortish, curly-straight hair, at least one piercing, some kind of lame-ass tattoo and a 5 o'clock shadow that's perpetually stained on his face. They usually have jobs as bar backs or waiters, and they take pride in the fact that they get along with everyone. Weird thing about this is, they say they always get along with everyone and that they're "lovers, not fighters," but they always have some kind of story about how they "totally fucked some guy up."

Typical dudes—in this case, two of them. Both of them squeezing Katie between their clean, black leather-clad shoulders. They don't wear the "badass" kind of leather jackets like you find on bikers. These guys wear the clean, shiny, classy leather jackets that usually cost as much as a new set of tires. And Katie is smiling open-mouthed, laughing at everything they have to say. I shouldn't be surprised. Katie seems like the type who might fall for the crap that comes out of a pair of lips sitting atop a soul patch. The one guy on her left keeps touching her knee every time he laughs. Katie isn't saying anything, which means he's laughing at his own jokes. He's probably telling some anecdote about how he and his buddies started the night stoned and drunk and ended up skydiving with the pope, or some random bullshit. That's another telltale sign of a dude—they always have some kind of random story to tell, and usually it doesn't have anything to do with whatever it is they were previously talking about. The most notable thing about "dude" stories is their structure. They usually start off with inebriation, and always have some kind of random ending.

She sees me as I walk towards her and waves to greet me, making sure not to interrupt the dude's story. The dude is rambling, talking about how tight he and his "boys" are. I think he's telling some story about being chased by cops or something. Dudes always have some story about escaping from cops.

"Yeah, so we just ran like hell! I kept running, but my boy, Rufus—get this—Rufus turns a 180 and clocks the cabby right in the beak!" Dude says. "Then we got back to my place. We smoked the rest of that dime and passed out. Never got caught."

"No shit!" Katie responds. I can't tell if she's just humoring him or not. "I always wanted to try to skip out on cab fare." She has?

Dude is now silent. His sidekick on Katie's other side is just laughing at whatever comes from this guy's mouth. Some dudes keep guys like him around (it never hurts to have someone around who you can rely on to laugh at your whim). Dude's hand is planted on Katie's knee—does she realize that? Does she care? She doesn't want it there, does she?

"When did you guys get here?"

"Huh?" I murmur. "Who, me?" I know she's talking to me, but I play dumb, keep my hands in my pockets and look at everything in the room but her.

"Yeah...you just get here?"

"Been here for about a half hour. Was talking to Hal for a little."

"Cool. Where're your friends?"

"I don't know...probably caulking their ass cheeks shut."

"Cool," she says with a laugh in her voice. She introduces Dude, but I don't listen for his name; he's always going to be Dude to me.

"Yo...sup?" he asks, sticking his fist in my direction. I look at it for only about three seconds before I hesitantly pound my fist into his. Ugh.

"Oh!" Katie bursts out of her mouth. "Stay here a second, Kal! I'll be right back!" With that she jumps up and trots out of the room, leaving Dude, his sidekick and me all alone.

It's quiet at first, with me lighting a cigarette and pacing my eyes back and forth around the room, as if I'm looking for something. Dude gently nods to the muffled music coming from out the hallway and downstairs. Finally, the inevitable comes: Dude tries to start small talk.

"Yo," he says, reaching out and gently tapping my arm. "This is my boy, Gunther," he says, pointing at his sidekick. "We grew up together."

"Oh, yeah?" I say, allowing myself to be sucked into a whirlpool of dribbling nonsense. "Where you guys from?"

"The city."

"Which one?"

"Philly."

"No shit. My mom is originally from there," I say. "What part?"

"Yardley," Dude says, sticking his chin up as he mutters

145

the last syllable.

"Yardley?" He doesn't know that I know where Yardley is—which is almost 30 miles north of Philadelphia. In short, he lives nowhere near any "city." In fact, Yardley is an upper-class, almost rural area.

"Yeah, Yardley," he says. He gives me some kind of thug-like glare; I think he's trying to intimidate me. I hate kids like this: guys who go to college and use that opportunity to totally brainwash themselves into being something they're not. They use the fact that most people don't know the truth about them—in this case, the fact that he doesn't live in the city—and totally exploits it to the point where they're practically developing a full-time mask.

"You know this girl pretty well?" he asks, referring to Katie.

"We hang out."

"You with her?"

"No…not really."

"No shit…cool, cool," he says. "She with anyone?"

"You know, I'm really not sure," Shit. I should say she is. I should say she's with me. I don't want this piece of twat-scum stealing Katie from me. I don't know if I deserve Katie and I don't know what kind of guy she deserves, but it's not Dude.

"Nice…" he says. "I'm going to be all over that tonight." Gunther snickers at the comment and Dude nods with a cheesy, cocky smile, not knowing how high he just made it on my shit list.

It takes a while, but Katie finally comes back into the room. She stops on her way over to talk to some guy sitting towards the door who's holding, of all things, a martini glass. I'm assuming he's one of the gay ones.

The minutes she spends talking to this guy feel long enough to age cheese. I wonder if I should be excited or worried. I wonder if I should be thrilled or annoyed. The point has finally come where I feel totally numb towards all social interaction I have within my species. Between people verbally threatening me, like Fernando and the Fat Chick in Chip's class; people pestering me, such as Dutch and Lana; and people like Katie and Jill who are there to chip away at what's left, I'm seriously starting to wonder what the point is anymore. What does all this matter in "the big picture"? People like Dude over here—what's his point? What does he have to gain or lose in the grand scheme of things? People like Molly—where do they play into this whole thing? Even the people like Barry, Jay and Wally, who I've loyally leeched onto for the past few years—am I even going to recognize them in a crowd 10 years from now? I want to believe I will, but do I know for sure? People come and go. Some come and love you in their arms, only to stab and betray you with their every word and breathe. Some casually say "hi" to you each day on the way to class and turn out to be one of your fondest memories. Some come and hold you warmly and softly, only to leave you for their cheating, Latino ex-boyfriend. I look at my life with a general glare and realize something: I don't have a "big picture" to look at; I only have a bunch of mismatched pieces to a jigsaw puzzle. Is this why I can't get anything straight? Where do I fit into all this? *Do* I fit into all this? What if I'm the only piece of the puzzle that doesn't fit?

"Yo, bra," Dude says. "What you starin' at, man?"

"What?" I ask.

"You been staring at that wall for, like, five minutes, broseph!"

"Christ," I say under my breath, rubbing my eyes with my index finger and thumb. The Stare. It's getting more frequent lately.

"Okay! I'm back!" Katie beams, bouncy and buoyant like a schoolgirl holding gossip.

"Listen," I say. I look at Katie, still bubbly and perky for reasons unknown. Dude and his sidekick are next to her, shooting cooled-down glares ambiguously across the room at anyone who'll look at them. "I think we're going to get out of here."

147

"But you just got here…" she says predictably.

"Yeah, I know, but maybe we can meet up later?"

"It's because of the whole gay thing, isn't it?" she asks, almost sounding disappointed.

"Sorta…" I say. It's only half the truth. The rest of the truth involves me being too much of a fucking coward to stay here and risk having to watch me lose her to Dude. I'm such chicken shit.

"Is it that big of a deal?" she asks.

"No. I mean, for me it isn't. The other guys are a little weird about it…"

"Oh…"

"Yeah…"

"Well," she says, "do what you gotta do. I'll call you if I want to meet up with you later."

"Right…" I say, turning slowly. I can't focus on disappointing her. I have to focus on my friends. I need to focus on getting me and the guys out of here before we get into some kind of battle royale with 20-some-odd gay men. I keep a steady, arrogant sway and pace to my walk. I want to turn to see if Katie is looking at me. I want to turn to see if she cares. More than anything, I want her to come chasing after me.

"Kal!" she yells over the thuds and booms blasting from the stereo. My brain naturally freezes out all the talking in the background and focuses on her yelling at me.

"Hey." I act like I wasn't hoping she'd come after me.

"You're really leaving?" she asks. Girls like her probably aren't used to guys leaving them.

"I think so…" I should stay. I want to stay. I want to be with her. But I did promise the guys we could go to the bar. Then again, they don't need me with them to go to the bar, right? I could stay here on my own. I could walk Katie home, make sure she doesn't go home with Dude. On the other hand, Jill might be at the bar. It's Friday and her car was still parked at her place. The tennis team has a tournament, which means Fernando is gone, which means Jill is probably going out with her friends. Which means I could probably talk to her and apologize for that fight we had a few weeks back.

"C'mon! Stick around. I want to talk to you about the article," she says.

"The article?" I ask. For a split second, I thought maybe she had other interests in me.

"Yeah, and besides this party'll get better," she says, almost pleading. "And at least you know if you pass out here, you won't end up in any dumpsters or anything, right?" She brings up a good point. And do I even know for sure that I'll see Jill at the bar? No! And even if I do, she's probably still pissed at me. But still…Katie may be fun and good looking, but Jill is Jill. Then again, Jill isn't into me that way. But, I don't think Katie is either…

"I've got an idea." Katie makes a quick turn, jerking my arm by the wrist as she pulls me down the long hallway. We pass by a bunch of people. Some of them look at us as we pass, some don't. Their faces blur sideways as Katie whisks me down the hall.

"What are we doing?" I ask. I sound annoyed. Hope she doesn't pick up on it.

"Dancing."

"Come again?"

"I'm going to show you how to slow dance," she says, still bubbly.

"I don't need to know how to dance," I protest.

"Every guy needs to know how to dance."

"How do you know I don't know how to dance already?"

"C'mon, Kal." She drops my wrist and lets it go limp to my side as she tilts her head with an "are you kidding me?" kind of stare. "Besides, this is one of my favorite songs, and I always need someone to slow dance with to it." She points her trigger finger to the sky, suggesting I listen to the song. "Open Arms" by Journey. She slowly grabs the fingers on both my hands and gently places them upon her hips before wrapping her arms loosely around my neck.

"I never figured you for a Journey fan," I say, trying to hide my awkward chills.

"I fucking love this song," she says, glaring to the side of my head, almost as if she were avoiding my observation. I can't help but notice yet another side to Katie. This is almost like a young, teenybopper version. The type who believes in bubble gum-flavored ice cream and romance. The type who would've paid to see *Titanic* four times while it was in theaters.

"I didn't think you were much into slow dancing, either." Stupid. I should keep my mouth shut. She's going to realize I'm nervous.

"I'm not really," she says, focusing on me. "I only do it when I'm here and when this song is on."

"Is there something special about this song?"

"No," she says in a dreamy kind of haze. "It's just a good song."

"Okay..." I mumble blindly.

"You know," she begins, shaking off her temporary, dream-like state, "it's weird how comfortable I feel around you."

"What do you mean?"

"A few weeks ago you were just some kid I had class with who was accused of attacking a girl. And here I am now, bringing you to parties with me and slow dancing to cheesy '80s love ballads," she observes. "It's just funny. I feel like I can be myself around you, which is nice."

"And who's that?" I ask, trying to sound clever.

"Who's who?"

"Who's the real you?"

"What do you mean?"

"Well," I begin, feeling as though I already regret saying something that hasn't even come out of my mouth yet, "you act a little different every time I see you."

"Is that a bad thing?" she asks, pulling her head back a little.

"No..." I say, looking for a way out of making this an

150

awkward conversation. "It's just different."

"Well, is 'different' such a bad thing?" she asks with a flirtatious charm.

"No," I answer.

She silently sways along with the music, her hips forcing my hands to bob in and out. She looks around at everything in the area but me.

"Besides," she finally says, "if you're a different person every time somebody sees you, then it's harder for them to get to know you."

"Why's that so important?" I ask with a dumbed-down curiosity.

"Because if they don't know you very well, it's harder for them to get bored of you," she admits slowly, looking down as if confessing to a priest. Figures. I should've expected this. She has issues. All girls have issues. This probably has something to do with her ex, which means she still loves him, which means I have no chance in hell. Lovely.

"So why just here then?" I ask, hoping to change the subject.

"What do you mean?"

"A minute ago, you said you only slow dance when this song comes on and just when you're here," I remind her. "So why just here?"

"Oh," she blurts with a hint of surprise at my question. "Because this is when all the guys slow dance downstairs."

"What?!" The shrill alarm in my voice is enough to scare the skin off of a rhino.

"Yeah," she says, slowly taking a step behind her, "all the guys downstairs slow dance. That's why I brought you here, so you wouldn't have to worry about them trying to grope you or anything." She raises a quick eyebrow at what can only be described as horror painted across my face. "Why? Is something wrong?"

"Kal!" Wally runs up the stairs, each foot hitting the steps with the force of an anvil. "We need to get going!"

"What's going on?"

"Dude, it's Dutch…"

"What…?" I say as traces of confusion weave their way into my voice and thoughts. "Wally, what happened to…"

"Me, Barry and Dutch were just standing around, hanging out," he explains, "and then some dude tried going cheek-to-cheek with Dutch, and…"

"What?!" I yell bolting down the stairs, subconsciously pulling Katie by the arm to come with me. We hammer our feet down against each step, easily maneuvering our way through each drunk lined up along the stairway.

"Which one is Dutch again?" Katie asks.

"The jackass with the giant ears," Wally replies.

We hit the bottom platform of the steps to find a small huddle around Dutch and some blonde kid in a pale blue button-down shirt.

"I'm not fucking gay!" Dutch yells.

"Then why did you pull your balls out?" the blonde asks innocently.

"Because I was putting them on the keg!" Dutch explains to an angry mob of homosexuals. "Not because I wanted to hug some butt-fucking dance queen!"

"Why would you put your balls on the keg?" a confused voice yells from the crowd.

"It's my thing!" Dutch whines, as if it were common sense. "That's what I do!"

"Fag!" Someone yells from the crowd.

"I heard that!" Dutch circles his eyes around. "Who fucking said that?"

"Yo!" I yell as Barry approaches. "What the fuck happened?"

"I don't know. I guess Dutch is gay now, or something," Barry slurs out in a drunken stammer. "We just saw some dude trying to slow dance with him when Journey came on."

"Ugh…" I say.

"See?" Katie says, nudging me. "Aren't you glad I showed you how to dance upstairs?"

I look around to notice that everyone in the room is staring at Dutch like their eyes were loaded Magnums. Their looks sharpen as Dutch continues with his homophobic speech.

"See that? Fag, fag, fag," he says, pointing around the room at each of the guys around them, as they slowly advance towards him. "Oh what? Now you're going to kick my ass? Why? Cuz I know your little secret? Huh?" He rambles on, making less sense with each word. "What? You guys going to work me over now or something? Pound my ass or something? Stuff my mouth full of cock to shut me up? Huh? Just like in jail?"

"What's he talking about?" Hal asks me, creeping up from behind.

"No clue," I respond.

"He's just in shock," Barry suggests.

"He's making my guests a bit uneasy," Hal states in a polite but firm way. "Not to mention how insanely offensive he's being in the process."

"Yeah…" Barry says. "I think it's time we left anyway."

"Great job, guys." I mumble. "Way to fuck up any chance I had with Katie. Spectacular."

13

Open-heart Perjury

I'll never understand the idea behind the college professor. I understand the idea of someone who is paid to pass on knowledge and experience, but the term for that is "teacher." I understand the purpose of someone who is paid to keep track of class participation and grades, and they're referred to as "administrators." While the college professor may have traditionally covered the same tasks as both of these other professions in the past, I don't think they do anymore. At least not in the same way the parents of Berkshire University students are expecting when they fork over thousands of dollars each year.

I think about this every Monday morning, when I'm in Chip's class for the first—and sometimes only—time of the week. I don't drink on Sundays, or at least I try not to. The withdraw leaves me with a head full of unfinished thoughts that scatter off the insides of my skull like BB pellets bouncing off a brick wall. Right now the main thought that has been occupying my brain is how Katie is still willing to talk to me after the little display of homoerotic tension that went on at Hal's last week.

I watch Chip while he sits on his desk, the tips of his leather cowboy boots scraping against the floor. I don't know what he's saying, and I don't care. Most professors, they tend to be laid back and just shit random anecdotes out of their mouths each morning; Chip is no different. I can understand

154

this. It's hard to have any real sense of direction when you're instructing a class full of hangovers on the finer points of something as useless as communications. The weird thing is that I'm not in class—I'm in his office.

From what Katie's learned by asking around, Connie Ward was one of those few people at this school who actually had some potential. She was one of those girls who would've probably kicked ass if she went to an Ivy League, but she was screwed repeatedly while her family danced along the poverty line, leaving her no choice but to go to the one college she could afford: Berkshire.

Connie apparently had a tight relationship with Chip, who was her academic advisor. Usually advisors are assigned to each student in order to provide them with inaccurate info about picking classes, only to yell at you for choosing the wrong class when they know damn well that they talked you into taking that class in the first place. There's a reason I haven't seen mine in two years. People like me fit into the majority at this school. People like Connie, on the other hand, tend to be in the minority since they have strong, almost paternal relationships with their advisors. At least that's what Katie said she learned from asking around. Which brings me to somewhere I never wanted to be—in a no-holds-barred, "Barbara Walters Special Interview" with Chip.

"You guys want to light a j?" Chip asks. He's so casual about it that he doesn't even bother looking at us when he does.

"You serious?" I ask.

"I'll smoke!" Katie says, looking at me with a shrug and a "when in Rome" kind of smile.

"Can't we get into trouble for that, or something?" I ask.

"Nah," Chip says. "I rule this school."

"How's that?" I ask.

"Look at me," he demands. He points to himself with both index fingers. "I'm damn near 60. Who's going to accuse a 60-year-old college professor of smoking pot in his office?"

"Touché," I say, but he doesn't listen. He's too busy rolling up a joint. His office is small. It barely fits his desk and the two giant bookshelves that he has primed and loaded with books on every imaginable subject. Who the hell does he think he's fooling? He didn't read all of them.

"So," Chip says before he licks the joint, sealing it, "why me?"

"Excuse me?" asks Katie in a professional voice.

"Why me?" he asks again. "Why are you guys interested in talking to me about Connie?" Katie and I look at each other. I roll my eyes towards her then towards Chip. She needs to remember that she's the journalist here, not me. She's the one who should have the answers to little questions like this. But instead, she stares at me the same way Chip does. They both expect an answer out of me.

"Well," I start, "you said in class once that Connie was one of your best advisees. We thought maybe you knew her better."

"'Knew her better' how?" he asks, breathing in through his closed teeth. The joint is lit and smoldering in his hand. I wonder if it is still cool to say "joint"? It sounds like a clichéd word someone would say if they had no clue about drugs. Have people come up with a new word lately?

"We just heard that she looked up to you," Katie says, reaching for the joint Chip has stretched towards her. "That and since you were the one who started raising money to help her out, we thought you would be a good place to start when it comes to piecing together what happened to her."

"I'm trying to prove I'm not an attempted rapist," I add. "So if you could help us out, that'd be swell."

"Oh yeah…" he says, as if a light bulb just popped over his head. "You look just like that guy in the poster," he adds.

"I know."

"That must be fun," he says in a low voice, "having people randomly point and whisper about you as you walk around the area."

"It's awesome."

"So," Katie says while holding the smoke she just inhaled inside her lungs. "What can you tell us about Connie?" She exhales. A cloud bigger than my head fills the air.

"Hmmmm," Chip says, taking the joint back from Katie. "Well, what can I say? She's a good kid. Always had her stuff done on time, she was never late to class. Always polite and courteous." He takes a long drag on his joint, breathes in, exhales and starts again. "She was kind of your typical 'sad, poor college student' story. You know the type: Too smart for community college, too poor for private school, she fit the mold of a typical Berkshire student with a haunting accuracy. She had a thing for puppies, I remember that. She always talked about getting one of those yippy, little puppies...crap...you know the ones..."

"Poodles?" Katie suggests.

"No, but they were kinda like that."

"Chihuahua?"

"Nah...it wasn't so...'ethnic.'"

"Yorkshire Terrier?" Katie asks. "That's what my aunt has," she adds with a giggle. "Awww! I miss little Belle-Belle!"

"Belle-Belle?" Chip asks, passing the joint back to Katie. "That's a fucked up name for a dog."

"But she's so cute!" The two are quiet and stare at each other for a while before cracking up.

"See?" Chip says, looking towards me with a suddenly sober face. "I told you I rule."

Christ, this isn't going anywhere.

"Katie?" I try getting her attention. "Katie!" I yell.

"Yo!"

"Don't you have anymore questions?"

"Oh yeah, that's right!" she exclaims, trying to repress her giggling. "Soooooo...so, so, so..." she says, trailing off a bit. "Tell me about you and Connie."

"I just did," answers Chip, with a smile full of fake charm.

"Yeah, but tell me more," she requests. "Did you guys see a lot of each other? Did she come by a lot?"

157

"Not as often as I'd like you to, sweetie!"

I wonder if "Dudes" are just younger versions of all the "Chips" in the world.

"Awwww!" Katie says, reaching over and gripping my wrist as she looks at me. "He called me 'sweetie'!"

"Seriously, I don't think I have anything to share that can help you out," he says. "Other than pointing out the fact that your buddy here looks a lot like Suspect Numero Uno." He glares at me. The look is similar to the one he gave me back when this all started.

"Okay!" Katie beams. "Well, I'm gonna call you if I think of anymore…stuff…okay?"

"Far out," he replies. Who the hell says "far out"?

Katie packs up her stuff while Chip continues to smoke away. He's got a relaxed, iced-down glaze over his eyes, the quintessential look of a stoned, teenage hippy listening to a Strawberry Alarm Clock record in his dad's basement.

When we leave, he closes the door behind us almost too quickly. It nearly nails me in the ass.

"I think he knows something," I say as we slowly walk down the hall.

"Kal? I mean, just, like, c'mon, okay, Kal?" Katie says, her lips twitching in slow motion.

"What?"

"I dunno!" she says. She's gone. "What do you mean?" she asks with a sigh, trying to get her senses back.

"He just gave me this creepy look," I say. "He gave me a look like that when this all started."

"So?" she groans. "You never looked at someone before?" Her voice drags and stumbles with each word.

"You don't get it. It's a weird look…"

"So you think he had something to do with it?"

"When I was in Luther's office, he mentioned that he and Chip were talking about the whole Connie Ward thing," I say. "Why would they be talking about it?"

"So, they're drinking buddies," Katie says, trying to collect as much of herself as possible. "Of course they're going to talk about shit like this when they're drunk."

"How you figure?"

"Because...I don't know..." she says, as her battle to fight the buzz comes to a disappointing end. "You are such a sweetie!" she says in a playful voice, resting her hand on my shoulder. "That's why I'm gonna help you. Let's go break into Chip's office and look for clues, Scooby-Doo style!"

"What?"

"Dude...I'm stoned," she confesses.

"Oh! I forgot to tell you!" My excitement delivers a puzzled glare to her face. "Spaz texted me just as we were stepping into Chip's office. He dropped off that report today—the one that apparently proves I'm innocent. I didn't read it yet, but maybe we can find something in there!" Her half-closed eyes widen with shock and a smile cracks open on her face. She opens her mouth, hopefully prepared to deliver some rational thought.

"Okay..."she says. "Wanna go to the cafe?"

14

Thursday Night Lights

I wonder if anyone can hear me burp. I did, like, four times, and they were pretty loud. Nobody turned to look at me. One dude kind of looked like he heard, but he didn't. It's early, and I'm feeling pretty shred up. Been a shitty day. Days like this hurt.

My eyes are watering and my nose burns. The bar is filled with that weird smell, like a mix of mildew, stale beer and expired cleanser. The music in the background is blurring and mixing with the noise coming from a crowd filled with strangers. Each breath I take is weighed down with the smog left in my lungs from almost 15 cigarettes. My hand is the only thing keeping my arm up. I mean, my arm is the only thing keeping my hand up...or my head, or something. I don't feel like thinking or being awake or any of that right now.

Other people's elbows brush up and greet my arms casually as random strangers smuggle themselves between me and another person, trying to make their way towards the slowly crowding bar. I'm the only person actually sitting here. I've been here for a while, I think. One particularly aggressive elbow decides to let me know that it wants to occupy some of the space I've owned for the past however many hours.

"Hey," I say. The guy with the elbow is big, has a lot of facial hair and a hat. "Hey!" I say again, a little louder. He's got the back of his neck facing me. There's a really long hair sticking off his neck and I really want to pull it—not because it'd hurt him, but just because it's annoying me for some reason. "HEY!" I yell. I elbow him back.

"Yo, dude!" he yells. I didn't think I hit him that hard. "What the fuck?"

"I said 'Hey'..."

"Yeah, I don't fuckin' care, dude, you knocked over my dip cup." His voice is kind of low, but kind of not. It's muffled by the snuff in his lip. I notice his arm is about as wide as my head.

"Right..." I say under my breath. He can't hear me over all the noise.

"I'm fuckin' talking to you," he says, bending inward, being sure to be caught in the corner of my eye.

"You say the f-word a lot..." I tell him. His beer-soaked breath is reflecting off my face. He's wearing a baseball cap with "Carhart" embroidered across it. He's got some twang in his voice. I think he might be a hick or a townie.

"You gonna fuckin' apologize or what, dude?" he asks.

"Luke, calm down!" I hear coming from a tall, dark-haired girl on the right.

"No, man, fuck that!" he says to her. "He's a dick!"

"Dude, I had a long day, can you please stop saying 'fuck' so much? You sound like Jeff Foxworthy with Tourette's..." He grabs me by the shoulder, gripping onto my jacket. Almost effortlessly, he pulls me off the stool and throttles me to the ground. I hear him mutter something about me being an asshole on my way down to the floor.

"Owwwww...." I mutter. "You broke my ass bone." The room spins slowly and the air becomes thinner with each breath. A small audience forms; they circle around us like piranhas. The tall dark-haired girl is holding the hick's arm, trying to pull him away from me.

"What?" he says. "You getting' up, motherfucker?"

"C'mon, man..." I say. My voice is soft and trembling. I feel my stomach churning with bile and burning itself raw.

"Can't you keep the threats a little more PG? Unemployed locals bring their kids to this bar." I say as I stumble to my knees, my ass feeling as beaten as it'd be after a prison orgy.

"Keep your mouth shut, pussy!" he yells, yanking his arm from the dark-haired girl's grip and palming my forehead. My back crashes onto the ground, and I slide a foot or two as he tussles me back down. This time, my head bounces off the concrete.

Getting up will just end up with me being thrown back on the ground, so I'm thinking I should just relax. My arms spread across the pale, chilly concrete floor as I look up. More people are crowding him, telling him to stop. He's pushing some other kid in the face now—better him than me. That's when I feel more tugging on my shoulders.

"Okay, get up, Sugar Ray," Doug says, trying to help me to my feet. I manage to get up, only to sit down again on the stool where this all started. Some large bouncers are escorting my new, aggressive friend out of the bar. I reach into my pocket and pull out a crumpled cigarette.

"When did you get here?" I ask, lighting up.

"I dunno..." Doug says. "A while ago, I guess. How about you?"

"I don't know...same, I guess." My neck limps up, my head sways involuntarily.

"You drinking tonight?" Doug asks.

"I guess," I say, pointing to a half-full pint. "You here alone?"

"Nah," he says. "Bunch of us are in back." He casually pays the bartender and picks up a full glass.

"Cool."

"What're you doing here? You alone?"

"Yeah," I say. "I came pretty early...like, 4ish, I think."

"4?" he asks. "You know it's, like, 11 now, right?"

"One of those days," I say, knowing that excuse will only get me so far with some people. Not Doug, though. He's in a constant drunken state that prevents him from taking most conversations very far. Someone could get drunk from drinking his blood. Could a vampire get drunk from drinking an alcoholic's blood? I always wondered that.

"You should've called me. I would've come with you," he says. "I didn't do shit all day."

Things are quiet for a few seconds. Doug looks straight ahead into the crowd that fills the middle of the bar. His eyes stay half shut.

"Yo," he says, breaking silence, "is it true you took everyone to a gay party the other night?"

"It wasn't a 'gay party,'" I say. "It was just a party at a gay dude's house. And everyone there was gay. And making out. But it wasn't a 'gay party.'"

"Right," he says. "I'm sure Dutch loved that."

"Of course he did. There's a reason why he was waddling the next day." That's probably the cleverest thing I ever said.

"I think he is gay," Doug says, lighting a cigarette.

"Why?"

"Why else would he call everyone else gay?"

"But you call everyone gay, too."

"But that's because everyone I call gay is gay, like Dutch," he explains. "So, what made you come here at 4?" he asks.

"I don't know. Would it be too cliché if I said girl problems?"

"Probably."

"Oh. Well, that's what it is."

"Yup, they suck," he says with a sigh, seeming more sober than he should.

"Yes, yes they do." It's quiet for another minute or two before he digs deeper.

"Is this because you're too much of a fag to fuck that girl from the newspaper?"

"Well, yeah, her, but someone else too. Remember that girl Jill I used to date?" I raise my head and look at him as he nods. "Okay, so I got this thing from Spaz that was supposed to prove I didn't attack that Connie Ward chick, right? So, I finally get it, and it's a small report filled out with public safety detailing everything I did and said and shit."

"How'd they get that?"

"That's the thing. Jill filed it with them."

"Why?"

"She saw the wanted poster and she probably thought she was doing some kind of favor for me. She went and sealed my alibi." I catch myself chattering at a fast pace. I stomp out my cigarette and light another.

"No shit…"

"Yeah."

"But that doesn't make sense…"

"I know."

"Why would they just take her word for it? If you were the guy they're looking for, how do they know you didn't just send Jill down there to lie for you?"

"That's the thing," I say. "It's what's in the report." He looks at me with a puzzled glare. "The Admiral needs a shot of Jack," I say to the bartender as I wave my index finger. I turn back to Doug. "It's because of the type of report it was."

"What?" he's jittery with anticipation, waiting to hear the rest of the story. It's the most animated I've ever seen him. "What was in the report?" He looks at me with concern, his normally half-closed eyes now open. "What type of report was it?"

"It was a disturbance report, Doug." The corner of my eye catches the bartender reaching my shot towards me. I turn and snatch it from his hand, pouring it down my throat. Things get blurry and I gag.

"Wait, hold up," he says. "Why was she filling out the report?"

"She was reporting a disturbance. I was the disturbance."

"What kind of disturbance?"

"I don't know. It's like…I dunno. It said all kinds of shit, like I was grabbing her ass and her friend's ass and making jokes about some fat chick. Typical shit," I explain. "Apparently, the Admiral left her a bunch of drunk voicemails at around the same time that the whole Connie Ward thing

164

happened, which she used to prove I couldn't be attacking Connie."

"The Admiral strikes again," he laughs.

"Yeah. This might actually be the only time that my drunk dialing actually paid off."

"Wait…I'm confused," he says. "Why is this a problem? It's somehow enough to take you off the hook, right? And it's not like they can do anything because you grabbed some ass and drunk dialed her."

"Well, here's the thing. First, I still want to think I can patch things up with Jill. Her little walking, talking piece of Spanish Harlem is going to fuck up again, hopefully for the last time. Then, ideally, I was hoping me and Jill could pick up where we left off."

"Okay…"

"But, if I'm getting all drunk and acting like an asshole, I'm just as bad as the douche she's with now."

"Right…"

"Not only that," I continue, "but I think I got some kind of thing for Katie, and she's going to want to see this report." He nods silently. "First off, she already told me she only likes me as a friend, but I think she was drunk, so I don't know. But anyway, if she sees the report, she's also going to think I'm a douche and want nothing to do with me anyway." I stop to catch my breath. "Am I making sense?"

"Okay…" he starts, "let me see if I follow. You're all worked up because you think that you may have ruined your chances with two girls who want nothing to do with you sexually?"

"Hmmm," I grunt. "It sounded a lot more romantic in my head." I drop my head and face the ground. Doug's eyes return to their neutral, half-open state, the rest of his face is buried under a baseball hat and four days of stubble and scruff. "See, I just don't know what to do," I say. Doug doesn't respond. He keeps fixated on the dance floor in the middle of the place. "It's like, I got these girls. They both kind of like me in one form or another. Neither of them wants to go the distance. And then I sit there and think about why—and here's the real depressing part—I realize that I'm a drunk, an alleged rapist and, like, a million other things, and it's just really annoying. And the thing I really hate is that there's no sign of it getting better. Remember high school? Fuck that, remember last year? Think of all of us last year. Did we ever complain about shit? We just went around, had a good time. Now, it's all about all this outside shit— these outside issues, like confusion and misdirection and awkwardness and lack of self-control, which is cool 'cuz I understand that's normal. It's just annoying, you know? It's like before, we had all this outside, annoying shit, but there was hope for change. Now what? I mean, I'm starting to think that the reason I—not just me, but all of us—the reason all of us drink so much and sleep all day is because we're just too friggin' scared. We're too friggin' scared and stupid to look to the future, because we know we're all totally unprepared, and we're going to get eaten alive, not by the 'real world' but by life in general, and it sucks. It just sucks, plain and simple. And I just get really fed up, not just because this is all true, but because this floods into my head anytime I think of my love life. I mean, how shitty do things have to be for..."

"Wait!" he says, staring forward and sticking his index finger up. "I just realized something!"

"What?"

"Lesbians..." he says as he lowers his index finger downward, pointing towards the dance floor. Two girls—two girls so hot and slutty looking that they can only be 18—are grinding into each other and making out. "Nice," Doug comments with a twisted grin. "What were you saying? I zoned out," he confesses.

"Nothing. I wasn't really talking about anything special..."

*   *   *

At the risk of sounding like a teenage girl writing poetry for her English 101 class, the streets in this small town have a very unique energy to them on Thursday nights, one so crisp and effervescent that you can almost taste and define the flavor of excitement as you breathe it in and let it stroke your tongue. Scattered clumps and crowds of people meander up and down Street Road, their anticipation somehow bellows louder than their voices. There's a kind of enthusiasm in this town on a Thursday that simply can't be compared to or matched by anything I've seen yet in my uneventful life. The energy that surrounds the streets is a lot like a pizza with a ton of toppings—while it's enjoyable as a whole, you can still taste and sense each individual ingredient that makes it up. You can sense the anticipation of the young, ambitious freshman guys while they walk to some party, hoping to bring home anything but their virginity. You can feel the awkward lust and attraction between two complete strangers, drunk and rushing home to have sex before their roommates get back. You can feel the cloaked nervousness of a senior class trying to deny the fear they have of graduating and moving into their parents' homes while they are locked in low-paying, dead-end jobs. You can even feel the jubilation of the once-thin, now-overweight freshmen girls who're going to use being drunk as a legitimate excuse to eat an entire pizza by themselves at 2 o'clock in the morning.

The weird thing about Thursday's unique feel is that it's unmatched by any other feeling, any other day of the week. For some reason, with college students anyway, there's something that's just so much more appealing about going out and having fun on a school night instead of on the weekend. School night? Who the hell am I kidding? There's no such thing as a school night anymore when you arrive at college.

The school clock tower, erected over the giant marble arches of the administration building, rings downhill and echoes through town. It's midnight. I never thought it was possible to drink myself sober, but here I am. The worst part about this is having the disabled physical coordination that comes with being drunk, but not having the jovial, inflated sense of self-esteem that I need in order to drown out the other issues in my life, such as Jill.

Small, scattered groups of people mingle outside of Ball Park, a pizza place five minutes from Dill's. This is a regular intermission spot for the confused, wandering souls locked in drunken mediocrity on the streets of Berkshire.

"Broseph," I hear yelled to me as I walk my way through. I know it's the Dude from Hal's party, I know he's talking to me, and I know if I keep walking, acting like I didn't hear him, he's going to yell at me until he gets my attention.

"Hey," I say.

"My man…" he says, slowly stretching his arm forward, pointing his fist at me as a greeting. "Give me some chumba."

"What?"

"Chumba, bra, chumba!" he says, shaking and emphasizing his fist slightly. "Give me some poundage, Kevin."

"Kalvin," I say, hesitantly returning his greeting with my fist.

"What's the word, bra?"

"What do you mean?" I really hope there's a better reason for this conversation than small talk.

"You partying?" he says.

"No," I say. "Just drinking."

"Keen," he says. His head moves and sways like ocean waves, allowing him to survey the area. I can't see his eyes because he's wearing sunglass—at night.

"Why do you have the sunglasses, Dude?" I ask. My voice is condescending. I feel like I'm his father.

"Good question," he says, flopping his longish-shortish hair around with some quick turns of his neck. "But," he says, "a better question might be 'Why shouldn't I have sunglasses?'"

"Because it's after midnight."

"Keen," he says, lowering his glasses with his left middle finger. They reveal blood-shot eyeballs wrapped in red,

168

crackling veins. "I got my smoke on, and hard, brotha."

"Right," I say.

"I believe you remember my dirt-pushing consigliere, Gunther," he says using his thumb to point to the tall, stolid ape who's been at his side this whole time. "We had to smoke, like, at least an ounce, man."

"Is that right…"

"You know how much that is, dude?"

"I don't know…sure."

"That's *a lot* of fucking weed, dude!" he says with a giggle cracking through his voice. He turns and nudges Gunther as he laughs, then points his fist towards him. They pound fists hard. "Yeah, bra, give me some chumba! Yeah!" He looks at me. "We smoke all the time, bra."

"Sounds fun." I hope something heavy falls on me…I need out of this.

"You should stop by later. We made a gravity out of a mop bucket and an empty bottle of Captain. Off the fucking hook, man."

I have nothing against getting stoned, I really don't. I spent the better part of my first three years here burned out like a broken light bulb. But I hate—and I mean HATE—boastful potheads. Boastful potheads can really only be found in college. For some reason, bragging about how much you smoke or how high you are just isn't cool in high school. Boastful potheads are characterized by a few telltale signs. First, obviously, they brag about being high. Second, they always have to tell you how much they smoked. It's not enough that you know they're stoned; they also have to tell you how much they smoked to get that stoned—which is usually some random, astronomically inaccurate amount. Third—and this is my favorite—they always have some kind of bong that is supposed to set them apart from all other stoners. Some restaurants have a "signature" dish; boastful potheads have a signature bong. They're particularly proud of this bong for one of two reasons: A) they designed and made it from scratch, or B) they have some kind of unique, exotic bong, like one their buddy picked up for them in Mexico, or something. And get ready for a long night, because they will tell you every—and I mean every—story and anecdote they have that even remotely relates to their "piece."

"Yo," Dude says, limply throwing his hand at my arm. "Isn't that your girl?"

To my left, I see Katie, bundled in a jacket and scarf, walking down the sidewalk alone.

"I want to hit that so hard," he says.

It doesn't take long for Katie to see us. When she does, a smile thaws her straight face and she paces a little quicker towards us.

"Hey!" she says, her tan cheeks rosy and bright from the clean, cold air.

"Hey..." I say.

"Word," says the Dude. Gunther simply nods.

"What're you doing here?" she asks, looking back and forth between Dude and myself. "You guys all here together?" she asks with a puzzled grin, pointing back and forth at each of us.

"Me and my boy, Kal, were just having a talk!" he says, slamming his hand onto my shoulder, his fingers digging deep enough to feel through my thick, black jacket.

"Yeah?" she asks, looking at me. "About what?"

"About how you and him should make your way to my place tonight, maybe drink some beers, take a few hits off of Pietro," he says.

"Pietro?" Katie asks.

"My gravity bong."

"Okay," she says. "But why'd you name it 'Pietro'?"

"It's Russian for 'Peter,'" he says.

"Yeah, but why..." I ask before he cuts me off.

"It's Russian, bra, Russian," he says, shaking his hands towards me to emphasize whatever retarded little point he has.

Katie and I shift our eyes towards one another, taking relief in each other's confusion.

"I think I'll pass for now. Me and Kal are getting something to eat first." My first reaction is to say something like "We are?" in some innocent, dumbfounded voice, but for the first time in a while, I relax and play it cool by keeping my mouth shut. "Maybe after we're done, or something."

"Clutch," he says. "Gunther!" he yells, snapping his fingers. Gunther moves for the first time in about 20 minutes and reaches into his back pocket, pulling out a pale, yellow business card. "My card. When you two are done, you call me. We'll talk."

"Sure," Katie says, politely. She turns towards me and rolls her eyes.

With that, Dude and his manservant stand up from the wall they're leaning against. Dude winks, taps his heart and points at Katie as he walks away.

"What a joke..." she says.

"I know, right? I mean, seriously, what kind of tool gives out business cards?"

"Shut up!" she screams defensively. "You know I only have those cards because I'm with the newspaper!"

"Awww!" I say, with as much fake sympathy as I can find. "You know I'm just messing with you..."

"I hate you."

*   *   *

Katie is already working her way through two slices of pizza by the time I sit down. She handles her food like any girl does in the presence of other people: very dainty-like. She folds each slice, then holds it by pinching the crust area between her thumb and combined index and middle fingers, letting her ring and pinky fingers flail outward like wind socks. She plunges her teeth into the bottom of the slice, then pulls her head and hand back in opposite directions, stretching out a thick line of mozzarella. After severing the cheese strip with her front teeth, she opens her mouth into a tight circle and breathes in cool air in order to cool down the gooey cheese and warm, sweet sauce.

"Hmmm," she says with satisfaction. "I've been craving this all night."

"Were you staying in tonight?"

"Yeah, I was planning on it," she says. "Actually, I was trying to get started on your story."

"Oh yeah?" I ask. "How's that been working out for you?"

"Eh. It'd be nice if we knew what the real story was."

"What do you mean?"

"Writing about how you're innocent is only a small piece of the story," she says before repeating her whole bite n' chew routine all over again. "It's not really a complete thing unless we figure out who actually did attack Connie."

"Gotcha," I say. My stomach is burning—a casualty from the war brewing in my stomach between digestive fluid, alcohol and a ¼ slice of pizza. My nerves don't make things easier. Jill—I only think of Jill. I've been good to stay away from her lately. I feel kind of stupid obeying Fernando's threats, but I just want to make things easier for her. I don't want to be that guy who pesters her while she's trying to pursue a relationship with another guy. Still hurts, though.

"Let me ask you something," she says.

"What?"

"What do you want to be when you grow up?"

"You mean now, or what I wanted to be when I was a kid?"

"Both."

"That's a little random, but okay." She giggles with a type of innocence you only see in children, just like she did at Hal's. This may actually be the only time I've seen Katie act the same way twice. "Well, right now, I'm not a hundred percent sure what I want to be."

"This is, what, your fourth year?" she asks. "Cutting it a little close, aren't you?"

"Yeah, I guess. I don't know. There was a lot of stuff I wanted to do, but I can't because of money and stuff."

"Like what?"

"Christ…where do I start? Doctor, teacher, lawyer—all the lame typical stuff."

"Cool."

"But now, I don't know. I've been thinking about switching over to social work or something. I don't know why. Just seems cool."

"Makes sense, I guess, in a really disorganized way," she giggles and it rings over the crowd like music. "What about when you were a kid? What'd you want to be then?"

"Batman."

"Batman?"

"Yeah." She's caught me at a good time. I feel sober enough, but my judgment is still clouded by hours of drinking. Deep down, I know I'm not completely sober, and I know I'll regret opening up like this later.

"Why Batman?"

"You kidding me?" I ask, joking around. "Batman is friggin' awesome. But then I realized that if I wanted to be Batman, my parents would have to be killed and I wasn't real big on that."

"Awwww," Katie says, laughing and adding a weird, jovial kind of sympathy to her voice. "That's cute. You close to your family?"

"Yeah, sort of. I'm kinda close to my parents, anyway. Not my older brother, Moose."

"Moose?" she asks, twitching an eyebrow.

"Yeah, Moose. He's a dickhead."

"Ooooookay," she says. "So how old were you when you stopped wanting to be Batman?"

"I dunno. Eight maybe? That's when I wanted to be Spider-man instead."

She stops drinking from her straw with a jerk, smiles and chuckles at me. I don't think it's real, and I wonder if she's humoring me. Then again, it sounds sincere enough.

"My older brother was really into Spider-man when he was a kid, too" She wraps her lips around her straw. She sees me with a smile and returns one while she sips.

"That's cool. My brother was mostly into cocaine, so I kind of tried to stay out of his hobbies."

"Oh," she says. The smile falls off her face and is replaced by a compassionate lift of her eyebrows. "I'm sorry."

"Don't be. He's retarded. I just laugh at it." She nudges her head backwards, knocked off a bit by what I said. "It's not a big deal. He just does shit so stupid it's funny. Like last year, he got really drunk at my cousin's wedding and head-butted my mom because she tried cutting him off."

"And you laughed that off?"

"Eh...guess you had to be there."

We're quiet. My pizza's cold already, but I'm happy about it. It's nice knowing my pizza is cold because I've been enjoying myself with her.

"So," she asks. "Want to go get high?"

"Huh?"

"Let's go to your new best friend's place and take him up on his offer!" She picks up Dude's card from the table and waves it in front of me.

"Nah. I'm good."

"Aww! C'mon! I don't want to go myself!"

"Yeah, so you bring me down with you..."

"Pleeeeease?" she begs. "If I go alone, he's going to try to sleep with me again!"

"Again?" Oh, Christ... "When was the first time?"

"He kept trying all this cheesy shit to get me to go home with him after Hal's party."

"You didn't, did you?" My fear gets the best of me and I don't think to hide the panic and fear in my voice.

"Hell no! I told him you were my boyfriend."

"You did?"

"Yeah...you don't mind, do you?"

"No...but I told him before that we weren't together."

"Yeah, I know," she says. "I just told him that me and you were fighting."

"Listen, I'll be honest with you, that weird lord/manservant thing him and his buddy got going on kind of freaks me out."

"All you have to do is drink their beer and pretend to be my boyfriend," she says. "Please?"

*   *   *

Dude insisted on us coming over but told us to wait until 1:45ish. Katie and I agreed that we're both skipping Chip's donut-enriched Friday morning class tomorrow. The bars are starting to empty their numbers onto the streets, making this part of town the place to be for the next 20 minutes. At about this time every week, Street Road has the glow and emotion of a street carnival. Jubilant drunks dance and sway toasted about the town like street clowns. Designated drivers try to settle down rowdy friends like lion tamers. Really sad and desperate ugly people try to make one last stand, hoping someone will think of them as something more than freaks and take them home. Everywhere you look has something to see. The best part is Katie. She walks with a kind of stride that radiates her good mood. She nods her head and smiles at everyone who walks by, still keeping her mind focused on our conversation.

"Were you really that worried to show me the public safety report because your ex-girlfriend was in it?" she asks, still smiling.

"No, I was worried to show it to you because it said I was harassing her. I figured if you saw that, you'd think I was a dick."

"Nah. I've seen you drunk. You're harmless," she says, looking at me. "Stupid and annoying, but harmless."

"I'm working on it."

"Calm down, I'm just messing with you," she says. We're quiet as we take a few more steps. A lone girl power-walks in our direction with her arms folded. She's crying as she shoves her way between Katie and I. We don't pay attention to her. Nobody in Berkshire pities girls like that after their first week.

In fact, the lonesome girl walking home crying has become something of a staple here. There are always at least a handful of them to be seen each weekend. Usually, it's because they got all drunk and slutty and put themselves in a stupid situation with a guy too drunk to do anything but upset them. Most people find it hard to feel any sadness when they see them walk by. Actually, the only sad part about the situation is that most people find this funny and have a little bit of a laugh when they see the lonely, crying girl walking home. Girls like that should know better. After all, if you're going for a night on the town wearing a hand-kerchief for a shirt, you should be smart enough to realize that the guy you're with is getting you drunk and bringing you back to his bedroom to do more than check out his black light posters.

"So…" Katie says, interrupting my insensitive train of thought. "Were you two real close?"

"Me and Jill? I don't know. I guess we kinda were, in our own, weird way."

"How so?" she asks. I squirm a little as I walk and take a deep breath through my teeth. "You don't have to talk about it if you don't want to…"

"No, it's okay," I say. "We weren't together all that long…maybe a little more than a month. But I guess we were still pretty close for a couple dating a short time like that."

"What happened?"

"Her ex-boyfriend."

"Oh."

"Yeah." I look away, pretending to pay attention to something else. "It was my own fault, I guess."

"Why?"

"When we met, she was on the outs with him because she caught him cheating on her. When we started dating, I should've realized I was just a rebound."

"That's not true," she says the tone of her voice thickening with assertiveness. "First off, it's not your fault. You liked her, she was single, and you did what was right for you at the time. Second, a month is a long time to be with a rebound, which means she probably had at least some real feelings for you."

"Yeah, I guess."

"Some people are too blind to see a good thing when they have it."

"Thanks."

"And you know she's only hurting herself in the long run. Her boyfriend is probably still an asshole—a leopard can't change its spots, you know?"

"That's true," I say. "I don't know, I feel kind of guilty about the whole thing because I was immature about it."

"How so?"

"After we broke up, she tried really hard to be friends with me. Most people when they break up with you just say the whole 'let's be friends' thing out of courtesy, but she really meant it. She tried really hard to talk to me and stuff and I just threw it back in her face."

"You still talk?" Katie asks.

"Well, we did up until a few weeks ago. Kind of. We kind of got into a big thing about how I was acting immature about the whole 'being friends' thing."

"Hmmm," she says. She's got something brewing in her head. "Maybe she still likes you. Maybe she still has feelings for you."

"I doubt it."

"Maybe she realized you weren't such a bad catch. Maybe out of the two of you, she realized that you were more than just some partying frat guy with too many hours logged at the bar. Maybe she realized you had potential for a good thing and wanted to take things slow."

"Maybe not."

"So all those guys you hang out with," she says, changing the subject. "Are they all in your frat?"

"Yeah. The guys you met were."

"You guys don't seem like typical frat guys."

"We get that a lot," I say. "It's probably because we're

too lazy to have parties and stuff anymore."

"How's that?" she asks with a laugh.

"We don't really try to get anyone else to come over. We just get shitfaced and forget about it," I explain. "Our parties usually suck. That's why we barely ever have them anymore."

"Eh," she moans out. "Could be worse. At least you're not one of those creepy frats like Sig Chi."

"I know...I heard those guys are date rapists."

"You'd fit right in," she chuckles.

"Is this the place?" I say, trying to derail the conversation. I don't feel like talking about my problems anymore.

"11 East...yup."

11 East stands tall before us. Its brick veneer is crumbling. The building itself is warped and slanting right. Next to the building is a creek that's washing away at the ground and foundation the building is settled on. From the outside, the place looks ready to be condemned. At the bottom of the building is a green fire door. Dude told Katie that normally you need a key to get in, but he had everything covered, and he does. It's propped open by a CD that falls to the ground when we open the door. It's one of those CDs everyone gets in the mail—the ones that offer about 458,708,505,830 free hours of AOL.

The first thing I notice is the staircase. It takes me a few minutes to understand what I'm looking at, and at first I think I'm still drunk. The steps are completely slanted. Katie walks up first, leaning against the wall where the banister once was. She trips a few times going up, so do I.

Dude said his place was upstairs. The first thing I notice when we get up there is the low lighting, which is provided by a lamp laid out on the floor. The light reflects dully off of the warped hardwood floorboards. I trip over broken chairs and beer cans as I blindly follow Katie into the next room.

"You know where you're going?" I whisper.

"No," she whispers back. Funny how people just naturally whisper when they're in the dark.

"Remember, this was your idea," I remind her.

"Oh, blow me."

We make our way to a hallway that's also missing lights. I can hear beer cans being kicked around as we shuffle our feet cautiously. I grip the back of Katie's collar as she bravely plunges forward. We finally make our way towards the only other room in the place with any lights.

"Brohan Guttenberg! Welcome to the crib!" I hear as we step in. Dude is standing tall in yet another dimly lit room, arms outstretched in opposite directions, as if he's waiting for one of us to hug him or something. He's wearing jeans and a white t-shirt. And he still has those goddamn sunglasses on! There's a steel-framed bunk bed behind him. Gunther is fast asleep on the top.

"Hey," Katie says, "where's your bathroom?"

"What the hell you doing?" I whisper.

"What?"

"It was your idea to come! Don't leave me here!"

"I'll be quick. You'll be okay alone here, big man."

"Down the hall, make some lefts and you'll be there," Dude says.

Katie leaves in a hurry. Dude drops to the floor and sits Native American-style behind a small coffee table.

"Glad you decided to party, bra," he says, busily scurrying his hands across the table, moving stuff around its surface. "I wanna talk to you while we're alone."

"Okay..."

"Bro, I just want you to know, man, Katie, she is, like, all yours. I won't try and hit that."

"Right."

"I know I said earlier I'd hit that, but I won't. I ain't gonna touch your steak, brotha." His words slur. He's high beyond all methods of reasoning. "And besides...I got me some Hanna to plug tonight, ain't that right, baby?"

Dude's glare is focused behind me to a futon with a girl sitting on it. Her head hangs between her knees, bobbing like a buoy over a short, plastic wastebasket.

179

"Hanna, Kyle. Kyle, Hanna." Dude says.

"It's Kalvin." She says nothing. Her feet start to jitter and her bobbing goes faster, gradually picking up pace. Then it happens. Her jaw drops open; vomit flushes out as if she was an old-fashion water pump. The puke lands perfectly into the bucket, splashing against all the puke that's been collected already. Katie walks in just in time.

"Oh my God!" she yells. "Are you okay?!"

"She's stellar," Dude says. "She's just emptying herself out before me and her proceed with 'The Magic.'" Katie huddles close to me, and I feel her tremble. The expression on her face is caught somewhere between nervous laughter and a panicky cry as she looks at me before we both look at Dude. "I'm talking about sex!" Dude says, shedding light on the meaning behind his phrase, "The Magic."

"Are you okay?" Katie repeats frantically to Hanna, who waves her arm at Katie.

"I'm fine," she groans, spitting some more slime into her puke bucket.

"So…" Dude interrupts, "you two gonna make some 'magic' tonight, too? Cuz you can do it on my buddy's bed if you want." Katie tightens her lip as her brow lowers under the weight of her anger. Her eyes fix themselves on the coffee table where Dude is sitting, forming out little lines of coke with an ace of spades.

"What is that?" Katie growls through her teeth.

"It's candy, babe," Dude says.

Katie is pissed off when she turns to look at me. She was creeped out before, but now she's just plain angry.

"Hey…I know you…" I hear from behind as I feel a soft tug on my sleeve. Hanna is leaning against her thighs with her elbows, her face staring up at me. She has pale skin under tussled, blonde hair. She'd be kinda hot if I couldn't smell the bile on her breath.

"From the wanted poster?" I ask.

"Yeah," her voice shakes and cracks.

"Kal!" Katie yells, "I want to leave! Now!"

"I know you didn't attack Connie..." Hanna mutters, smiling as she sways her head in figure 8's.

"You do?"

"Kal!" Katie pulls hard on my arm. I wobble and catch my balance by grabbing the nearby doorframe. Dude is strapped by the nose to the coffee table, escaping the building without even leaving the room.

"Yeah..." Hanna says. "I know because I saw the guy who really did it..."

"What?!" I ask. "Who? Who was it?!"

"This guy..." she slurs. "He was tall..."

"Kal," Katie injects, "she's drunk off her ass. She doesn't know what's going on..."

"But what if she does?" I ask. "He was tall. What else?"

"Kal, she's halfway passed out. She probably doesn't even remember her name!"

"I want to go now," Hanna says. She sways backwards and tries to swing forward, using her momentum to get her off the couch. "Take me home."

"Fine." A sense of responsibility fills Katie's voice as her face sags with compassion. "Help me get her up, Kal."

"Yeah..." We each take one of Hanna's arms. Her hands are clammy and glazed with a cold sweat. Hanna takes some control of her body once she's on her feet, using Katie and I as crutches every few steps.

"Hey! You can't take her!" Dude screams, enraged and fueled on coke. "That's mine! I'm supposed to be fucking that tonight!" I don't even acknowledge him with a look, but Katie decides to pause and flip him off. Why do people give the finger anymore? Is anyone really *that* offended by it anymore? "Gunther! Get them!" Dude yells, turning around and poking at his dormant behemoth. "C'mon! Wake your fat ass up and get them!"

*   *   *

"My roommate and her boyfriend'll be here soon," Katie

181

says. My ass is frozen to the stone step in front of the building. I want nothing more than to be able to move, but Hanna is passed out cold on my shoulder. Small strings of puke and drool bridge the gap between her mouth and my jacket.

"You think she was telling the truth tonight?" I ask.

"About seeing the guy with Connie? I doubt it."

"Still," I say as I wonder about the situation "that's a pretty random thing to lie about, even for someone as wrecked as she is."

"I didn't catch where she lived. Did you?" She's changing the subject.

"Nope. What should we do with her?"

"I don't know." She sits down and mashes herself close against me. She's warm. A fragrance of dried peaches lifts from her hair and wraps around my head. "I guess she can stay on my couch."

"That's not a problem?" I ask, lighting up a cigarette.

"Shouldn't be." She reaches over silently and pulls my cigarette from my mouth. "I'll talk to her tomorrow when she's sober. See if she's telling the truth." She takes a drag and passes the cigarette back in my direction, keeping her eyes focused ahead of her.

"Thanks."

"Anytime." She turns and whips her hair off her shoulder, smiling at me in the process.

"I appreciate what you did for me up there, too."

"What?" she asks.

"Getting on his case for the coke. You didn't have to do that."

"I know." She smirks out the side of her mouth.

"It was still pretty cool of you to do that though."

"Let's see," she says, "you don't smoke much pot, you don't do much coke, you don't have a lot of wild, crazy parties and you don't try to date rape women," she says, counting the list off of her fingers. "You've got to be the dorkiest fucking frat guy I know."

182

"Ummm…" I say bewildered. "I don't know what to tell you. I get really drunk a lot…does that count for anything?"

She doesn't say anything to me. She wants to, I can tell, but she doesn't. My stomach moves and quakes. Her fragrant, peach scent intensifies as it shoots up my nose, blasts through my sinuses and tickles my brain cells. Shocks and tingles go down my spine. Our heads are turned, facing one another. She's breathing out through her nose, and each exhalation smoothes its way over my upper lip like a soft breeze, just as our lips push together with an almost inert force.

The inside of my stomach folds over itself and tightens when I realize I'm kissing her. My nerves fire into high alert; I almost panic. It's been a while since I've done this sober. I think about sliding my tongue in but she beats me to it. Her tongue is warm and wet as it gently pries open my mouth and slips its way through. I drag my tongue over hers. She pushes her whole body towards me, and I try to take her all in, until Hanna's head gets in the way. Shit…how do I do this? Katie is pressing and pressing harder against me. I nudge towards Katie, but Hanna's head rolls slightly off my shoulder. I move back, away from Katie, and Hanna's head'll fly backwards and plummet towards the cement.

"Oh my God, Katie!" a shrill voice echoes over a frozen engine block, struggling to warm up in the frosted night. "Are you hooking up with a guy who has a girl passed out on him?"

The voice comes from a petite girl in sweats and a knit hat coming from the passenger side of a Ford Taurus. Some big, tan guy—possibly a Samoan—is dressed just like her and coming from the driver's side.

"Okay, this is that girl I told you about that's crashing with us," Katie says to her roommate, ripping her lips from mine. "Help me get her up," she whispers to me. I don't need to. Before I can figure out what's going on, the Samoan and the little girl are helping Hanna off of me without saying a single word.

"You sure you don't mind?" I ask.

"It's not a problem," she says. "I had fun tonight."

"Good," I say with a strain as I stand, rubbing the frost off my ass.

"Did you?"

"Have fun?" My voice quivers. The wind chill collides with my nerves and excitement, making me shake like a dry leaf stuck under a windshield wiper. "Yeah, definitely."

"Good!" She grabs me by the collar, reeling me in like a fish. "Call you tomorrow..." she whispers before giving me one last kiss.

"Ready?" asks Katie's little friend.

"Yeah," Katie says without looking at her. "Bye..." she says to me, falling into the back seat next to Hanna.

I watch the cherry-red tail lights drive off as a cloud of exhaust covers the road. I drag another cigarette out of the crushed box in my pocket. My hands shake too much, and lighting the thing becomes as complicated as surgery. Moments pass before my legs are calm enough to move again, and all I can think about is Katie and her lips. I haven't felt this good in a long time. I haven't felt this good since I kissed Jill like that.

15

Good Vibrations

Completely sober, I'm a little taken back by last night. I hooked up with Katie—and she was sober! Holy crap. Just saying that in my head feels amazing on so many levels. I hooked up with the Hot, Liberal Arts Chick. I'm fucking awesome.

I was a good mile or so from my house after Katie's friends had picked her up. I declined a ride home. I felt like being the lone, misunderstood college student waltzing home in the early hours of morning, pondering the deep aspects of life. But instead, once the high I got from kissing Katie wore off, I reverted back to lazy, slightly drunk Kal. Dutch and Doug's place was nearby. I climbed in through the only unlocked window in the place, which happened to be above Doug's bed. He was hammered from his long night of staring at lesbians. When I climbed in and fell on him, he got startled and threw me off his bed. I crashed to the floor, just after I crushed my head against his bedside table. Of course, he was in such a deep sleep that he doesn't remember any of it, and wondered why he woke up to me passed out and bleeding on his bedroom floor.

"The fuck were you thinking, retard?" Dutch asks as I recapped my break-in. "You're an ass."

"We keep our front door unlocked, you know," Doug said.

"You're an ass," Dutch repeats. I feel like my parents are

yelling me at after waltzing in drunk. Dutch is acting like my angry father; Doug is playing the defensive mother.

"What?" I ask. "You want me to fucking apologize?"

"Calm down…it wasn't a big deal," Doug says. Creepy.

Apparently, Doug and Dutch also thought it was a good idea to get drunk last night just to skip class today. Most of the students in the campus community probably agree. These two decided to dedicate their day to watching the *Godfather* trilogy. At one point, I may have thought it was ingenious that they planned their day to the minute, as not to get to Happy Hour late. But for some reason, it feels a little trivial. I kind of hope this is just a phase, but at the same time, I hope it's not.

"You're bleeding again," Doug says. Blood creeps and squiggles its way down from the gash on my forehead and into my eyebrow.

"Doug," Dutch says, sprawled out along a couch and focusing on the TV in the center of the room. "Go get me a pizza."

"Screw that," Doug says in a lazy voice, reclining back into an easy chair. "You get a pizza."

"You're such a fag! Why won't you go get a pizza? It's for both of us!"

"I'm not a fag…you're a fag!" Good comeback, Doug.

"Get my pizza!"

"At least I don't go to gay parties," Doug says.

"Fuck you!"

"You were probably all there, making out with dudes and stuff, rubbing their balls and letting them put it in your ass…"

"Yeah, you'd know, fag," Dutch says, as they start what's the first of probably many arguments about who's gayer. I tune it out because I've heard it all before. All I can think about is how nice and big their place is. They could probably have some kick-ass parties here, but they refuse to. They're "those guys"—the ones who have an awesome place but refuse to utilize it.

"…suck my dick," Doug says, a little pissed about something Dutch said.

"Yeah, you'd like that wouldn't you?" Dutch responds.

"Not as much as you!" The age-old debate over who's more likely to be gay continues. Luckily, my cell rings with salvation. It's Katie's number on the ID.

"Hey," I say, walking out of the room. I don't want her to hear the newest chapter of "Fag-Gate" going on in the background.

"Hey! Am I waking you?" her tone is positive and her voice rubs like silk along my eardrums. "How was the walk home last night?"

"It was fine," I say. "Actually, I didn't go home, I crashed at a friend's place."

"I see," she says. "Which friend was that? The one I had to show my boobs to, or the one who single-handedly offended all of Hal's friends?" Her tone is sarcastic and playful—a good sign. That means she's probably not feeling weird about last night.

"The second one. Dutch."

"Gotcha," she says with a small laugh. "So, what're you up to?"

"Nothing I can't get out of," I say. "What's up?"

"My one sports reporter quit on me and I need to cover a roller hockey game, which is probably going to suck. Want to come with?"

"How can I say 'no' when you do such a good job of selling it to me?"

"Well, it starts in 20 minutes, so get your ass down here."

"Sure."

"I mean it, Kal! I talked to Hanna this morning before she left. You need to hear what she said!" The tone of her voice is weird; I can't judge if it's good news or not.

"I'm on my way."

*   *   *

187

I should be wondering what Katie has to say about her talk with Hanna. I should be anxious, maybe even nervous, but I'm not. I've got my mind on other things, like what the hell I'm going to do when I see Katie. Do I kiss her? What if yesterday was just a random thing she did? What if she thinks I'm a horrible kisser or I had shitty breath or something? What if she changed her mind about me overnight and I go to kiss her and she turns away? Or even worse, what if she humors me and gives me a really awkward "just friends" kind of peck? Crap. Now I am nervous, just not about the right things.

Katie is sitting by herself on the one side of the bleachers that border the roller rink. There are about 10 other people there, too. Katie moves her book bag when she sees me coming. She pats the spot next to her, inviting me.

"Hey," I say while sitting down. I'm frozen, and my eyes are dry and itchy. What do I do?

"Hey," she says, taking the initiative and giving me a full kiss. It looked so simple for her. I feel like a little bitch for even worrying.

"So what's going on?"

"Okay, get this..." Her voice is jittery. "Hanna told me who the old guy with Connie was...you ready?" I don't say anything because the truth is that I'm not ready. Now that I don't have to worry about kissing Katie, I'm finally starting to worry about this situation. "She said it was Chip!"

"Chip? As in our teacher, Chip?"

"Yeah!"

"No shit!"

"That's what I said!" she yells. "But I had her look at a picture of him in the yearbook to be sure. Not only that, but Amy, my roommate, is a waitress at Dill's. She said he's there almost every night for last call, and he's usually with at least a couple of students."

"So does that mean Chip did it?"

"Can't say for sure, but it looks that way," she says.

"Hanna said her and a bunch of other people saw the two of them leave together that night at closing, which is right when the incident happened."

"Whoa…"

"And the fact that he didn't mention anything to us when we talked to him makes things look more suspicious."

"I knew he was hiding something!" I proclaim. "That explains why he offered to smoke us up when we talked to him. He wanted to dumb us down enough to take his word on everything."

"Wow…" she says. Her jaw is hanging like a marionette. "This is huge…"

"But why me?" I ask.

"What?"

"Why me?" I repeat. "If Connie was attacked by Chip, then how come she described a guy who looks like me to the police?"

"I don't know," Katie says sympathetically. "Maybe she's scared to accuse Chip. He's a pretty big member of the community."

"It doesn't make any sense…"

"I know," she says, looking towards her shoes. "And that brings up something else we need to talk about…"

"What?"

"This is obviously a lot bigger than we thought," she explains. "If we're going to keep this up, things are going to get really hard. We may have to accuse someone of a serious crime; it won't exactly be a holiday." She reaches towards me and put her hand over mine. "You need to decide if you actually want to keep going through with this."

"Well, we can't just stop," I say. "If he did this, that means he attacked a girl and he's going to get away with it…we have to at least tell the police."

"Kal, the police probably already know about it."

"How's that?"

"This is a small town. There are only eight cops and most of them probably know Chip. Hell, for all we know, they could even be his drinking buddies."

"You think so?"

"Kal, they're townies, but they're still cops. They've talked to all the same people we have and more. If we figured it out, they must've, too. That means we'd have to take it higher than the local cops." Her hand starts to rub mine. Her touch is soft and warm. "Not only that, but Connie is obviously avoiding us. Without her backing the whole thing up, all we have is a suspicion."

"You're right. You're completely right…"

"I know it's hard to grin and bare something like this, but we don't really have a choice." She squeezes on my hand and looks at me. "But, if you want to keep going with this, I'll stick with you."

She's right. I have to make a choice. But what do I do? I have no desire to take this further, but I don't know if I can let something like this sit on my conscience.

It's hard to think about this here. The roller hockey game is moving fast and the noise is drawing my attention.

"S-s-shoot the d-d-damn ball!" yells some guy with blonde hair and glasses who's been benched. He's fully dressed for the game, but it looks like he hasn't been put in yet. "C'mon you p-p-p-pussies! Y-you look like f-f-fuckin' s-s-scrubs!" That stutter is really pissing me off. He looks like he's going to have a heart attack.

"Okay," I say to Katie. "You're right. This is only going to get worse. We should quit while we're ahead."

"You sure?" she asks, the tone of her voice swells with compassion.

"Yeah," I say. "I'm sure." She looks me straight in the eye and smiles. Connie Ward and the rest of the world disappear for that short moment. "We can still hang out though, right?" I say, trying to lighten the mood.

"Of course!" she says, kissing me on the cheek.

"*Oh, my God!*" screams a shrill voice. Stuttering kid is lying on his back, shaking. "Jeremy!" yells a short, brown-haired girl from behind us. Katie and I watch silently as she runs down and meets a crowd of people gathering around him.

"He's going into diabetic shock!" someone yells. "Somebody get him some chocolate! Fast!"

"Hey," Katie says, taking my attention away from the situation. "Let me buy you lunch. It'll cheer you up."

"What?" I ask. "Shouldn't you be down there for this? Like, reporting on it or something?"

"Nah," she says. "I'm the assistant editor. I'll just make someone else do my dirty work later."

"Okay," I say as we both stand up and collect ourselves.

"Shouldn't I pay though?" I ask as we walk away. "Isn't the guy supposed to pay?"

"Nah, not always," she responds. "Besides, I have to pay for you. You're my little bitch now!" Wow...that's just degrading. Now I know how all those girls in those rap videos feel.

16

Support Structure

"It was only my third game of the season. I would've never guessed it'd happen to me. Not then. Not during my senior year," says the lanky guy with the dark-blonde hair. "I didn't care that I was playing defense, you know? I didn't care. I was just happy to make varsity. It was going to be a good year."

"That's a good start, Aaron," says Dr. Romita, her hair tied tightly behind her head. She's thin for an older lady. She's got a button-down shirt that's opened and flexing a hefty supply of cleavage. Not bad for someone who's got to be pushing 50. "What happened next?" she asks.

"I don't really want to get into the accident itself..." Aaron answers.

"Aaron, you've got to learn to talk about the accident," Dr. Romita says casually, her eyes focused on the clipboard in her hands. "It's pointless to try to get over something like this if you can't even talk about it."

"You're right," he admits. "It was really my first time playing D. In lacrosse, defense and offense are totally differ-ent. I went to charge this guy—he was a skinny, little guy—I had no idea how things would've ended if I went after him." He lifts his head and stares around the room. He darts his eyes across the eight other people in the room. They freeze on me for a second. His brow sinks as he tries to recognize me. His hand rubs and massages his forehead before he talks again. "The kid flat-out leveled me. His head hit my chest like a cannonball," he says as he rubs his head some more. "My mom said I was blacked out for almost five minutes."

"Were you awake when you got to the hospital?" Molly asks.

"Sorta. I can't remember much of it," he responds.

"Why the hell did you bring me here?" I whisper to Lana, who's to my right.

"You said you were seriously considering social work as a major," she responds.

"So?"

"'So?' So this is the kind of stuff you'll be doing if you switch over," she says. Lana and Molly assist Dr. Romita with this support group. I think it's called "Outpatient Care." It's a group for people who've had surgery and feel somehow, I don't know, violated because of it. Apparently, Molly and Lana took what I said to heart last Friday at Happy Hour. I was on such a trip with things working out between Katie and I the past few weeks, and I was too stupid to keep my mouth shut. Katie's put my whole life into a weird sort of order. Ambition has never been my thing, but for some reason, when I think of Katie, I have this urge to, I don't know, do stuff. Of course, maybe I should've thought things out a little more before I told these two about that. They haven't shut up about going with them to their stupid support group ever since I got all drunk and yappy about switching to social work.

"...I would've never played that season if I knew it was going to cost me two ribs!" Aaron whines out. He drops his head onto Dr. Romita's shoulder as she glides her hand through his thinning hair. "I feel so empty without them!" he screams. Crap...I probably should've been listening to whatever he just said. But damn, Dr. Romita's boobs look good.

"It's okay," she whispers in his ear, patting his temples gently. "You know, Aaron, God took a rib from Adam and created a woman," she says, grasping his shoulders and pushing him away slowly. "He only took one rib and did that

193

much good. Imagine all the good that can come from taking two of your ribs!"

"What?" I yell. Everyone looks. Whoops.

"Shut up!" Molly whispers, as she elbows me.

"Does anyone else have some support to offer Aaron?" Dr. Romita asks, slowly moving her head, scanning for volunteers.

"Well," says a short, dark-haired girl as she raises her hand. "When I had my surgery, I felt empty afterwards, too."

"Thank you, Nicole. Can you please explain?"

"Umm…well, I had this thing in my uterus—something called a fibroid. Apparently, like, most girls have them or something, I don't know. But mine—mine really hurt!" she says, raising her voice with a fake kind of anger. A ghostly chuckle echoes through the circle for a moment.

"You had to have a C-section to remove it, didn't you?" Dr. Romita reminds the group.

"Yeah. It was crazy…" Nicole remembers aloud. "I mean, wow. It was like I gave birth. Only instead of a kid, it was a grapefruit-sized fibroid." She's quiet. Everyone stares at her except me. The silence is so awkward that I feel my knees shake. Everyone else is patient, waiting quietly for her to continue. "But I don't know…it's weird, y'know? Like, I know this thing had to be removed, right? And I know…I know it had to be taken through a C-section, but still…I still feel…weird," she says. "I feel like someone came into my house and stole my old VCR. I mean, I don't use my VCR or anything anymore, but I'd still be pissed if it was taken from me…"

"Wow," I say in a voice just loud enough to be considered anything but a whisper. "That's really fucked up." Angry stares follow.

*   *   *

"How'd you like your first taste of social work?" Molly asks with one hand on my shoulder. It's unusually warm out today, and the black in my jacket sucks in the sunlight and heat like a fat chick slurping spaghetti. Then again, it is March.

"I didn't."

"I didn't think you would," Lana says out the side of her mouth while she lights a cigarette.

"I guess it just isn't my thing," I say, mimicking Lana as I light my cigarette.

"Whoa, wait..." Molly says. Her and Lana look at each other briefly before looking at me. "What's up with you today?"

"What do you mean?"

"You're kinda chipper."

"So?"

"First off, you're *never* chipper. Second, if you were ever chipper, it wouldn't be after wasting your time listening to other peoples' problems for an hour," Molly says.

"It's a nice day out. I'm in a good mood."

"And?" Lana asks.

"No 'and,'" I say.

"Did you finally get over your Jill issues?" Molly asks. There's a tone in her voice that resembles sarcasm.

"What Jill issues?"

"C'mon, Kal!" she says. "You've been a mess ever since she broke up with you and went back to dating that guy on the tennis team." I'm shocked that she can read me like that. I look at Lana. She just nods. Of course, she already knew that my problems went back to Jill.

"Okay," I say, "maybe Jill had a small part to play in how I've been acting the past few months."

"A small part?" Molly bursts out. "You've been a drunk, self-loathing mess since it happened. I mean, that *is* why you were acting that way, right?"

"You told her?" I spit out as I shoot a glare towards Lana.

"No..." Lana responds in a meek voice.

"She didn't tell me anything, but you did just now with that little outburst." She's got a wry smile smeared on her face. She loves it when she gets the best of people.

"Sorry," I say to Lana.

"It's okay," she says, smiling and tilting her head all at once.

"So is it true?" Molly asks

"What?" I respond. "That I'm over my issues? Yeah, I guess so." My lips remember the soft pressure put on them by Katie's lips and all they can do is curve and smile.

"Cool," Molly says casually. "So I take it you two haven't talked since her boyfriend threatened you?"

"Nope."

"Probably for the better, right?"

"Maybe," I say. "Maybe not."

"What do you mean?" Lana asks, sharing the concerned spotlight with Molly.

"I kinda want to ask her about that report she filed with public safety."

"Why?" Molly says with squinty eyes and a confused voice to match.

"I dunno...closure?"

"That's so stupid," she lets out in a slow voice, exhaling smoke and shaking her head slowly.

"I don't know. It's going to bug the hell out of me unless I ask her about it."

"But why do that to yourself?" Molly's voice rises up. "What if you go there, you talk to her, rekindle all these 'issues' you've been going through, and find yourself buried in your own filth and depression again?"

"Then I'd look a lot like that friggin' pig you're keeping shacked up in my place."

"First off, leave Thor out of this. Second, don't change the topic. You know I'm right." I look away from her as she's about to go on. I know she's probably right. I just don't want to believe it.

"Don't you think so, Lana?" she asks.

"Kal, I think you should do what you need to do," her voice is sweet and gentle as it fills my ears. "Just be careful."

"I can't believe you're condoning this!" Molly turns her concern towards Lana.

"You asked what my opinion is, and I gave it," Lana says, dropping her expired cigarette.

"Christ!" Molly blurts out. The two of them begin to fight. I just sit back and enjoy the warm weather. It's nice seeing the first warm day of Spring after a hard winter. It gives you a new perspective and kind of lets you know that a new phase of life is kicking off. For once, even if it is only that first thawed-out, warm day, life seems to have a way of working out.

Around the back of the building, I hear a riding mower charge across the grass for the first time in months. The smell of fresh, chopped grass fills the air and covers the default stench of cow shit. Spring has hit Berkshire hard, and the town is going to react with a bender—that's usually what happens in towns like this. Warm weather = drinking. Then again, so does cold weather. Okay, maybe weather has nothing to do with drinking motivations. I wonder what I used as a motivation to drink before I met Jill. It seems like years ago now. Wow. Times like this would usually lead to the same thought process: I'd think of Jill, I'd replay the first time we met, our first kiss, etc, then I would get depressed and feel a need to drink to the point where my mind's eye got too buzzed to see my memories without a thick blur. For the first time in a while, I don't feel that way. I don't feel my blood shaking inside me, waiting anxiously for more booze to drown out the last of my functioning cells. All I can think about is Katie. When I put her on my mind, the mix of cigarette smoke and cut grass mix together and smell better than a $1000 perfume.

"The hell are you all giddy about?" Molly asks.

"What?"

"You're all smiley and giddy…what the hell's wrong with you?"

197

"I don't know what you're talking about."

"Does it have to do with that girl you've been hanging out with?" Lana asks.

"What girl?" I know she means Katie, I just don't want them to know about her yet. It is kind of embarrassing admitting that a girl makes me feel this good. Especially after they've seen me so invested in Jill only for that to go downhill faster than a gimp that slipped in mud.

"Oh my God!" Molly screams. "Did you fuck last night or something?!" Her smile shows off the same kind of pride my parents had when they found out I got accepted to a school that didn't have the words "community college" in the title.

"I got to meet up with the guys," I say.

"Oh my God! You did!" Molly yells, trying to avoid my changing the subject.

"Don't you have class soon?" Lana asks, making it obvious that she's trying not to step all over my privacy, unlike Molly.

"Skipping it." I respond.

"For what?" Lana asks.

"Drinkin.'"

"Didn't you just say you were over all that?" Molly asks, her smile sneering into a weird, condescending type of concern.

"What?" I ask. "I can't drink when I'm in a good mood?"

"It's only, like, 1 o'clock," Molly argues.

"So? It's my fraternity's 'in-service day.'"

"In-service day?" Lana asks.

"It's an excuse for all of them to skip class and drink during the day," Molly explains. "Retards..."

"Have fun in class, girls!" I say. I hope the enthusiasm in my voice doesn't make me sound gay.

"Ugh..." Molly says. "Whatever. Be careful." She drops the last of her cigarette and reaches out for a hug.

"Yeah," says Lana, "don't get in any trouble or anything." She follows Molly's lead and hugs me tight. "Don't

198

call her when you're drunk," she whispers in mid-hug.

"Who? Jill?"

"Or this new girl…" she pulls away slowly. The look she gives makes me feel like I'm wearing a suit of armor. She taps my sleeves and straightens my collar. "Have fun."

*   *   *

"Dude," comments Doug, who came as a late edition to our festivities. "Why do all really hot girls date mechanics or construction workers or something like that?" His tone is slurred. He's got his back on the cold, shadow-covered grass in our back yard. The springtime sun starts to duck behind the horizon as 5 o'clock comes around and brings a chilly, early-Spring night with it.

"Cuz they're all manly and shit," answers Wally. "College guys aren't."

"Bullshit," says Jay. "I'm manly. I've got a car,"

"Chicks dig guys with trucks," adds Barry, who's sitting in a lawn chair. "Look at the fat kid who lives next door to us. He's got a truck. It's the only way he can get any poon." Barry throws a can onto the ground, watching it bounce and roll away. "It's not fair to the rest of us who have cars. That's why it's my civic duty to pass out and puke in the back of his truck."

"You doing that tonight?" Doug asks.

"We'll see. The night's young."

"Yo," asks Dutch. "What're we doing tonight?" I could set my watch to when he asks that every night. $5 bucks says someone answers with a gay joke.

"What's your rush?" Jay asks. "Got some dick to suck or something?"

"The cafeteria's open," Wally says. "Wanna go drunk?"

"We did that yesterday," Barry answers.

"So?"

"What're you? A fucking freshman?" Dutch yells.

"Technically," Wally says. "I only have, like, 25 credits."

199

"But you've been here for three years!"

"Yup," Wally replies after he drags a long burp from his mouth.

I think this is the first time in months that I hung out and got drunk for a reason not motivated by anger. And it's nice—almost kind of refreshing. And the best part? I haven't had "The Stare" or any assaults by my 16-year-old inner child in weeks.

Life is good.

"I can't believe we're graduating in a month," Barry says, prompting a discussion on the matter.

"Maybe you are," Jay says. "The rest of us got another year of getting shitfaced and scaring girls."

"Rub it in," Barry says, almost regretfully.

"You guys find jobs yet or anything?" Doug asks.

"Nope," answers Barry.

"Nah," Dutch says. "I'm gonna take my time. I've got a good job already."

"At Foot Locker?" I ask.

"Better than that fucking job you got!"

"I don't have a job right now."

"Exactly," Dutch responds. Everyone laughs. They have a right to. Up until a few weeks ago, I was a joke.

"Hey, Kal," Doug says. "You ever do that newspaper thing that that girl with the boobs wanted?"

"Nah," I say. "Wasn't worth my time."

"You're not worried about it anymore?" Barry asks.

"Nah, no reason to be," I say. "It's been almost two months since that wanted poster went up. It's old news now."

"That was friggin' hilarious," Wally says. "You were skitzing about it. That was awesome." He's right. It's weird in retrospect how much more...I don't know...calm I am now.

"We're running out of booze," Jay mentions, throwing another can into the pile.

"So get more," Dutch says.

"You fucking get it," Jay says. I just turn my ears off as

best I can for the upcoming argument. If I resist throwing my two cents in, maybe they'll forget I'm here and not nominate me to go.

"Whose phone is that?" Barry asks ambiguously. It takes a minute before I realize it's mine. Shit. Jill.

*　　　*　　　*

"Hey," she says. Her voice unlocks an overflow of warm sensations in my brain and queasy shakes in my stomach. She looks humble as she stands in the doorway of my bedroom. Humble and hot. She's got on a pair of tight jeans, a tight t-shirt and a tight windbreaker to go over it. She's got the "tight" look nailed down. "Can I come in?"

I lie on my bed with my hands behind my head as pillows. I don't want to make eye contact with her, not yet. I just keep focused on the flies, which are still humping on my alarm clock.

"I don't know," I say, half sarcastic. "Do you have a signed permission slip from the conquistador you've been dating?" If this was some kind of duel—and in my opinion, it is—I'd be leading 1-0.

"He can be kind of possessive," she says. I think she's trying to segue into a joke. I don't let her.

"'Kind of possessive?'" I ask. "I'd be surprised if he hasn't pissed on you to claim you as his territory." Not my funniest joke, but it's enough to knock her down a peg. 2-0.

"He told me about when he came over here," she says. "I'm sorry he threatened you."

"I'm sorry you're submissive enough to let him." Submissive—that's a good word. Definitely worth a bonus point. 3-0.

"It wasn't my idea. He did it behind my back."

"I know. I think he mentioned that right before he threatened to bleed me."

"You still mad about it?"

"No."

"You sure?" she asks sincerely, as she slowly steps into my room.

"Positive."

"Good. I was afraid you would be," she says as she sits on the foot of Wally's empty bed. She's quiet. All she can do is smile half-assed at me. Crap—she gets a point for being the "bigger person." 3-1

"I'm sorry about that fight we had last time we talked." 3-2. Crap.

"Don't worry about it. It was over a month ago. I'm over it." The apology brush-off—easily one of my best moves. 4-2

"I have to admit, I expected you to call me after that," she says. I keep staring. "I wanted to apologize then, but you never called. I was like 'Oh my God! Did I really offend him that mu…'"

"Is this what you needed to talk about?" I ask, interrupting.

"What?"

"You said on the phone that you wanted to come over because you really needed to talk to me. What for?"

"Can you sit up please?"

"Why?"

"I'd feel more comfortable." Her voice cracks halfway through her last word. She's barely holding together a sad face. Tears are going to pop from her eyes like they're water balloons. I was hoping this had something to do with the report she filed. I want to ask her if it is, but my stupid sense of "compassion" makes me ask something else: "What's the matter?" I finally ask.

"Kal," she says with tears swelling up. "I'm so sorry."

"Sorry about what?"

"Everything." She cries hard into her hands for a few minutes before I offer her a tissue.

"He cheated on you again, didn't he?" She just looks at me and nods. Damn. We made eye contact. That's a one-point penalty. 3-2.

"Yeah." Her bawling starts to sound almost rhythmic.

"I'm so sorry, Kal."

"Why?" I say, rubbing her back, feigning compassion. "You didn't do anything to me."

"I shouldn't have picked him over you," she says, catching her senses.

"What?"

"I really cared about you. I still do. That's why I got so mad last time we met. That's why I got so mad about you avoiding me. I just wanted to be with you, I wanted to tell you I cared about you. But you'd never answer when I'd call." The water works start up again.

"This confession doesn't have anything to do with you being dumped for another girl, does it?"

"Kal, I loved you..."

"Huh?"

"I loved you. I went back with Fernando because my parents liked him. They didn't like that I was dating a 'frat guy,' so I did the stupid thing and went with the guy my parents liked."

"Your parents liked a guy who cheated on you more than they liked a frat guy? They sound like good people..."

"I know I was stupid, and I know I was wrong and I know how all this sounds. I'm an idiot. I'm stupid for picking him over you, and I'm stupid for hurting you." Her face is a chapped red from all her crying. "I'm a stupid, fucking bitch for doing what I did and if you don't talk to me again, I understand. But the reason I came over here was to tell you that. Not to tell you that we broke up or that I want to get back with you. I didn't even come over to tell you how I felt about you. I just had to apologize because I know how much I hurt you." Wow. The Catharsis. That just blew the game out of the water. If I could calculate a score, it'd probably be 3-9,865,439.

I'm expecting her to ask me for a response, like they do when stuff like this happens on TV. She doesn't. She just sits there until she can hold herself together enough to attempt to stand.

"Jill?" I say as she's standing up.

"What?"

"Don't..." I choke on my words in mid-sentence. "Don't beat yourself up about it. It's all in the past."

"Kal..."

"Seriously," I can't believe I'm saying this, "you did what you thought was right. You had to pick between us and you bet on a sure thing. A lot of people would've done that."

"I'm sorry I hurt you," she says, dropping her ass back down on the bed.

"Don't worry about it. If I didn't get hurt, he would've." I try not to choke on the bullshit dripping out of my mouth. "You would've hurt someone no matter what. If you went with me, you might've been at his place right now having the same talk with him."

"No, I wouldn't" she says. "I didn't care for him then like I cared for you." She squirms closer to me, slowly at first. Then she pounces, jamming her lips against mine, and it feels good. It feels perfect until I remember about Katie. I think of her and realize that I just got myself into some shit that I can't get out of without someone getting hurt. Fucking irony.

17

Someone to Love

"…that's about the whole story," I say. "No matter how I cut it, it comes down to one thing: Jill or Katie."

"Tough choice," he says in a low squeak. "Any idea who you're going to go with?"

"No idea whatsoever," I say.

"Have you tried making a mental list of pros and cons?"

"Yeah," I say, nodding. "About a million times over."

"And?"

"Nothing…nothing I can use to help me make the right choice."

"Let me hear it," he requests, showing an unusual amount of compassion—something I've never seen from him.

"Alright. Well, Jill is Jill, Katie is Katie—that's a pro for both of them, I guess."

"Okay, that sounded really cheesy, but go on."

"Jill I know pretty well. Katie has about 1000 different personalities, all of which are pretty unpredictable."

"Okay, one for Jill."

"I also feel in my own league with Jill. Katie…she's confident and smart. I kind feel like her retarded sidekick."

"Jill-2, Katie-zip. Go on."

"Jill means well, but her loyalty is questionable, obviously. Katie hasn't cheated on me, and I don't think she will since she's been cheated on herself."

"That's a good point."

"Jill's parent's hate me despite not knowing me. Of course, she seems to come from some kind of conservative, anti-alcoholic boyfriend upbringing."

"And Katie isn't?" he asks, drinking some water.

"I don't think so. Someone as liberal as she is she most likely has some pretty liberal parents."

"Good point, but you can't be sure."

"I know," I say. "Where are we at with the score here?"

"What score?" he asks with innocent eyes.

"You were keeping score between the two of them...y'know, with the pro/con list?"

"Sorry," he says, going for more water. "I suck with numbers."

"Don't worry about it. I should've been counting myself."

"See that?" he asks. "That's your real problem there, not this girl thing."

"What?" I ask, shifting in my seat. "What's my real problem?"

"I'll tell you in a second," he says. He gets up and walks around in confused circles as if I'm not there. "Hey," he says, finally stopping to notice me again. "You care if I crap here on the floor?"

"What?"

"Normally, I'd just dump it out, but since you're here I thought I'd be courteous and ask."

"I'm pretty shitfaced, so to be honest, I don't really care," I say. "It's your place, do what you want."

"I appreciate it," he says, squatting down. "What was I saying?"

"You were about to tell me what my 'real problem' is."

"Right," he says, finishing up. "Your real problem doesn't have anything to do with which girl to go with, it has to do with your personality."

"How so?"

"You put too much blame on yourself and not enough on anyone else."

"I'm not following..."

"Okay, well, ever since this thing with Jill started, you've been putting the blame on yourself. Instead of saying 'Fuck that bitch, I'm moving on,' you said 'I must've done something wrong for her to dump me.'"

"Bullshit..."

"Is it?" he asks. "You know Berkshire is a shitty town with a shitty school, right?"

"Yeah, everyone does."

"Then why do you blame yourself for having a shitty college life? Why do you blame yourself for not being able to do anything with your life?"

"I don't!"

"Like hell you don't!" he yells. "If you don't, then how come you spend half your time getting yelled at by a little 16-year-old snob that only you can hear?"

"You know about that?"

"Damn right, I do! And how come you can't go five minutes without getting locked into some kind of creepy, homicidal stare?"

"I don't know..."

"Because you blame yourself! You blame yourself too much on how you've turned out!" he yells, eyes lit up like Christmas trees. "Yeah, you need to take some responsibility in your life, but Christ, Kal! You spend so much time yelling at yourself for things out of your control that you need to create another version of yourself to lay the blame on for you."

"So now you're a shrink?"

"You know I'm right," he says, going for more water. Tangents must take a lot out of him.

"But I haven't had The Stare or anything in weeks! Not since...wow..."

"...not since you've been with Katie, which proves my point more." He's getting cocky, but I guess he has a right to be. "Since you've been with her, you haven't been thinking about Jill, you haven't been thinking about this Connie

Ward crap and you haven't been thinking about how much your life sucks. In short, you haven't had any reason to blame yourself."

"Wow…"

"Yeah."

"Oh, my God…"

"I know."

"You're totally right," I say.

"I guess we know who you should go with then, huh?" he says. "You care if I shit again?"

"Again?"

"Kal?" Barry yells up the stairs, surprising me sober…well, not really. I hope he didn't hear me screech like a girl. "Who're you talking to?"

"What?"

"You were just talking to yourself."

"No, I wasn't."

"Yeah, you were."

"I was on the phone." He knows I'm lying. A quick view around the room brings him to a new conclusion.

"Were you talking to the guinea pig?" he says, staring at me.

"Thor?" I say. "That's impossible." Did he hear the whole conversation?

"Right…" he says, turning to walk down the stairs.

"Are we going to the bar soon, or what?" I ask, hoping that deviates the subject enough to get him to forget I was just having an imaginary conversation with the pig.

"Yeah," he says, delivering another odd look before taking a step down the stairs. "Listen, it may not be any of my business," he says, looking at me from the side of his eye like a shark. "A lot of girls out there aren't worth getting drunk and retarded over. But the ones who are worth it aren't going to dump you for some douche bag and then expect you to take them back."

"Yeah," I say, surprised by his sudden insight. "Thanks, Barry."

I try to cling to a sense of balance as I stand up. When it's done, all I can do is stare at Thor, peeping his head out of a little plastic igloo in his cage. I guess Molly was right: It does help to talk to him. I feel so much better that I'm not even worried about the fact that I'm crazy enough to have a full conversation with a guinea pig. Looks like everything's coming up "Kalvin."

It's so quiet, I'm actually a little scared when I feel my cell vibrating in my pocket. It's Katie.

"Hey," I say, hoping my good mood is infectious.

"Kal?" she asks softly.

"What's up?"

"I…I just don't know…"

"Well, you don't have to answer it now. It was kind of a rhetorical question anyway."

"Listen, I don't know how to say this…"

"Say what?" That's also a rhetorical question. I've heard something like this before—only last time I heard it, it was coming from Jill a few months ago.

"Listen, can you come over? I think we should talk."

18

Disaster's Pretty Face

At first, when I look around, I don't remember ever being to this particular cornfield. Berkshire is covered in farms and cornfields, probably too many to visit even if somebody actually felt like doing so. This one is a little different than the rest, though. This one doesn't look like it has had corn, or anything for that matter, growing in it since the Reagan Administration. That's what makes it distinct for me; that's what helps me remember why I'm here instead of any of the other fields I could have passed out in last night.

"Hello?" Lana says through my cell phone.

"Hey." I try to act casual. "What're you up to?"

"Nothing. Watching TV."

"You done with class for the day?"

"It's Friday," she reminds me, "I don't have class today."

"Right," I say. "Would you want to do me a favor?" I freeze for a second halfway through the word "favor." I have to ask myself if I'm willing to do this to myself; more importantly, I have to make sure I'm willing to do this to her.

"Maybe," she jokes.

"Can you pick me up from somewhere?"

"Okay..." Hmm. So far, so good. "Where?"

"You know where the old, one-room school house is?" I ask. "The one in the middle of the cornfield? The one that's all beaten up that the townies give tours of?"

"Yeah..."

"There."

It's quiet. I wait.

"How'd you get there?" she asks. She already knows the answer, she has to. Maybe she's just giving me a chance to lie—a chance to avoid putting her into any state of concern.

"I don't know." I shoot it to her straight. "I guess I walked here, or something…"

"Last night?"

"I guess so."

"You slept in a cornfield last night?"

"Looks like it."

"Why?" Her meek, quiet voice can't cloak her mixed sense of confusion and anger.

"Why do you think?"

"I thought you said you were done doing that stuff!"

"I didn't say that."

"Yes, you did!" she yells. "The other day, remember? After me, you and Molly got out of that support group meeting, you said you were over your issues and you didn't need to drink yourself to death anymore!"

"I said that?"

"Something like that, yes."

"That doesn't sound like something I'd say." She lets out a groan on the other end of the phone.

"That's, like, five miles away! How the hell'd you get out there?!"

"I told you: I don't know. I guess I walked or someone dropped me off…"

"Who the hell would just drop you off in a cornfield for no apparent reason?"

"I don't know…the pope?"

"Jesus…" she grumbles.

"Or him, too."

"You're fucking unbelievable," she says, followed by a click on her end. I can't blame her for hanging up. She's only looking out for me, I guess.

I'm lucky I decided to wear my jacket last night. It's cold,

211

cloudy and waiting to rain. It takes a minute or two to remember that I put my smokes in my inside coat pocket.
They're crushed, meaning I slept on my stomach. At least
when I'm drunk and retarded enough to make my way out
to a field, I'm smart enough to sleep on my gut. My phone
rings before I light up. It's Lana, right on cue.

"Hi…" I try to act as humble as possible.

"I'll pick you up, but it's not going to be for a while."

"Why?"

"Because I was about to drop some books off at the library. You're just going to have to wait a few minutes."

"Thank you, Lana." I sound like a kid.

"Just be by the schoolhouse when I get there."

I shuffle my feet around in the dry dirt for a while as I
walk in shallow circles in front of the schoolhouse. I have a
bunch of random thoughts and memories from last night,
but they don't fit together too well. I remember getting completely destroyed at the bar. I remember walking to one of
the pizza places, but I can't remember which one. I'm pretty
sure I remember being kicked out. I think I gave Wally a
noogie at one point. From there it's a haze. I think I was in a
car at one point. Maybe I asked someone to bring me here,
maybe I walked, I don't know. I did come here for a reason
though: Jill.

Jill brought me here a couple of times while we were dating. She's cheesy like that. She liked looking at stars and
whispering sweet nothings and all that other crap that Julia
Roberts' movies have taught girls to expect from relationships. That didn't bother me about her, though. In fact, I
think the first time I realized that it didn't bother me was
when we were sitting out here. I think it was the night that
we came out here and it was too cloudy to see anything.
That was one of those nights where she actually cracked me
open a little bit. She did a lot of the talking most of the time,
and I just listened. But I think that night was different. I
think that was the night she fell asleep while I talked. Yeah, it
was. She has a tattoo on the small of her back—a little pic-

ture of a moon that she designed herself. She was talking about how it hurt, and I went on some tangent about how I didn't want to get a tattoo because if I were ever wanted by the police, it'd be easier for someone to identify me if I had a tattoo. Seems kind of ironic now, after being indirectly accused of assaulting someone.

It's weird thinking of little situations like that. In the time we were dating, I don't think I ever took her on a real date. Cheap bastard. I think the only thing that could be considered a real date was when I took her for pizza that one time. We went for "cheap dates" like walks around town and shit like that. She always smiled and seemed to like it. I never thought for a second that she didn't. She seemed as content as I was. I think one time she even said something about how it's nice not making a big deal about dates. She said she was happy just hanging out. For the last few months I thought it was a lie. I thought me being a cheap, drunk asshole was the reason she dumped me for Fernando. Her telling me differently yesterday has thrown everything into a weird perspective. She said she loved me. Maybe I love her, too. Tear-filled confessional moments like yesterday's have a way of making you realize odd things.

*   *   *

"So…" Lana says, breaking silence. It's weird how small talk can still be hard to force, even after you've known the person for years.

"So…" I return.

"What happened?"

"Last night?"

"Yeah," she says, "unless you literally did just get completely bombed and stranded yourself in a field for no reason."

"Katie broke up with me," I admit. It's hard, but after a few seconds I feel relieved to admit it.

"Katie?"

"Yeah. She's the new girl I've been seeing that I didn't want anyone to really know about."

"Oh. *That* Katie."

"Yeah."

"Do you care if I ask why?" Her voice is small and quiet as she risks opening me up.

"Sure," I say, "go ahead."

"Why?"

"Jill came over yesterday," I don't know if I'm just giving her an adequate background, or if I'm changing the subject.

"What? Why?"

"To tell me she loved me and she made a mistake with the other guy and that she wanted me back and stuff."

"How'd that go?"

"Pretty well," I mumble, just loud enough to hear myself over the screeching windshield wipers. Thick drops of rain bounce off the car and make a percussive echo under my voice.

"So you dumped Katie for her?"

"No, you're getting ahead of yourself." She glares over at me with a confused stare while quickly turning her head to refocus on the wet road. "I was going to, but Thor talked me out of it."

"The guinea pig talked you out of it?"

"I don't know. It was either him or Barry. I get those two confused." Her head tips back slightly, physically showing surprise. "Anyway, after I realized I'd be making a mistake going back to Jill, Katie called me. Told me to come over." She's quiet; doesn't even say "and" or anything to prompt me. She waits for me to tell the tale at my own pace. "So, I went over and she sits me down and tells me it's not working out."

"She flat out said it like that?"

"Yeah."

"Well, that's kind of respectable. Most people would probably have beat around the bush."

"Not her," I say. "She gave me every reason for what was

happening. She actually wrote them down and read them off to me."

"Ouch."

"Yeah…"

"What were they?"

"Well, her first—and probably favorite—reason is that she's now engaged."

"What?!" Disbelief soaks over her tone.

"Yeah," I say, lighting my fourth cigarette in a half hour. "Her ex-boyfriend came up the day before, somehow made up for whatever he did wrong and popped the question."

"Wow. Just like that?"

"Just like that."

"My God! I can't believe it! Was she serious?"

"Apparently," I say, keeping my face towards the window. I see a guy on a bike getting pattered by the rain. It makes me laugh for a second, but then I realize why I don't feel like laughing. "She had other reasons, too."

"Like what?"

"Well, apparently the only reason she was into me in the first place was because I was wanted for assault."

"What?"

"Yeah. 'I'm sorry, I just have a thing for bad boys.' Her exact words."

"Jeez…"

"Yeah. I guess it was kind of a turn-off when she found out I really didn't have anything to do with it."

"At least she was honest."

"I guess." She doesn't ask anymore, probably thinking she's exhausted my willingness to talk. The void of silence is filled by the swishing noise of her tires splitting through a puddle, splashing raw, cruddy rain water away from the car. "You know what the worst part about all this is?" She looks at me, eyes swelling. "The worst part is the whole mind fuck that's going on now. The aftermath that she didn't intend."

"Yeah…" she says. Her head's probably swimming, looking for ways to consol me. "Maybe this is just a phase. Her and her boyfriend broke up for a reason right?" She looks at me for a response I'm not willing to give. "She was probably just swept away when he proposed. I think if any of my ex's did that, I'd do the same thing."

"You would?"

"Yeah," she begins, "but then I'd realize why we separated in the first place, you know? Leopards don't change their spots, Kal. I'm sure this is just a little phase for her."

"'Leopards don't change their spots.' That's funny, 'cuz she said that to me about Jill once," I remember out loud. "And I thought the same thing about this situation at first. But then she decided to let me know that they consummated the whole thing—several times over again."

"Jesus! She told you that?!"

"Yup," I say with my voice scratched and raw from exhaustion and smoke.

"I'm sorry, Kal," she mutters as we pull up to my place. She puts the car in park before hugging me from her seat. Her chin digs into my shoulder. "I'm so sorry this had to happen to you again..."

"It's okay, Lana..."

"I just don't like seeing all this happen to you."

"It could be worse."

"I don't want to see you hurt yourself again just because someone else did it first."

"I wont." I push her out of my arms gently.

"I'm sorry. It just makes me upset. Seeing this happen to anyone sucks. It hurts even more seeing it happen to one of my friends."

"Why?"

"I don't know. Just does. I care about you."

"Lana...?"

"What?"

"You got me wet."

"You're such a dick," she whispers, smiling and wiping off a stray tear.

"Thanks for everything. But you really don't have to cry

about this, okay?"

She hugs me one more time and smiles as she pulls away. I rub her back gently for a second as I jump out of the car into the oncoming storm. The rain washes down on me and soaks into my clothes. Lana watches while I fumble through my keys with cold, wet fingers.

The house is warm, empty and surprisingly welcoming. My jeans reveal a darker shade of blue as the rain soaks through. My hair hangs and drips, heavy and wet. The warmth exits my body again and leaves behind chills when I notice an unfamiliar face sitting on our couch.

She jumps off the couch as she sees me, brushing off her ass as if she subconsciously knew she caught some disease by sitting there.

"Kalvin?" she asks. "Kalvin Gray?" She flaps her eyelids twice when she talks. She has a cat-like look to her. Her small nose, her big, angular eyes, the way her chin comes to a smooth point—everything about her just looks very cat-like. Her long, tan-colored sweater and soft blonde hair swing as she steps towards me. She looks warm and dry, obviously waiting here since before it started raining.

"Yeah, ummmm," I say, bumbling my hands, pointing them in different directions, subconsciously using them to show how baffled and awkward I feel at the moment. I realize she's in my house, and I have no reason to be afraid of her. She should feel awkward around me. "Do I know you?" I ask, sparing courtesies.

"Your roommates said you'd be back soon. They said I could wait for you…"

"Okay, but that doesn't answer my question," I groan, going through a pile of mail on the counter. I know none of it's mine; it's just hard for me to look her in the eyes while I'm acting like a dick.

"I came here to talk to you about something," she says, brushing the hair behind her ears.

"If it has anything to do with women being directly related to the Devil, I'm way ahead of you," I say, finally looking up at her for a glance before shifting my attention towards the couch as I plop down.

"My name's Connie Ward," she proclaims as she stiffens her back, "and I think there's something we need to talk about."

19

End Game

The hard, marble floor clicks and claps as the bottom of my shoes smack against it. Assholes. Fucking assholes…

The hallway seems longer than it has to be. Things are moving around me, but I might as well be walking on a treadmill. I'm not getting anywhere fast enough. I'm going to fucking kill those little shitheads…

The lady at the front desk is going to give me a hard time. She's going to want to know if I have an appointment. She's going to try and stop me from doing what I have to, and the best part is that she doesn't realize what she's stopping, what she's delaying. I'll fucking cut that bitch if she even tries to give me a hard time about this.

Okay, got to stop. Got to collect myself. Can't curse at old ladies…again. Okay. Relax, Kal, relax. Okay. I'm going to kill those fucking cocksuckers…

"Excuse me? Sir?" the secretary cautiously says as my foot jabs open the double doors of the waiting room. Squeaky hinges strain to hold the doors as they fly and bounce of the wall. "Sir, you can't…"

"I need to see Luther. Now."

"Oh," she says, slowly trembling back to her seat. "I, um, I don't think he's here."

"You don't think he is?"

"I'm not sure."

"You're sitting right in front of the only door leading out

of here," I remind the trembling old bat. "How can you not know if he's here or not."

"No, he's not here."

"He's not?"

"Yes...I just remembered. He's not here."

"I need to talk to him now."

"You'll have to make an appointment," she squeaks out of her lips. Her hand is shaking a pen across some paper. "If I could have your name..."

"Where is he at?"

"I'm not sure."

"Then look."

"Sir, please don't talk to me like that..."

"I'm not talking to you, I'm yelling at you! I want to see him, and I want to see him now!" Her frail neck looks like it's about to give as she drops her stare down towards the desktop.

"It says here that he isn't available until tomorrow."

"The hell he isn't!"

"Sir..."

"Get him on the phone for me."

"...if you'll just calm down..." Got to chill out. I can't give this lady a heart attack. I can't freak her out to the point where she's ready to call the cops on me. Got to play ball with her.

"Okay. Okay, I apologize," I say over heavy, deep breathes.

"Now, if we can just sign you up for an appointment..." she says, but my attention travels to the door to Luther's office.

"What was that noise?" I ask.

"What noise?"

"I heard talking."

"Talking?"

"Yeah," I say. "Coming from there..." It starts as a low mumble muffled by stained mahogany doors. It's louder with each step closer.

"You can't go in there," the secretary says. She yells it with just enough concern to earn her $11 an hour.

She keeps yapping while I wrap my hand around the icy, fake-silver finish of the doorknob. I hear Luther's voice. It comes though the door like a dull hum. I can't make out what he's saying. There's another voice in there with him—a guy's voice.

The secretary yammers on about how I can't disturb Luther. I don't care. This has to be done. But do I want to do it? When I open this door, one of two things will happen. I'll either close the door to the world of shit that my life has been drowning in or I'll open a whole new one. It all comes down to how much I want to do this. I've spent the better part of the last four years avoiding things I had to do because I didn't feel like doing them. Will doing this change everything for me? Or will I regret not leaving well enough alone?

Okay…I guess I have to do this. Got to take a few deep breaths first—can't go in there all flustered. Got to let him know how serious I am. Each breath I take is weighed down by a wall of carbon monoxide that has built in my lungs from being a smoker for the past seven years. Sweat trails from my palms and smudges along the silver doorknob. Here goes…

"Kalvin!" Luther welcomes me. His voice drowns out the creaking door. "How're you?" He smiles while leaning back in his leather-upholstered chair.

"Good afternoon, Kalvin," says Chip, sitting in front of Luther's desk. Only the side of his head is facing me.

All the piss and vinegar that fueled this trip immediately seeps through my pores and collects into a swamp right under my ass. All my nerves burn the inside of my stomach like a kettle fire. I'm left standing with nothing to say and a dumb stare to go along with it.

"Is everything okay?" Luther asks as he steps away from behind his desk. He keeps his eyes focused on me as he blindly walks to the side of his office where a small bar is set up. I can't remember why I'm here.

"You just going to stand there?" Chip asks. "Or do you

got something useful to say?"

"Calm down, Chip," Luther suggests in a fatherly voice. "Kalvin's probably just here to talk about his hunt for Connie Ward's assailant." He twirls a tiny, plastic stirrer around the rim of his glass, mixing whatever he just made. "Right?"

"I know what happened," I say. My knees regain feeling.

"Oh?" Luther says, patronizing me. He glances at Chip with a smile. They're like two cats about to play with a mouse before ripping into it. Right at that moment, a feeling blankets the room, and I'm given the impression that all three of us are immediately on the same thought.

"So you found Connie's attacker?" Chip says, smiling.

"It looks like he did," Luther answers, "which is great. But I'm more concerned with some of the minor details." He sits on the front of his desk, sipping from the tip of his glass, waiting for me to say something. "How did you find out about it?"

"Connie."

"Didn't you say earlier that you thought she'd go to him directly?" Chip asks Luther.

"Yeah," he responds. "But I didn't think it'd be for a while. At least not until finals week."

"I guess you called it," Chip says. I wonder if he forgot I was standing here. "See," he says, turning to me and re-membering I'm in the room. "I thought she would've sat on it until after she graduated. And I really didn't think she'd tell you of all people. I guess you called it," he says, turning back to Luther. "Then again, you were the one who slept with her. I guess you would know her better."

"That I do," Luther says, "that I do." He finishes his drink with a gulp and walks towards the bar to freshen it up again. The cocky smirk he's been wearing fades away with each step and reveals a dark grimace—the kind people have when waiting in line at the DMV. He looks pissed about something. "So," he says, mixing another drink, "are you going to stand there? You want a drink or something?"

"No."

"That's probably a first…" he mutters under his breath.

"How do you know so much about me?" I ask.

"Hmm…" Luther looks a Chip, who reflects the confused look back. "Apparently, I don't know that much about you. I didn't expect you to ask that."

"I asked you a question…" My fists clench.

"I know, and I'll answer it, but let me ask you something first," he says. "How much do you know?"

"Everything," I say.

"Everything?" Chip asks.

"Ev-ry-thing," I say. "You used me."

"Not quite," Luther says.

"We only used your appearance," adds Chip.

"Exactly. If we were 'using' you, we'd have slipped your name into the police report," says Luther, sipping again on his drink. "We thought we'd give you a break."

"You're not getting away with this," I say, my fist cocked in front of me. Chip laughs out loud as Luther tries to hold a mouthful of booze in while chuckling.

"Get away with what?" Luther gloats with a laugh. "It's not a crime to encourage an assault victim to identify her assailant."

"Maybe not," I say. "But it is a crime to attack someone, like you did."

"What?" Luther's smile drops to the ground with his jaw.

"I told you: Connie told me everything." I take short, shallow steps towards the desk. For almost a second, I feel halfway intimidating. "She told me about how you and her became fuck buddies after she met you at the bar. She told me how she tried to get out of your little 'relationship' once she found out you were still married, and how you were so pissed about it that you went ape shit and beat the hell out of her in a drunken rage."

"Interesting…" Luther says.

"And it gets better." My confidence builds higher with each word that flies from my mouth. "She also told me how you threatened to get her expelled if she told anyone. But it didn't end there, did it?"

"You're on a roll. Why don't you tell me?" Luther sighs out, looking at his watch. He looks bored. Or he's just trying not to break a sweat.

"You beat her so bad that you put her in the hospital. There was no way people wouldn't notice…"

"Bad*ly*," Chip blurts out.

"What?" I ask.

"You said 'beat her bad'," he says as he steps up from his chair and heads for the mini-bar. "You should've said 'beat her bad*ly*.'

"I thought you were a communications major," Luther comments. They're trying to distract me, throw me off. I can't let them.

"She was so beaten up that you couldn't let her go anywhere without an excuse. That's when you decided to call your friends on the Berkshire police department and got them to eat some bullshit story about her being attacked by someone who looked like me."

It's quiet for a few seconds after I talk. Luther holds his palm flat against his mouth, looking downwards in quiet thought. Chip nods numbly, as if he's going along with me long after I've finished talking.

"So…" Luther says, "Connie told you all of that?"

"Not all of it. She told me up until the part where you put her in the hospital. The rest I figured out for myself."

"Yes, well, don't give yourself too much credit," Luther says as he stands and paces around his office with tiny steps. "So my first question, I guess, would be, 'Why'd you come here?'"

"Because I'm giving you one chance to confess before I bring it to higher authorities."

"Oh?" he says with a giggle. "Not too long ago, the editor of the newspaper told me you dropped the whole case. So now, just because of some confused broad, you're going to bring all this shit over your head again?"

"When we decided to drop this whole thing, it was because we thought he did it," I say, nudging my head in Chip's direction. "We couldn't take it any further because there was nothing that could've been done, especially since we figured the police already knew about it."

"And now you think you can do something about it?" Luther snorts at me.

"Chip is a nobody. If I went against him, I'd end up only shitting on myself since he's just a lowly, unmarried, underpaid college professor. He has nothing to lose." My fists relax to my sides. "You, on the other hand, are a well-respected pillar of the Berkshire community. You have a family at stake, a sterling reputation and a $140,000-a-year paycheck. Not to mention that if the Board of Higher Education got wind of this, not only would you never get out of this shithole town, you'd probably never work for them again. Basically, after that, you'd also be a nobody. The best you could hope for is to become yet another lowly, unmarried, underpaid college professor."

Luther and Chip look at each other and collect their jaws from the floor. They expected a lot of shit from me, but not this. They never predicted this.

"Well," Luther says, finally collecting himself. "You certainly have me by the balls, don't you?" He's smiling. Why's he smiling?

"You know, Kal," Chip says, "it hurts me a little to admit this, but I'm a little impressed."

"Honestly, who'd have thought you had a spine underneath all that," Luther adds, pointing at me. "But you're forgetting one thing."

"I don't think I am." My voice sounds louder than anything that's ever come out of my mouth.

"But you are," Luther says, mixing yet another drink. "You're forgetting that even if you do take this to some 'higher authority,' even if you do find someone willing to listen to you whine, they'll never take you seriously." He turns from the bar and faces me dead on with a smile dark enough to scare the devil out of a possessed child. "After all, you're just some deadbeat frat boy with a marijuana, uh, I mean 'cheesecake brownie' addiction," he says, using his index and middle fingers to make quotation marks that bounce like bunny ears.

"What?"

"Did you really think I wanted you to eat that brownie just because my wife's a good cook?"

"Nice try," I say, "but I'm calling your bluff, Luther. I wasn't even high after I ate it."

"Doesn't matter," he says. "Chef Chip over here added just enough dirt to keep your piss contraband for at least a month."

"I used to make those all the time when I was your age," Chip adds with a grin. "Besides, do you think it was just a coincidence that I lit up while you and that little butt-slut from the newspaper interviewed me?"

"But I didn't smoke with you!"

"Doesn't matter. The door and windows were closed. You still inhaled enough to fail a test."

Shit.

"Not to mention that you're a problem drinker," Luther mentions. "Not only could I force a drug test on you and have you expelled—maybe even arrested—but I could find enough people to deliver a convincing enough argument to prove that your drunk opinion doesn't amount to shit."

"You don't think I'll bring this up after all that shit is flushed from my system?" I ask.

"No, we thought of that," Chip says.

"That's why you're going to be getting a visit this week from the Berkshire PD, who're going to want to take a 'sample' from you." Luther grins. "You know, just for safe keeping..."

"You agree to play ball, you'll never hear about that piss again," Chip says. "Of course, we'll have someone hold onto it though, just in case..."

This can't be happening. This can't be real. This was

supposed to make everything better. This was supposed to make everything right.

I can hear the two of them snickering. Luther keeps talking, with Chip chiming in every few seconds. I can't listen. My stomach hurts. It doesn't burn; it hurts. I can feel a load of piss brewing inside of me, trying to force it's way out. I can feel my life being sealed with wax and marked for mediocrity.

"You just closed every door that could have led you out of this shitty life," Little 16-year-old Kalvin says. Man, I was an asshole when I was 16.

"Kalvin," Luther's voice rings gently in my ears, at first, just before it starts to pound my eardrums like a gong. "Gray! I'm talking to you!"

"Huh?"

"What're you staring at?" Chip asks, genuinely confused. Dammit... The Stare... of all times...

"Why me?"

"What?" Luther asks.

"Why me?" I repeat. "Why'd you pick me? You had almost 10,000 students to choose from. Why me?"

"Because, Kalvin, you're a deadbeat," Luther says.

"There're other people who would've been a better fit." I say.

"True, but they're not quite like you."

"How?"

"You're a puppet," Chip says, sitting back in his chair once again.

"What?"

"You're an empty mess of a man, Kalvin," Luther says. "Look at yourself—you just float around town, not doing much of anything. You don't try to make anything of yourself; you don't try to do anything with your life. Hell, with the exception of that little fraternity you're in, you don't even get involved with extracurricular activities." He counts off each detail on his fingers. "You're not doing anything with your life, and that's what made you such a sure thing."

"When we realized that we needed a patsy, you're the first person who came to mind," Chip adds. "You were always at the bar drinking yourself into submission. When you weren't, you were making a dick of yourself in my class. In short: You were the right person, in the right place, at the right time."

"The hardest part was talking Connie into describing you as the assailant," Luther mentions. "But once she realized her future was in jeopardy, she was more than willing to blame you, my little pawn."

I can't follow what he's saying—not because it confused me, but because he's right: I am a pawn, and I'm not even willing to fight it.

"Think of it, Kal," Luther starts up again. I hate this prick so much right now. "You're not using your life, so you leave it open for everyone else to use. Me, Chip, Connie— we all used you. Hell, even that girl you were with…what's her name?"

"Katie," Chip answers.

"Right…even Katie used you. Everyone remotely involved in this situation used you." Luther says, sitting firmly in the seat behind his desk. "You're a puppet, Kal. A puppet left on the floor for everyone else's use."

I try to speak up, try to defend myself, but I can't. I keep choking on the realization that he's right. These two used me to stay out of trouble. Connie used me to confront them. Katie used me to find them. I am a puppet.

"Don't feel so sad about this, Kal," Luther adds. "Take it as a life lesson."

"You fought and you lost," Chip says.

"Now, if you'll excuse us, we're going to get ready to go to happy hour at the Toad Creek. Consider yourself lucky you got out of this with just a damaged ego."

I can't even look up as I walk out of the room. My feet drag along the plush carpeting, and I'm left with a tail hanging limp with humility. Those fuckers—they had this all planned from the start, and I jumped through every hoop they set up. Motherfuckers...

"And Kalvin?" Luther says, just as I make it to the doorway. "Remember: if you even try to bring this up to anyone ever again, I'll crush you."

"Rock-bottom hurts when you hit it at full speed, doesn't it, kid?" Chip adds.

20

Same As It Ever Was

"When I see this field fully stocked with so much potential, I get a little jealous," Luther says as a microphone echoes his voice across a football field full of young graduates. A dark gold tassel drips off the edge of his mortarboard. "When I see so many talented, young professionals ready to make claim of what they've earned in our society, I feel just a little envious that I'm not on this football field with you. Not because I wish I was only 22 years old again, but because I wish I was fortunate enough to have front-row seats for all the incredible changes that your generation is prepared to make to our world." I've seen flaming brown paper bags full of less shit than this.

It's been nearly a month since the Connie Ward situation came to a close. The cops came and took my piss, as Luther and Chip said they would. Since then, I've come to terms with everything that's happened. I was a little jaded at first by the situation. As much as I realized this school sucked, I never thought that someone like Luther helmed it. I told my parents about the whole situation. I didn't want Luther sending any kind of threats to them as a back-up plan. It just seemed best to tell them about the whole situation right away so there weren't any surprises. They surprisingly understood. I don't remember too much about the conversation. Unfortunately, the only part I really remember is the part of the conversation that seemed most cliché; the part where they mentioned that people like Luther are everywhere in the world. They said that people like him are what this country was founded on. Such a cliché, but it's so accurate too. I wanted to ask about people like me. I wanted to ask them about what happened to the people like me are who left in the wake of every shit storm caused by people like Luther. I was too afraid of what their answer might be.

"I wish I had more to do up here than gush," Luther continues. "People of your generation—you're outstanding judges of character. You would be able to tell if I was just standing here blowing smoke up your gowns. But, luckily, I'm not the type to BS. And I attribute my success to that. I wouldn't have made it into this spot on stage right now if I slinked and slipped my way like a snake. And neither will you." The irony of this situation is almost crippling. "What I'm saying is—and this is as blunt and simple as I can make it—is be yourself. Follow yourself and your heart. And most importantly, follow the path your heart paves for you. If you don't do that, you're lying to yourself and denying your own destiny." Part of me wants to suspect that he knows I'm in the crowd when he drips this shit show out of his mouth. "I guess what I'm trying to say is," he says, rubbing his mouth dry and showing a smile, "keep it real."

"Did I just hear that right?" Jay says, rocking his head back with shock. "Did he just say 'keep it real'?"

"I think he did," adds Molly. "That's not very professional."

"Trust me guys," I say, joining them and Doug as we lean forward against the fence edging along the back side of the field, "he's the farthest thing from 'professional.'"

"Did you ever hear back from the main office in Harrisburg?" Molly asks. Like all my friends, I told her about the situation. And like all my friends, I lied to her too. I didn't want them to think I was going to be a complete pussy that stood there and let Luther fuck me over until I was raw. I told all of them that I reported Luther to the State System for Higher Education in Harrisburg. Not my finest hour by any means, but whatever.

"No, they never got back to me…hey, can you see any of them?" I ask, changing the subject.

"I think I see Dutch," Doug says. "But it might just be some other retard with giant ears."

"We should've just got tickets for graduation," I say. "Wouldn't have to stand here bent over the fence this whole time."

"You're used to being bent over though," Doug says. "Fag."

"Fuck!" I yell. "What the fuck? Can't you guys ever think of anything funnier than fucking gay jokes?!"

"What's up your ass?" Molly asks. I look towards the three of them, waiting for one of them to make a joke answer to something "gay" being up my ass.

"It's just been a long fucking day," I explain. "That's all."

"It's only, like, 9 a.m.," Molly adds. "How can it be a long day? You've only been awake for 20 minutes!"

"Being awake has been kinda hard for me lately," I say, trailing off and hoping I don't come off too melodramatic. I notice Luther's voice going inaudible as he strides away from the podium. A blonde girl prances up to the podium, bubbly and buoyant. I think she's the student speaker. I'm pretty sure she was in my dorm freshman year. It's kinda shitty realizing that I'm watching someone who's been at this school as long as I have graduating when I still have another year yet.

"That girl's, like, a friggin' genius or something," Doug mumbles unprompted.

"How do you know?" Molly asks.

"My one teacher kept talking about her the one day," Doug answers. "She's supposed to have, like, all these awesome job offers and shit."

"Must be nice," I say. "Do any of these guys have any offers yet?" I ask about our friends.

"I don't know," Doug says. "I just hope none of them get any really good jobs and become ultra-rich. That'd piss me off." The one thing I notice about my friends and I is the bitterness that binds us. I think most friends are expected to be supportive of each other on some level, but my friends and I are knitted into a tight relationship based on wishing each other failure. I wonder if that's just something we do, or if other people are like that, too.

"Know what I'd do if I was rich?" Jay brings up randomly, waiting for someone to answer. "I'd pay for a giant mansion that'd have escalators and treadmills and shit to take me everywhere. I'd never walk again," he says to my silent friends and I. "That'd be awesome."

"I'm not surprised," I say.

"I'd buy a shitload of cars," Doug says.

"Very original," replies Molly. "I shouldn't talk. I'd probably just by a bunch of houses I don't need."

"I think I would use the money to fuck with people, too," Jay adds. "I'd wait till all the guys who ever pissed me off got married, and then I'd pay a young black actor, or an Asian actor or whatever, to go over to the wives of the guys I don't like and say that they're the guy's kids. Ruin their marriage and shit," he says smiling blankly into the distance. "That'd be awesome."

"I could see myself doing something like that," I say.

"That's the thing," Jay begins. "You got all these famous people and celebrities going around spending money on finding cures for shit like AIDS and cancer and necrophilia, and doing stuff to help people, but you never see anyone using their money to fuck with people like on soap operas," he says, finally looking at us. "I want to be that guy—the guy on the soap opera who fucks with everyone else."

"I don't think you need to be rich to fuck with people, Jay," I say as I eye Luther, sitting on the stage all proper and prim with his legs crossed. "People fuck with other people all the time. Usually the ones you'd never expect."

*   *   *

I knew this was going to happen. I've been preparing myself for over a month, but it still hits me harder than a bullet hits glass and leaves me in twice as many pieces.

It starts off simple enough with "Dear Kalvin." The rest isn't so simple.

Hey. I feel like I'm in high school again, writing notes to boys and everything. I'm tempted to write something like "What's ↑" and "NMH" and things like that. Anyway, I know I haven't returned your calls lately, and I'm sorry. I feel like a bitch for doing that, especially since I used to think you were a jerk for doing the same thing to me. Knowing you, you're probably paranoid that you did something really subtle yet stupid to piss me off, and you think that's why I haven't called you or emailed you or anything. That's not the case.

The thing is, I have some bad news that I've been meaning to tell you. God, I feel so shitty about this. I wish I could do this to your face, but I can't. I hate myself for being such a coward. I wish I could tell you how I do care about you, I really, REALLY do. I wish I could let you know how crazy I've felt since me and you started dating back in the beginning of the year, and how horrible I felt every time I realized I dumped such a sweet guy like you for someone like Fernando. Most of all, I wish I could let you know why I keep going back to him, especially when he hurts me.

I know that a few weeks ago, I told you I loved you and I told you me and Fernando were over for good. By now, you most likely realize that I've been talking to him again. God…I feel so shitty for never giving you a chance, Kalvin, I really do. You have to understand, no matter how sure of myself I am when I say I love you, I still don't feel the same as I do when I'm with Fernando. I know I might just be setting myself up to get hurt again—I seriously realize that—but I don't know what it is, y'know? I just don't understand what it is about him. I feel like I'm supposed to be with him. I feel like we're meant to be together. I'm so sorry, Kalvin. I know I'll always regret that I never said this to your face, but the truth is that I just can't.

I wish I could just end this letter here, but I can't. There's something else I need to tell you. Fernando is graduating, and he decided to move to Philly. He asked me to move in with him, and I said yes.

Berkshire isn't for me, Kalvin. I don't fit in here. I don't even know if college is for me. I know that sounds stupid after spending three years here, but I just don't know what's right for me. I guess that's part of the reason why I had so much trouble choosing between you and Fernando. Life comes down to choosing between what's right for you and what you want. It hurts me so much to say this to your face, Kalvin. I wish you knew how much I'm crying while I'm writing this. But at the end of the day, you and Berkshire may be what's right for me, but Fernando and this new life in the city is what I want.

I wish I loved you, Kalvin. I seriously do, and I'm so sorry.

Sincerely,
Jill

I've read it 100 times since I got it yesterday, but I still haven't let it sink in. I was waiting for something like this. I just thought it'd be more, I don't know, personal. But this...this is just shitty. Jill is out of my life, quite possibly forever. The only thing distracting me is the vibrations and the trademark Nokia ring tone pumping out of my pocket.

"Hey," Lana says on the other side of the phone.

"Hey," I respond. "What's up?"

"What're you doing?"

"Nothing. Just sitting around my place."

"Oh, yeah?"

"I should be packing up my shit. We're supposed to be out of here in two days." It takes me a minute to realize why she's really calling. "Shit, Lana..." I say in an indignant voice. "I was supposed to meet you, wasn't I?"

"Yup," she says. "Right after graduation was over."

"Sorry."

"Yeah. Don't worry about. I'm sure you'll be there the next time I graduate from college."

"What? Are you going to grad school or something?"

"No," she says. "I was just saying that to make you feel like a dick."

"I appreciate it," I say. "Did you just get back from lunch with your parents?"

"Yeah. What're you doing?"

"Still just sitting around my place," I say.

"Oh, right…I just asked that." She's quiet for a few seconds. She might be mad at me for not coming to say congratulations yet…oh shit…

"Congratulations!" I say, probably a little too late.

"Finally…I was waiting for that." I can hear a smile cracking as she raises her voice slightly. "Hey, I'm sorry about what happened," she says, the slight raise in her voice disappearing.

"What're you talking about?"

"That thing that happened with your ex."

"You know about that?" I ask. "How do you know about the note?" There's no way she could have found out. I just got Jill's note yesterday, and I didn't tell anyone.

"What note?" she asks. "I was talking about the thing in the newspaper." Whoops. I guess I didn't tell anyone about the note after all.

"What thing in the newspaper?"

"You didn't see it yet?" she asks. "Oh…"

"What?"

"I don't know…" she starts, trying to stall while she thinks of a way to change the subject.

"Just tell me, Lana," I say, showing some force. "What thing in the paper?"

"There was some little section somewhere in the middle congratulating their assistant editor on getting engaged." Katie. I was getting so re-obsessed with Jill that I was starting to think about Katie only eight times a day.

"Oh…" I say.

"You okay?"

"Yeah, I'm fine."

"I didn't mean to open up any wounds or anything."

"You didn't," I lie.

"What note were you talking about?" she asks, veering the conversation off course.

"Nothing important."

"You sure?"

"I don't know."

"Want to talk about it?"

"Not now," I say. "I feel like some drama queen bitch with all the moaning I've been doing lately."

"Well, you're coming out tonight, right?"

"Yeah."

"Maybe we can talk about it then."

"Okay."

"Right," she says. "I'll see you then, I guess."

"Wait!" I yell to her. My voice probably screams to her like a distant yell as she most likely pulled the phone away for a quick hang-up.

"What?"

"Congratulations again on graduating," I say.

"Thanks."

"I'm proud of you. Seriously."

"What?"

"I am," I say. "And while I'm at it..." my voice gags and chokes a little as I'm working my way into my next sentence. "...I'm really lucky to have you in my life. I really am."

"Huh?"

"Seriously. Thanks for being such a great girl and an awesome friend." She's quiet, like she's letting her brain digest all the mush around the sentiment.

"You're such a dick," she says.

"No, I'm serious!"

"That sounds like something out of a shitty movie," she says, casually brushing off my sentiment. She knows how hard saying stuff like this is for me. "I'll talk to you later, okay?"

"Okay." I can still hear her voice ring silently in my eardrum while I hang up.

It doesn't take too long for the doorbell to start buzzing. I didn't even know we had a doorbell. I'd look through the peephole on the door, but Wally drew a giant dick around it in permanent marker. He drew it at just the right angle so that the peephole looks like the eye of the cock—he's talented like that. I feel stupid looking though it. I know the drawn image of the dick isn't going to piss or jizz on me or anything like that, but it's still weird.

"Hi..." I hear as I open the door. Connie is standing humbly in jeans and a Berkshire sweatshirt, her oval, cat-like eyes staring wide at me.

"What's up?" I ask.

"You don't care that I'm here, do you?"

"Why would I?" I ask, swinging the door completely open as I turn my back to her and return inside the house. "Come on in."

"Thanks," she says, slowly stepping in. I plop on the couch just as she completely submerges herself into our living room. She stares around the room, observing the discarded cigarette packs and broken beer bottles. It doesn't faze her much.

"So..." I say, lighting a cigarette, "what's up?"

"Are you guys living here over the summer?" she asks.

"Nope. Why?"

"It's just really messy here," she says, continually observing the room. "Shouldn't you guys clean up?"

"We'll get to it," I say, joining her in the realization that we're essentially standing in a junkyard. "Eventually."

"Oh..." she says. I can see her eyes tremble and dart as she fishes through her brain for a way to start small talk. "So, where you guys living next year?"

"Down off of Street Road. About a mile from campus."

"Where at?"

"Down by the gas station," I say. "I'm moving in with two of my fraternity brothers."

"That's near where I live."

"Awesome." She's a sweet girl. I shouldn't be sarcastic with her. "So what can I do for you?"

"I wanted to come by before you left town," she says. Her voice is low and mumbled.

"Well, you don't have to worry about that," I say. "I'll

probably be living in my new place most of the summer."

"Oh..." she says. She's saying that a lot. "Can I sit down?" she asks, looking at the spot next to me.

"At your own risk."

"Thanks." Her ass lands on the soft, decrepit cushion. "I just wanted to apologize again."

"You don't have to."

"I want to," she says. "What I did was wrong. I could have ruined your life," she says, fumbling her hands against each other, looking at the floor.

"Well, you didn't," I say. "Besides, it was kind of messed up already. I probably wouldn't have noticed."

"Okay," she says quietly. "Is everything okay?" I look at her when she asks. "I don't mean to pester or anything, but you look kind of..."

"No," I say. "You're not pestering. Don't worry about it." She looks at me silently, as if she took what I said as the opening to some list of sad trifles and complaints.

"I know you don't know me, but..."

"Yeah, I can talk about it if I want, right?" I say, cutting her off. "That's what you were going to say, isn't it?"

"Yeah." Her head sinks down. I think we're both feeling a sense of regret over the last thing that came out of our mouths.

"I'm sorry," I say. "It's been a rough couple of days...or months..." I'm silent for a second. My mind fills with thoughts and my lips try to hold all of them back as best I can. But they can only take so much pressure from my mind before they give. "Have you ever just really cared for someone? I mean like really, really cared for them?"

"Like love them?" she asks.

"Not so much love. I mean, yeah, love, but beyond that. Like really, really, cherished them so much that it almost hurts you inside because those feelings you have for that person are just that intense?"

"Yeah..."

"But at the same time, you just can't love them because

there's something stopping you? There's, like, some road-block stopping you. You care for them so much and it eats at you. But the thing is, they don't have that same affection for you, and because of that, you can't say that you love them, even though you do. But the thing is, you can't admit to yourself or anyone else that you love them because knowing that you can't have them will just, like, completely destroy you."

"Yeah, I think I understand," she says. "Do you mean like there's another person in the way, or something else?"

"Both!" I yell. My own enthusiasm knocks me back. "It's as if not only do you have to deal with the fact that there's this other person between you and the person you care for, but also this other issue. Like, as if that person isn't meant for you. Like they're either better than you, or they're meant for better things? And the more you start to care for that person, the more complicated things get. Do you know what I mean?"

"Yeah," she says, in a tone so clear that it almost scares me. "I know exactly what you mean." That's when I realize who I'm talking to, and all the stuff she's been through with Luther. She obviously got hurt from this whole situation, too—a lot more than I did.

"Yeah, I guess you do. I'm sorry," I say. "And I'm sorry for dumping all of this on you. Believe it or not, I never talk about my problems like this."

"It's okay, don't be sorry," she says. "I came here to apologize to you."

"You really don't have to."

"Yes, I do," she says. "I remember when Chip and Al came up with this plan," she starts, still looking at the ground under her feet. "It was when I was in the hospital, after he hit me. All they kept talking about was framing this guy who was in Chip's class—which was you—and how it was the perfect crime because nobody would give a shit because everyone would've just thought you were some jackass."

"They weren't far off," I say.

"I just felt so bad," she continues. "I'm so sorry, Kalvin. I really am."

"Okay," I say, "but look at it this way: you guys really didn't ruin anything that wasn't already broken. If anything, I learned some shit from the whole situation."

"Like what?"

"Well…" I begin, remembering what Chip and Luther said to me while they were tearing into me once I found out the truth. "Let's just say I learned that just showing up in life isn't enough." With that she finally looks up at me for the first time in the conversation, only to give me a confused glare. "Just don't feel bad about all this, okay?" I ask.

"Okay…" she says, humbly.

"If you feel that bad about it," I add, "you can take me out to lunch sometime, okay?"

"Sure." A small smile cracks out from both sides of her mouth. We both stare at each other for a cool minute, allowing the void of awkward silence to fill the room around us. Her soft eyes glow. I guess it's true: Sometimes just talking about things does help. Or maybe she feels better just because she realized that the two of us walk on common ground. She had her love problems with Luther; I had mine with Jill and Katie. Either way, it's nice to feel the knots in my stomach tightening with small traces of self-satisfaction from doing the right thing. "I should get going," she finally says.

"Okay."

"Thanks for letting me apologize again."

"Anytime."

"I'll call you about lunch then…" she says, with a small smile while she closes the door. A date with Connie Ward. That's just funny.

It's weird how things work out sometimes. I vaguely remember the day when I came home and sat in this living room with Barry and Jay and everyone, getting taunted for looking like an accused rapist. Three months later, I feel just as vulnerable, and I may or may not have a lunch date with the girl I was accused of attacking. It just happens so fast—the weeks go by so quickly when you spend each day sitting around bitching about how shitty your life is while waiting to drink. I'm sure a smarter man could make some kind of metaphor out of that, saying something about how life goes faster when you let it waste away. I'm not the metaphor type.

As strange and aggravating as the last few months have been, I have these weird pangs of regret. Not the kind of regret that comes from making a mistake, but more like the regret that comes with closure. That strange sense that you feel once something is over; that odd feeling you have when you're looking back on something and you realize that maybe it wasn't that bad. Maybe I didn't have such a bad time the past few months. I guess that sense of regret I feel isn't coming from not doing something the way I would've wanted, but more from realizing that everything that happened did happen because I needed it to. Maybe the regret I'm feeling is not feeling as positive about it then as I do now. Or maybe I don't know what I'm talking about. Maybe I'm just a fucking retard after all.

The End

A preview of
What Ever Happened to Kalvin L. Gray?
from Michael P. Ferrari's second book
Training the Problem: Stories and a Novella

(Available March 2010 from **Blue Room Publishing**)

When I woke up, my mouth was the typical desert I'm used to in the morning. The air was dry and dusty in my little shit storm of a bedroom.

I swung my hand around, trying to find some water, but nothing. Just crumpled cigarette packets, mangled and crushed beer cans and the standard half-empty waters I've come to use as ashtrays over the years. I was hoping I'd grow out of this kind of wake-up scenario by now, but nope.

I lay back down, stared at the crusty white drop ceiling and waited for death by dehydration—my only real alternative to actually getting out of bed. Well, what counts as a bed for me. Since moving out of the dump on Cohen Street, I've scored a sweet apartment with my own bedroom. But the move trashed my bed. Thanks to a rain storm and the slippery, sweaty hands that came with my hangover, I ended up dropping my mattress into one of the mud puddles that can be found throughout Berkshire University year round, rain or shine.

I'm sure if I still had a girlfriend or something, she'd probably motivate me to find some kind of bed-like apparatus to fall into each night. Or at least wash the pile towels I've been using as a bed. But I'm the perpetual college bachelor, and because of that, I forfeit simple pleasures like sanitation.

My name is Kalvin L. Gray. Imagine a portrait of the stereotypical poor college student, pour a couple unnecessary pints of alcohol into his bloodstream and put a comic-book thought bubble over his head with the word "Duh" in it, and there I am.

I spent the rest of the hour trying to wake up. When I finally did, I stood, bent my abnormally squeaky, 22-year-old joints and opened the bedroom door to move on with my life.

The hallway to my apartment stunk of summer, and not in the good way. Summer smells usually contain a few whiffs of green tree leaves, the odor of fresh-cut grass and the smell of cool thunderstorm rain approaching from far off on the horizon, but not in my place. The sun turns the 140-year-old building into a pizza oven, taking the smells of our rotted-out floorboards, our deteriorating carpets and our crumbling drywall and baking it into some kind of scent that probably resembles Cerberus's anus.

Hmm…"Cerberus's anus." I should remember that for my English Comp class.

When I got out into the living room, one my roommates, Wally, was already on the couch, lying shirtless and scrawny on his stomach.

"Meh," he greeted me.

"Hunh," I nodded back.

I fell into the broken-down couch we brought with us from the last place on Cohen Street. It was one of those hand-me-downs with springs so old that they were lazy about holding my ass when I plopped into it.

"Shit, man," Wally groaned, staring at the 12 o'clock news on the TV. "Shit."

"What?"

"I hate the first night back after summer break."

"Why?"

He sighed and pushed himself slowly up with weak and creaky elbows. He kneeled on the couch, pointing at his khaki-colored cargo shorts, which I just noticed were the same ones he had on last night. With both index fingers he traced the smeared mess of piss that stained through his pants over night.

"Jesus…"

"Yeah, man." He lay back down. "This is why I can't get shitfaced in the summertime. Something about the heat makes me piss myself when I'm drunk."

"Maybe you should put a towel down or something," I suggested.

"What's the point? When I piss myself, I bring the pain. This cushion realizes that now, and it's never going to be same. It's dead to the world."

He talked a little more about his damage-inducing piss spree, but I didn't pay attention. My mind was on the fight I had with Connie Ward, my brand new ex-girlfriend. In the same covert way it always does, my brain started sneaking little bits and pieces of my memory back together, gluing together a picture of last night that was otherwise smashed by my boozing.

"Shit," I said. "Was Connie at the bar last night?"

"No," Wally groaned. "No. Wait. Yeah, she was."

"Dammit!"

"What?"

"I think I yelled at her when I was shitfaced."

"So?"

"I think I yelled at her for ruining my life with that fake-ass police sketch she gave of me when she got assaulted last year."

"Cool. Go you."

"No way, man. This is bad."

"Why?" Wally perked his head up enough to face me. "You guys are broken up. Plus, it's not like she did you any favors by telling the police sketch artist that the guy who attacked her was you just because she wanted to cover up her fuckfest with the president of the school." He paused. "Fuck her, man. Move on."

"I'm over her. Trust me: I moved, and I'm on."

"Bitchin'." Wally's head fell back down to the couch.

It wasn't true, obviously. Connie was the third in a trifecta of college broads who felt that fucking with me was sport in the same way fox hunting and polo are to the rich. I'm a guy, and even though we denounce that kind of shit from women, we're biologically engineered to crave it at the same time. Did Connie fuck me over by dumping me after that whole act of almost getting me arrested for attempted rape? Absolutely. Was I better off without her? Definitely. Was I over her? Maybe, maybe not. People—guys and girls alike—never get over the person who fucked them over until we start dating the next person in line who's ready to do it.

"We should probably start drinking soon," Wally said.

"Why?"

"Because we're too healthy as it is."

"I don't know," I said. "After all that shit that went down with the police sketch and people thinking I may or may not have been an attempted rapist and all that, I think I'm going to at least try to act more grown up."

"Didn't you try that last semester?"

"Yeah, but I kept passing out by allies and in dumpsters anyway."

"Oh," he grumbled. "So you're saying it didn't work then?"

"It's going to work this year."

The hall leading to our front door was long and isolated from the rest of the room. It carried noise too well, and I could hear footsteps getting muffled into the stained, thinning carpet. "Police in the house," said a new voice.

Wally and I raised an eyebrow at each other as two Berkshire cops came in; one was fat and falling apart, the other was young and short with thick, chub-covered muscles. He wore a face that screamed "Napoleon Complex."

"The door was wide open, so we let ourselves in," said the fat cop, who hung his hands from his belt.

"Are you Kalvin Gray?" the younger asked me. "We need you to come with us."

"Huh? Why?"

"We need to bring you to the station. You've been identified by several witnesses for committing several misdemeanors over the course of last night."

"You've got to be shitting me…"

"That sucks," Wally said as I walked out with the cops. "So much for changing this year…"

To be concluded in *Training the Problem: Stories and a Novella*, on sale in March 2010 from **Blue Room Publishing**!